Ivory Tower

Thomas Fahy

This book is a work of fiction. Any references to historical events, real people or real locales are used fictitiously. Other names, characters, places, and incidents are the product of the author's imagination, and any resemblance to actual events or locales or persons, living or dead, is entirely coincidental.

For my students

Part I

A View from the Basement

Part II

Climbing the Tower

Part III

In Memoriam

Part IV

Reparations

Part I

A View from the Basement

1
Spontaneous Human Combustion

No one expects to see a dead body and a penis at 6:30 in the morning. At least not in the Humanities Department. On a Tuesday.

I've never been here before staff and students and sunrise. I've never been here without drinking enough coffee for two. And I've certainly never been here early enough to discover a body in the main office. The old dead guy wears a pinstripe suit and powder blue shirt. His rust-colored fedora has a Frank Sinatra tilt, and a white handkerchief peeks out of his breast pocket. In short, he has a fashion sense completely out of place for the 1970s hell scape of the Humanities Department. Lemon-scented linoleum hallways. Oak paneled walls and olive-carpeted offices. Recessed lighting designed to jaundice the skin. It's an aesthetic only the terminally ill or the already dead could appreciate.

"Hello?"

I kick his leg. Twice, to be sure.

He's dead, all right. I've read enough coroners' reports to know he hasn't been here long. Not without stiff limbs, emptied bowels, or the smell of decay. The wrinkles on his ashen face appear etched into the skin, and his eyebrows sprout tufts of cotton. Purple-grey lips hang open to reveal a few bottom front teeth.

Compared to him, my black slacks and matching loafers scream "Clearance Aisle." The puffy, full-length winter coat I consider practical would be labeled homeless chic by most. Even J. C. Penney would disown my white dress shirt. Without a shower or sleep in over twenty-four hours, my auburn, shoulder-length hair resembles beached seaweed, and my eyes sting with dryness. I can't deny the simple fact that this guy looks better dead than I do alive.

Oddly enough, I know how to handle this situation. I shouldn't, but I do. Someone has to call the police. The coroner needs to be notified. The body moved. Family members and funeral directors contacted. Internment arrangements confirmed. State and internal documents filed. Death certificates mailed. I know because I fill out this kind of paperwork five nights a week at the Haverton County Morgue.

The indignities of being a graduate student in the humanities are too long to list in a single-volume work. Take the desk drawer stuffed with rejection letters for academic jobs. Take the snickering that comes with getting a PhD in Native American history when you're white. (For a while, my friends even called me "Mayflower," "Moon Cricket," or whatever Native American slurs for white people they could find online.) Or take the demoralizing part-time job to nurse your debts and pay your bills. To be fair, the nightshift at the morgue has the advantage of being quiet, so I don't have to make small talk. I can also write. That's what graduate school does to you. It makes you grateful for a job that gives you time to do work on top of the work that actually pays. To spend more time with the dead than the living. To toil on a dissertation that fails to get you a job—three years running.

One day I expect the title of my autobiography to read *Eat, Pay Rent, and Kill Yourself* by Anastasia Landers Shaw.

2

I storm out of the office as if the dead guy just pinched my ass. I'm not even supposed to be here, I remind myself. Last night, my dissertation director, Professor Riggs, asked if I would proctor her 7:00 exam. Such requests are not optional in the world of higher education. Or the mafia. Your dissertation director holds your life in her hands. She makes sure your project gets approved with the least amount of torture from your committee. She helps ready your writing for publication. She pens recommendation letters and reaches out to colleagues at other schools on your behalf. In short, at the end of this torturous journey, she ensures that you don't move from part time to full time at the morgue.

That is why I am here at 6:30 in the morning. That is why I came directly from my nightshift at work. To do her job for her.

Muttering with the fervor of the mentally ill on a New York City subway, I walk upstairs to the office of the department chair, Professor Hinks. Why is this my problem? Shouldn't he be protecting us from indentured servitude and dead bodies? At least in the department.

Hinks makes a point of letting everyone know he eats kale and gets to campus at five-thirty to swim—though I'm not sure either are things to be proud of. At least I know he'll be here. I can picture his face with the precision that comes from taking a class with someone for an entire semester. You learn every detail from fashion sense to body movement, tone of voice to facial expressions. Even their smells become familiar—the mixture of coffee, tuna-kale salad, chorine, and aftershave. Beneath his curly, salt-and-pepper hair, he wears an expression of perpetual surprise as if waiting for you to say something interesting while expecting disappointment.

When I reach the fourth floor, I find his door slightly open, spilling a cone of yellow light into the hall. All of a sudden, my stomach gets rock heavy. Maybe it would be better if he finds the body himself, I think. He'll have to go downstairs eventually. No, tell him. I'm just the messenger. It's not like I killed the guy. I'm giving him a chance to have the body removed discreetly. I should get rewarded for my thoughtfulness, my poise under pressure, my dedication for being here so early to proctor someone else's exam. I can already imagine the gratitude, the new bond that will exist between us. I'm almost smiling when I push open the door.

I recognize the look of perpetual surprise as I begin to speak, but something is wrong. Familiar but different—like coming home to find your furniture rearranged. I recognize the desk and paneled walls. The poster of John Coltrane's *Blue Train* album cover. The tightly packed bookshelves. And I recognize Professor Hinks.

Sort of.

The bottom of his forest green shirt is unbuttoned. So are his signature black jeans. His right hand moves up and down in front of his navel. In the gap between realizing what I'm seeing and what his body aches to finish, a surprising amount happens. He lurches forward, trying to snap the chair back to a ninety-degree angle. But he is too close to the desk. Hinks's right knee smashes into it, suspending him midair. He yelps in pain, reaching for his knee, and that's when he lets go of his member—a fully-swelled, inverted mushroom sprouting from a pair of red silk underwear.

I'm staring at the department chair's package, or it's staring at me, for what feels like an eternity. For some inexplicable reason, I can't turn away. It's like watching a Trump press conference or an episode of *The Bachelor*. I'm too stunned to move. I can only hope for one thing.

Spontaneous human combustion.

The chair falls into place with a loud crash. Hinks grabs both sides of the desk, yanking himself forward until his chest smacks onto the surface. His frantic movements knock over almost everything. A shrapnel of paperclips, pens, and papers litter the floor. The phone crashes on its side, one button blinking as if someone were on hold. And a thick document lands at my feet. Instinctively, I pick it up. Part of me wants to clean the entire mess, as if channeling Martha Stewart will somehow erase the last few seconds.

"Out!" he barks.

I close my mouth in what feels like slow motion and place the packet of paper gingerly on his desk. That's when I notice the words—"Dissolution of Marriage. State of Connecticut Superior Court"—at the top of the page.

I close the door behind me with cartoon-like exaggeration, as if nothing could be worse than a loud noise after seeing your boss masturbate at work. I don't want to linger. I don't want to hear the chair squeak as he stands up to buckle his belt and tuck in his shirt. Or worse, finish the job. I hurry down four flights of stairs for the exit.

Outside, the icy air stings my cheeks. I take slow, deep breaths to calm my thundering heart. What happens now? I try to convince myself that Hinks won't come up with some excuse to throw me out of the program. That he won't destroy my career before it even starts. That I'll be able to wear silk again.

I guess I should get something out of the way right now. I've never watched anyone flog the dolphin before. No judgement if that's what you're into. For me, it's a bit like synchronized swimming or extreme competitive crocheting. It just doesn't soften my butter.

I look at the grim stone slabs that make up the courtyard of the Humanities Department. It is as inviting as a Soviet-era prison. You have to turn a corner and walk thirty meters between two brick buildings before seeing any sign of life. But what does it matter in the middle of winter? The trees have shed their leaves. The dead grass has turned soggy. No birds sing. Only then does it occur to me that I didn't get a chance to tell Hinks about the body.

Damn.

Before I can decide what to do, before I can calculate how many years of therapy I'll need after this morning, the girlish tippy-tap of heels echoes around me. I know who they belong to before she turns the corner—Professor Tiffany Riggs. I'm surprised to see her since she asked me to proctor her exam. Maybe I'm just surprised to find someone alive or clothed around here. Even in the cold, she looks radiant. Most people in the department compare her to a real-life Barbie doll. She has long blonde hair, dusky blue eyes, textbook posture, and a svelte figure. The list doesn't stop there. Ample bosomed (totally fake), good-smelling, nicely proportioned, and successful by any measuring stick. In short, she's a total nightmare.

And did I mention that she's fucking my boyfriend?

2
Some Assembly Required

Do you ever feel wistful at IKEA? Maybe it's just me, but my vision of the afterlife is an IKEA showroom. Not the self-service warehouse, maddening furniture dollies, and checkout lines that charge you for a bag. I mean the sample rooms. Rooms that can evoke old world elegance or contemporary hipness. Rooms painted in dark greens, bright yellows, or boyish blues. Solid lines of shelves against a cascade of circular ceiling lamps and floor rugs. And have you seen what they can do with 118 square feet? Imagine living in a world where everything takes up the right amount of space and surprises you with its efficiency. Where everything is affordable and unbroken. The IKEA showroom always makes me feel one end table away from having my shit together.

Then again IKEA furniture never looks quite as good at home. Even as you sort through the boxes of Cubist particleboard and accessories, you know the finished product won't compliment your finely honed aesthetic of college furniture and crap from your parents' garage. The instruction manuals begin with six pages of dire warnings in languages you don't understand. The rest appears drawn for small children with limited motor skills. The step-by-step instructions seem foolproof—until you get cocky and skip ahead, until you use the wrong screw and damage the particleboard, until you spend ten minutes looking for a piece that was under your ass the entire time. That is when you remember IKEA would have assembled it for a small fee.

Enter Brett Bergin.

Brett works in the assembly warehouse at IKEA. Most people don't get to see the unsung heroes who perform magic with a *songesand* bed frame or *björksnäs* chest, but they can build IKEA furniture with a speedy precision that Henry Ford would admire. Within the day, it will be delivered. Finished. Flawless. And ready to use. But let me warn you about a danger not mentioned in any IKEA instruction manual. Brett Bergin can shatter your heart into lightbulb-thin pieces.

Brett moved to this tiny Connecticut town for me, for my dream of pursuing a PhD in history. He took a job at IKEA less than a week after we found an apartment together. He always loved making things, building something functional out of nothing. Or maybe he just loved me enough not to care about the nine-to-five grind.

For a while at least.

I had never lived with anyone before, so I was unprepared for an apartment complex that resembled a HAZMAT facility to bring me such joy. I was unprepared to take pleasure in divvying up dresser drawers and closets, to see him filling up so much space and wanting to give more. Is this what I had been missing? The closeness? The unexpected laughter? The bursting fullness in my chest?

Words fall short, so the IKEA catalogue became our lexicon. Most couples settle into nauseating nicknames for each other like "Muffin" and "Pumpernickel." Determined to be cleverer than that, we went with random IKEA products or made up Swedish-sounding words. He'd call me *Sockerbit* (box with lid) if I was lost in my head with work or *Blåbär* (blueberry) if he wanted me to stop talking and just kiss him. I called him *Plunkerhead* (an Ana original) after every bad joke or *Torkis* (laundry basket) if he needed to pick up his dirty clothes off the floor.

And almost every night before bed, like a man befitting his porn star name, Brett Bergin would slip under the sheets and say, "Hi, I'm from IKEA assembly. I'm here to loosen your *flagernaven*."

It was our version of Swedish foreplay.

Brett moved out fourteen weeks and five days ago. It is strange what you remember about someone who is gone, what still turns you on about him. The swing of his arms. The tilt of his head while chewing food. The faint nectarine scent of his skin. For me, I just couldn't get enough of Brett's hands. The joints of each finger, knotted and bony. The pointed mountaintops of his knuckles and its peach fuzz slopes. Fingers arched like the chiseled marble of Bernini. Sometimes, I still feel the impression of them on my skin. The heaviness of his palm pressed against mine. The callused roughness of his fingertips against my face, my neck, my breasts. He had this way of pulling me toward him, arm around my lower back that made me short of breath and nearly lifted me off the floor. At those moments, I was close enough to feel electricity from the lightning bolt scar under his chin. I was close enough to lose myself in the black hair beneath his throat or to look up the alpine-ridged nose into his Caribbean-blue eyes.

Now, he sleeps with my dissertation director in her bigger, larger, softer bed. He has sex with her firmer, nimbler, bigger breasted body—no doubt on sheets with a higher threat count and surrounded by matching throw pillows. Professor Riggs doesn't own the kind of furniture that gets assembled by the Bretts of the world. But that doesn't stop her from fucking them.

Bitch.

She first met Brett at a dinner party for graduate students in the middle of October—"a mix and mingle soiree," she called it with all the pretentiousness that comes with the word "soiree." Brett was my plus one. It was her first time hosting this annual event for the department and my first invitation to her house. On the way there, we got lost trying to navigate her sprawling suburban neighborhood. Each street, blotted with blood-red leaves, spilled seamlessly into the next, and the rolling lawns were wider than our apartment building. In my rush to get out the door, I'd forgotten my phone with the address, so we argued about whether her house was on a street named after a tree or a President. It turned out to be Colonial Drive. We found it only because one of my friends passed us on the road, and we followed her the rest of the way.

Parked outside Professor Riggs's house, we stared for a moment at its two-story brick exterior with black-shuttered windows and white columns. I couldn't fathom such luxury. Rumors floated around the department about a rich husband who died under mysterious circumstances. It's the kind of speculation that comes from small-minded envy. Naturally, I wondered if she ran a high-end escort service or sold election data to the Russians.

"Please let it be an escort service," Brett replied with a wink before we stepped inside.

As a species, the humanities graduate student is a peculiar one. It keeps odd hours, staying up until two

11

or three in the morning to write papers. It tends to suffer from a Vitamin D deficiency for spending too much time in libraries, coffee shops, bars, and, in some cases, mortuaries. It consumes fast foods, eschewing more wholesome approaches to sustenance such as cooking, and it prefers smoking, drinking, and getting high to exercise. In short, the graduate student's masochistic existence of self-doubt, loathing, and unpaid labor survives on a diet of fleeting compliments ("Nice job on that Civil War essay") and false hopes ("I hear the job market is looking better this year"). But along the way, nothing placates this creature and boosts morale more than free food and drinks. Particularly alcohol.

Professor Riggs's bacchanalian feast was designed to make us think of graduate school as the best decision of our lives. The open bar had a white-coated bartender whose nametag read "Flannigan." His crooked smile matched his crooked crewcut, and he reminded me of college swimmer with his long limbs and shiny face. We were chums by my third glass of pinot noir, and he christened me "Ana Banana." I called him the "Flann Man." Similarly dressed servers walked through the room with trays of hors d'oeuvres: prosciutto wrapped melon, salmon with capers, Szechwan dumplings, whipped cheeses, and fried crab cakes. To be honest, it didn't matter what was on the plates. We inhaled all of it. We ate like starving prisoners and recently released POWs. In short, we ate like graduate students.

And we drank. The Flann Man served them up, and we downed enough liquor to put a small winery out of business. Hinks, with pants firmly fastened, hovered by the dessert table. Molten lava cake with hazelnut ice cream, in case you were wondering. Almost everyone drank steadily.

Not Brett. He never liked having more than a couple of beers. He wanted to experience things "clear-headed," as he put it. I had never met anyone so capable of living in the moment, of finding pleasure in the details of everyday life. He watched basketball games with the focus of a coach. He went running without listening to music. He lost himself in conversation—about classic cars, butterfly migrations, the worst horror movies of the 1980s. The subject didn't matter. You see, Brett did not straddle life like I did. Half in the present, half terrified about the future. Half enjoying the moment, half worried about the next paper to grade or job to apply for. I longed for that type of immediacy. It was one of the things that made me love him. Even through my wine-hazed buffoonery, I could see that Professor Riggs recognized this about him too. Like Brett, she stayed clear-headed, sipping only one glass of white wine throughout the evening. The noise of fifty or so guests gave her every excuse to stand close to him while they spoke, to graze his shoulder after every laugh, and to hook strands of silky blonde hair behind her right ear. At the time, I felt pride. He was going home with me, I thought even as the room started to get fuzzy.

I was too drunk to have sex that night. Maybe that was the beginning of the end for us, leaving him to dream of her while I snored off a bottle or so of wine. Maybe he noticed that I took the wooden figurine of an elephant from her bookshelf before stumbling out the door. If so, he'd chew me out the next morning when I was sober enough to feel ashamed.

Or maybe he just fell in love with someone else.

I didn't find out until much later that she ordered a piece of IKEA furniture to be assembled and delivered the following day.

Bitch.

3
Tequila Mockingbird

After proctoring the exam and spending hours in the library, I head over to Tequila Mockingbird—the town bar for graduate students. The parlor resembles a Victorian reading room. Floor-to-ceiling mahogany bookcases crammed with hardbound books. (The books are real. I've checked.) Dark leather couches. Chairs huddled around small tables, and a gas fireplace across from the L-shaped bar. In the back room, two full-length bocce courts take up most of the space. Here you'll find the literary-themed décor you'd expect from a place owned by a former PhD student in English. Black-and-white photos of Edna St. Vincent Millay in Greenwich, James Baldwin by the Seine, Charles Bukowski giving you the finger. Next to the jukebox, there is a display case with a 1937 Woodstock typewriter and a first edition of *To Kill a Mockingbird*— too conspicuous to swipe without going full *Mission Impossible*. Not that I haven't thought about it.

Today, an interchangeable trio of sporty, middle-aged guys plays a game. The balls thud against the decomposed granite and grind to a stop against the backdrop of Billie Holiday's music.

With just enough people at two o'clock for some guilt-free drinking, I peel off my puffy coat. I've gained weight since Brett left. My hips push against my pants, and tonight I'll find red lines around my waist. I know better than to worry about weight and breast size and armpit hair. I teach feminist theory to my students, after all. But sometimes, I wonder how long it takes to

15

unlearn a lifetime of looking in mirrors to find flaws, to find things to dislike about yourself.

As I head over to Yumi at our usual table, I can't help but notice that she could be carried away by a strong breeze. Jean overalls hang loosely on her rail-thin body, and she sits like a baseball player, leaning forward with her shoulders somewhat hunched. Her black hair, which falls in waves to her shoulders, has blue highlights. Two margaritas with salt-kissed rims rest on coasters, and she reaches for one as I plop into a chair. An empty "Call Me Ishmael" shot glass sits on the table.

"I ordered for you," she says with her perfectly straight, white-toothed smile. "I'm surprised you didn't make a beeline for the bar after your close encounter with Hinks."

"It wasn't open." My fingers stiffen just thinking of all the texts I sent about this morning. "He's going to kick me out of the program."

"After creating a hostile, sexually charged work environment? Please. He could lose his job for swinging that thing around the office—"

"Ladies," Doug trumpets as he reaches the table. His Dolby Surround Sound voice suits his lumbering body, which towers somewhere north of six feet. He has a broad face with brown eyes and the kind of pale skin that burns red after an hour on the beach.

"Jerking off to divorce papers?" he asks. "Where are the pics of Japanese schoolgirls when you need them?"

"Classy," Yumi says, more playful than angry, but I catch a hint of both in her tone.

Doug thinks of himself as a witty smooth-talker, but in reality he's just a smartass who knows how to push buttons. For Doug, dishing out shit is a sign of love, even if it sometimes feels like acid reflux. As he sits next to Yumi on the couch, the cushion sinks deep enough to pull them close together. Anyone within shouting distance can see they are going to have sex. Doug is the kind of guy you either want to punch or fuck. Or both.

"So, who's the dead guy?" he asks before glancing over my shoulder to try to catch the bartender's attention.

"No clue," I reply, "but it's strange. He wore this amazing outfit from the forties, as if the office was really important to him."

"Well, he isn't the first person to contemplate suicide in that dump," Doug says as he stands. "I'm getting a drink. Need anything?"

We shake our heads. Yumi bites her lower lip as he takes long, heavy strides to the bar. Even as we sip our drinks, she watches the way he jokes with the bartender and leans against the counter, casual and cool.

While Doug waits for his order, Kavita arrives. She is wrapped in a white trench coat with a dark green scarf, and she waves at us before joining him. Tall with striking brown skin and shiny raven hair, Kavita has the posture of a dancer—the kind that makes everyone else in the room feel a little bit shorter and sloppier. She and Doug have been sleeping together for over a year. *"Totally casual,"* they call it, as if we lived in Southern California, but Kavita seems to be the only one who doesn't notice the spark between him and Yumi.

When they get to our table, the four of us toast to the sound of bocce balls cracking against each other. The sporty guys cheer in the back, and Billie Holiday starts singing about traveling all alone.

"So, what did I miss?" Kavita asks, both hands around her glass as if it's a warm cup of tea.

"The usual," I mutter. "Penises and Asian porn."

"L—O—L."

Kavita never seems in a hurry even when it comes to language, which makes her use of texting acronyms in conversation odd. Each letter comes out so slowly that it would be faster and far less painful if she just said the words: L—M—K (Let … Me … Know). T—T—Y—S (Talk … To … You … Soon).

"Seriously, it must have been horrible," she continues, "and sad. To have nowhere to go but that building. I never want to end up like that."

We sit for a moment in the kind of silence that comes from being able to picture ourselves as dusty, forgotten academics with nowhere to die but a department office. My phone, which has been face-up on the table, suddenly brightens with an email.

"Jesus," I say, half-dazed as I down my last sip of margarita. "Hinks wants to see me. Now."

"I'll go with you," Kavita says. "We all will."

Yumi grabs her purse. Even Doug nods, but unlike them, he doesn't move. I can tell he'd rather stay here and flirt. Who can blame him? He is sleeping with one of them and about to sleep with the other. I might as well go to bed with an orthopedic knee pillow for all the action I'm getting.

"No. This is my problem."

"Are you sure?" Kavita asks.

I nod. The truth is I can't let them come. Hinks can't know I told anyone about this morning. It could blowback on them in any number of ways. Not enough classes to teach next year. A lukewarm recommendation letter. A repeat performance.

"Good luck," Doug says a bit too quickly, and he turns to Yumi and Kavita with a smile. "Ladies, shall we fondle some balls?"

With a quick pivot, Yumi slaps his shoulder—clearly pleased with any excuse to touch him. As they gather their things to move to the bocce courts, I tuck the "Call Me Ishmael" shot glass in my bag.

That's when Doug clears his throat. I tense, thinking he has caught me, but he gestures to the front door instead. My eyes follow. I recognize the familiar stride and the arm-swing right away.

"Brett Bergin," Doug announces. "Private Eye."

•••

I practically push Brett back through the door, furious that he would step foot in here, furious that he knows where to find me. Of course, I am being irrational, but I can live with that. I am the one who first brought him to Tequila Mockingbird. I am the one who introduced him to Doug, Yumi, and Kavita. And I am the one stupid enough to move to a town with a population smaller than a Walmart, a town where it is easier to run into someone than to avoid him.

I can sketch Brett's muscular, athletic frame with my eyes closed—even when it is hidden beneath the burgundy Gore-Tex coat I got him last CHK. (That's pronounced "chuck" for Christmas-Hanukkah-Kwanza. We didn't want to shortchange any holiday, so we insisted on getting each other three holiday cards every year.) Though I can't see his sandy blonde hair beneath the hood, I know it is mussy from running his fingers through it at work and wiping his forehead with the back of his arm. Dark stubble hides some of his lightning-bolt scar, but I've traced it with my finger a thousand times. More.

I thought the pain in my chest and the scooped out hollowness in my stomach would be the worst part of losing Brett. I was wrong. The worst part is not being able to claim ownership anymore. Those are my lips to kiss, my eyes to gaze into. That is why I can't stand seeing him here. This is my place. I have to hold onto something.

Outside, the slate-gray sky drains the color from Haverton's utterly forgettable downtown. Two blocks of sun-bleached yellow siding and sandblasted brick. Peeling signs for storefronts like "Haverton Hardware," "Nico's Pizzeria," and, of course, that staph infection of coffee shops, Starbucks—like no one else in the country knows how to overcharge for a latte so we need two on every block. Carbon copies of this Main Street can be found in almost every New England coastal town. For a moment, it makes me wonder if Brett and I are any different. What if some version of us is about to have some version of the same post-breakup fight in another town? What if we are nothing more than the Starbucks of broken couples?

"Why aren't you at work?"

I can't believe that is the only thing I can think to say to him, but it is. I keep both hands deep in my pockets, and I am shaking a bit from the cold. The biting air seeps through my slacks and stings my ears.

"I only have a few minutes. I need to tell you something," he begins, head down and eyes at his feet. Not a good sign. "Tiff wanted to tell you, but I—"

"Tiff? Did you say Tiff?" I snort, the involuntary unattractive kind. Tequila burns inside my nostrils. "Jesus. Give me some room to puke all over myself. On second thought, stand real close."

"Come on, *Bekant.*"

"Don't IKEA-word me!"

His face hardens. "How many times do I have to apologize?"

"How long do you plan to live?"

I deliver the words with a ruthlessness that surprises even me. In truth, I am fighting with the only weapon I have. Brett's kryptonite is NGS (Nice Guy Syndrome), and I've gone Lex Luthor on him since the breakup. He detests not being perceived as nice. It drives him crazy the way some people can't stand Lacto-ovo vegetarians or people who say "next on line" instead of "next in line." (If you're not literally standing on a line, you're in line. Deal with it.) Brett can get the worst service in a restaurant imaginable— ignored, passed off to different waiters, served the wrong entrée with a strand of hair in his soup. Sure, he'll complain, but it's the kind of "aw-shucks" complaining that ends up with him apologizing and shaking everybody's hand.

He doesn't want the stink of our breakup on his skin. He doesn't want to see the way my wounded eyes have turned to smoldering anger. And he sure as hell doesn't want to hear any more spiteful questions about their sex life. Is it Olympic-caliber fornication with harnesses and a pommel horse? Is it a morning romp

21

without a hint of bad breath? Is it shower sex that actually works?

Oh yeah, I go there. Way too often.

"It just happened," he mutters. Once again, NGS has taken the fight out of him.

"'It just happened'? That's what guys say who aren't clever enough to lie or honest enough to tell the truth."

I stop. In fairness, I would rip off his clothes and make love to him on the sidewalk right now if he said "Tiff" was the biggest mistake of his life. Maybe that is the worst part—still wanting him so badly. It is awful discovering new worsts every day.

"I don't mean us. I mean we," he begins again. "Tiff and I. Tiffany and I. We are. We're … pregnant."

I can't hear my own breathing because I'm not breathing. I can't feel my heart beating because it probably stopped. It's just taking my brain a few moments to come to terms with my sudden, tragic death. The words came out of his mouth with the monotone you'd expect from someone reciting a predictable celebrity headline on Twitter: "Kim Kardashian Posts Picture of Boobs." "Kim Kardashian Posts Second Picture of Boobs."

You don't shatter a life together and start a new family in fourteen weeks and five days. With a woman twelve years older than you. Do you? Apparently, yes. Apparently if you're Brett Bergin, you're screwing more than IKEA furniture.

I can't be here in front of a bar without drinking. I can't be here in front of Brett without kissing him. I need to do something. I imagine delivering a devastating line and storming off like the wronged woman in a movie about a wronged woman who gets a better guy, better career, and better apartment by the closing credits. Instead of a clever retort, I yell the only thing that comes to mind.

"Asshägen!"

4
Smooth Vibrations

It feels good to storm away from Brett—even if the only thing waiting for me at the Humanities Department is Professor Hinks with his pants buckled. Fingers crossed. The distance is too far to maintain my pace as a disgruntled power-walker, but if Brett decides to chase me, I want him to work for it. He won't. Not a chance. But I can't help looking over my shoulder.

Damn.

Slippery brick walkways wind past trees with rainwater-stained bark and colonial buildings that evoke the Ivory Tower alchemy of a liberal arts education. White columns and stone steps. Brick buildings and bell towers. The campus of Haverton makes it easy to imagine tweed-jacketed professors smoking pipes and talking with intellectually-engaged students about philosophy, politics, and poetry. The interior of these buildings tells a different story, though. Missing paper towel dispensers in Humanities. Buckets for the leaking ceilings in Music. Mold in the Pequot and Gallaudet dormitories. And food poisoning that hospitalized three students just last week.

Beautiful on the outside, rotten on the inside. Like academia itself. Like my relationship with Brett.

I am not thinking about the pregnancy, about the real human being that will be created because Brett left me for Tiffany. How can I? It's easier to imagine receiving a MacArthur genius grant or an ambassadorship to Italy. No, I'm thinking about what I always think about after a close encounter of the Brett kind. Our life together. Though I have no desire to go there, I'm thinking about the beginning, about the first time.

It started the way so many fairytales do: with a vibrator and twelve helium balloons.

•••

Three summers ago, I found myself in charge of assembling a gift basket for a bride-to-be I didn't know and organizing a bachelorette party I wasn't invited to. My friend from home, Stacey, was maid of honor for a gal pal she hadn't seen in years and who, from all accounts, was so uptight she couldn't draw a map to her own vagina without asking for directions. Stacey wasn't much better, so orchestrating a bachelorette party terrified her. Enter Anastasia Shaw—fearless caller of male strip clubs and explorer of bargain bin items at Emporium Erotica. For the gift basket, I had been instructed to get something fun.

"Like a fireman calendar or a power tool."

"To do what with?" I asked, horrified but intrigued.

"Like I don't know. Something funny," Stacey replied. She was using the word "like" ten times a minute back then, and any talk of sex turned her fifty shades of red.

Naturally, I purchased a nine-inch purple vibrator and a dozen helium-filled pink pussies. Each pink pussy balloon was supposed to resemble a cat's head with two small ears on top and black whiskers radiating from a triangular nose in the center. It was artistry only a third grader could admire. Of course, I should have ditched the party favors for matching pink hats and a protest march, but Stacey was counting on something porny.

I tied the balloons to a picnic basket on the passenger seat of my 2004 sea-foam green Toyota Corolla—a hand-me-down from my mother that looked as stylish as it sounds. Inside the basket, I put the Pussycat Turbo 2000 alongside an eggplant, some bananas, and a card that read: "A picnic any pussy can enjoy." Stacey would tear it up, of course, but I wanted to see her face when she did.

The sunny June afternoon made the air heavy and hot. The car's air conditioner hadn't worked in years, so if I didn't want my pink pussies to float away, I could only open the windows a crack. I was wearing a mustard yellow sundress that stopped above my knees and brown ankle-strapped heels that boosted me to roughly 5'7. The dress complemented my green eyes and tan skin, which has always gotten me mistaken for Hispanic or Italian. It was one of the few times I thought I looked good. Sexy, even. I placed the Pussycat Turbo 2000 on my lap and fumbled with its base to insert the batteries. I had never owned a sex toy at that point, so this was new terrain for me.

Sitting in a parking lot in a car filled with pink pussy balloons and holding a purple vibrator the size of a hothouse cucumber can raise a lot of questions about your life. Why am I here? How did I become the go-to person for sex toys and vegetables? And in case I never get an academic job, is Emporium Erotica hiring?

Suddenly, the Pussycat Turbo 2000 roared to life with buzzing fury. I dropped it as if stung by a wasp, and it dove onto my lap.

"Jesus!"

I grabbed it but couldn't find an off-switch. The sticky latex contraption gave a high-pitched whine. There was only one button on the bottom. I pushed it, but the speed increased from fast to supersonic. I tried wringing it, turning it over in my hands, shaking it. Nothing worked. I tossed the Pussycat Turbo 2000 on the passenger seat and started the car. I needed to hurry. Stacey was expecting the gift basket almost fifteen minutes ago.

The quickness of the expressway agitated the balloons, and when I changed lanes, the Pussycat Turbo 2000 sprung to the floor beneath my feet. It buzzed and flopped around angrily. There wasn't anything I could do. I needed both hands on the wheel for now. Just until the exit.

As I eased onto the off-ramp, the sharp curve made everything in the passenger seat shift again. Pink balloons bonked against my arms and face. The basket fell to the floor, and I pressed hard on the break. The car barely slowed. I tried again, but something was wrong. The Pussycat Turbo 2000 was directly beneath the pedal. I looked down and pumped the break with more force, hoping to dislodge the vibrator.

That was when I hit the car in front of me.

I thought the airbags had deployed, but it was just several pink pussies pressing against my face and upper body. I pushed them aside as best I could.

"Bastard!" I yelled, as if a good scolding would teach the Pussycat Turbo 2000 a lesson.

A knock on the window startled me. I looked up. The man's face glowed in the white sunlight, his brow furrowed with concern. For me.

"Are you okay?" he asked without a hint of anger.

I nodded. Then I realized that a purple vibrator was sputtering at my feet. I swatted away a balloon and got out of the car with as much dignity as a person caught with a basket full of Emporium Erotica could muster.

I blathered apologizes, more humiliated than sorry, more shaken from his good looks than the accident. I didn't know what else to say. *The damage was minor. I couldn't have been going more than ten miles an hour. Nothing to worry about.* But he was the one who said all these things. I was barely listening. I was taking him in. The lightning bolt scar beneath his square chin. The broad shoulders and glistening, ocean-blue eyes. Hair resembling a sandy beach. He said something about working at a body shop nearby, his dad's place. He'd be happy to take care of my car.

"No charge," he added.

We were still standing by my Corolla, and in truth, I hadn't even looked at the damage. I couldn't take my eyes off him.

"We're running a special this week," he continued. "Free auto repair for the first person who hits me."

"Sounds like a winning business plan," I said. I wanted to feel charming and witty.

"I'm Brett. Brett Bergin."

"Seriously? That's a real name?"

"My parents wanted Clark Kent, but it was taken."

I couldn't believe it. I was flirting. We were flirting. With each other—even after I smashed into him, even with the Pussycat Turbo 2000 buzzing inside my car.

"With a name like that, you must have some superpowers," I said, trying not to slouch or appear too eager. "Apart from finding clients for your dad."

"Nope," he said with a toothy smile. "That's about it."

I laughed. All I wanted in that moment was to keep the conversation going, to convince myself that he really wanted to see me again, to drive recklessly for the rest of my life.

"Brett Bergin," I said. "I think that would be a good name for a porn star."

He glanced inside my car. "Of course you do."

•••

Hinks leans against the window frame in his office. Fully clothed. He holds a file in his hands and wears the same forest green shirt, black jeans, and, I presume, red silk underwear. He has a thin, wiry frame, and his curly, salt-and-pepper hair resembles rows of tiny springs. His office has been restored to its pre-masturbatory neatness. Papers stacked on the desk. Phone in its cradle. A stapler next to the "Vegetarians Party Till the Cows Come Home" coffee mug.

"Thanks for coming," he says with the sincerity of someone who knows I had no choice. Small, silver-rimmed reading glasses make his nose appear pinched and swollen. He wasn't wearing them this morning, not that I was focused on his eyewear.

"I'd like you to find out the name of the man who died in the office. Here is a list of faculty and staff who retired within the last fifteen years or so. I've crossed out people I know. I think this would be a good place to start."

He hands me the file before sitting down and turning his attention to a student paper. He stares at it with an intensity that has everything to do with getting me out of the office. I know this because student prose does not read like sexting or a WikiLeaks document. It gives everyone the same expression of bemused pain and utter defeat—a kind of indigestion caused by the realization of how little your students have been paying attention.

I watch him for a few moments without moving. Sure, I am grateful both hands are on top of the desk, but I am pissed that he hasn't apologized and that he wants to christen me the Miss Marple of the Humanities Department. I haven't been asked to sit, so I'm still standing in a buttoned-up winter coat that gives my body the shape of a wine barrel. Sweat beads on my forehead, and a sticky dampness forms in my armpits.

"Why me?" I blurt out.

He lifts his head slightly. "You still work at the morgue, right? I figured you could check his name against this list without much trouble. If he's one of us, even from a long time ago, I'd like to take care of the arrangements, to hold some kind of a service."

His sincerity takes me back to classroom Hinks, to the Hinks I know and respect. To the Hinks before this morning.

"We all deserve a proper goodbye," he adds before returning to the paper.

I turn around but don't take more than a few steps before he calls out.

"One more thing—"

Here it comes. The muttered apology. The "let's-keep-this-between-us" plea. The "I've-always-been-a-hands-on-guy" joke.

"Devon University called. Your preliminary application impressed them. They want to bring you to campus for an interview," he says with a genuine smile, with genuine pleasure that one of the department's students has found a moment of success on the job market.

My legs turn to Jell-O, and my skin must go a shade of Cherry Lemonade or Berry Blue because Hinks looks worried.

"Of course," he adds quickly. "I told them that you're one of our best. That they can do no better."

I mutter some kind of thanks before finding the strength to walk again. I pick up speed with each step as I move down the hall. He is letting me know that he won't use this morning against me—provided I don't go to Human Resources or start trending hashtags like #handyhinks or #hinkykinky. He is reminding me of the power he has over my future. Message received.

But that is not why I'm going to vomit. For the second time today, I rush down four flights of stairs and into the stone courtyard. I manage to get outside without losing the flimsy contents of my stomach.

"I'm screwed," I mutter aloud.

This is probably as good a time as any to tell you that I started pretending to be Native American five months ago to get a job.

And it seems to be working.

5
Lightfeather

It started the way most great ideas start. In a bar. On the third round of bocce ball.

That day, Yumi played with the accuracy of an assassin, and nothing made her happier than knocking Doug's balls as far away from the pallino as possible. Nothing made Doug happier than watching her ass while she did it. Black tights clung to the curves of her legs, and she wore a tight, "I don't do math" T-shirt. Purple lipstick and fingernail polish matched the streaks in her hair. *My fall color,* she had explained earlier that day even though it was still August.

"We're screwed," Doug proclaimed, gesturing toward me. He was so ordinary looking that you would expect him to be the spokesperson for white bread or an extra in a Judd Apatow movie. "Universities can't hire us. Too much whiteness."

Kavita spat up some beer with a laugh. The floral pattern of her beige dress reminded me of Victorian upholstery. Like Doug and I, she had just come from teaching her first class of the semester.

"I'm serious," he continued, moving to the head of the court. Even in khaki pants and a white dress shirt, his bulky body made him look more jock than professor-in-training. He picked up a ball and tossed it underhanded, putting it on a collision course with one of Yumi's. They connected with a loud "smack."

"Poor disenfranchised white people," Kavita said. "Centuries of colonial exploitation have left you with nothing."

"Damn straight."

"What if I sent two applications to each job? One as me and one as a Native American version of me?" I blurted. The questions spilled out of my mouth as if I had already formulated a plan, but the idea hadn't occurred to me until that moment.

Everyone was silent.

Doug sipped his beer. Yumi picked up a ball. And Mel Tormé crooned "No Moon at All" through the jukebox.

"As a middle finger to the system," I added.

"Well, you'll need to change your name," Doug said while Kavita sidled next to him. "What's your middle name?"

"Landers." I took a sip. The beer tasted warm and flat in my mouth.

"Sounds like an office supply company."

"My family thanks you."

"How about something with an indigenous flair?" he asked. "Like 'Gentle Breeze' or 'Bubbling Brook.'"

"W—T—F?" Kavita swatted Doug's shoulder. "Can you be more racist? She's not an air freshener."

Yumi downed the rest of her drink. "I'm thinking 'Bear That Growls.'"

Doug nodded with approval, and the plan evolved from there. If Native American Ana could get some job interviews while Non-Native American Ana could not, I would write an anonymous editorial for *The Chronicle of Higher Education* about the fact that our universities would be better served if we hired African Americans and Native Americans to teach Shakespeare and the Ana Shaws of the world to teach ethnic literature. If we did not anchor our efforts to diversify faculty with identity politics. If we sent a message that real diversity is about challenging our own assumptions about difference, not reaffirming them.

I continued to wax poetic for a few more rounds of bocce and beer before deciding to replace "Landers" with "Lightfeather." I had already used my middle initial in a publication, so it would be easy to make the shift. I could even change my name on a recent journal acceptance to "Ana Lightfeather Shaw."

Later that night, buzzed with beer and my own sense of brilliance, I told Brett. He worked days, which usually gave us a couple of hours together between the end of his shift at the warehouse and the start of mine at the morgue, but I had lost track of time at Tequila Mockingbird. Concocting a new identity will do that to you.

Brett sat at the edge of our bed on the green-and-white checkered comforter. Like all of our furniture, it came from IKEA. He called our bedroom set the "Cozy Cucumber" with its white, wall-mounted shelves, black reading lamps, and ivy-colored dresser. I was drying my hair with a dark green *vågsjön* towel when I stepped out of the bathroom. I wore only a black lacy bra and matching Hanky Panky panties. I was feeling feisty. I wanted to turn him on. I wanted him to think about my body when I was gone.

Of course, the more I thought about him thinking about me, the less I cared about Lightfeather. The more I wanted to do some deep-sea fishing in his pants.

"You're going to do what?" he asked.

"I'm going to pretend to be Native American." I moved in front of him, placing my hands on his shoulders and easing my knee between his legs. Maybe I could be late for work. "To make a point."

"A point about what?"

I wanted him with an urgency I hadn't felt in months. It was odd how the routines of life dulled desire—dirty dishes and unpaid bills, leftovers and late shifts. But now I wanted him to grab me by the waist and pull me on top of him. I wanted him to reach for my breasts. I wanted to see the bulge of his jeans stiffen.

He put his sandpaper fingers on my hips, but instead of sliding them inside my panties, he gently pushed me back and stood up. He was a good six inches taller, so I always found myself eye-level with his lightning-bolt scar. Keeping an arm's length between us, he stared at my face, as if my nearly naked body wasn't right in front of him for the taking.

"I don't understand you."

"Ditto." My voice was tight, pissed that didn't lust for me the way I did for him at the moment.

"It feels wrong."

"Jesus—"

"You've practiced some of your lectures on me," he pleads. "You talk about the brutality of that history all the time. Stolen lands. Relocation."

It was amazing how quickly my body temperature went from horn-dog hot to freezer-burn cold. I wrapped the towel around myself.

"What do you care? It's not like you're giving TED talks on race at IKEA."

The sting of my words made his eyes narrow.

"I can be a good role model for my students as Lightfeather," I continued. "I can still teach and inspire them."

With one long stride, Brett stepped over to the dresser and surveyed my array of trinkets on top. He grabbed the Unisphere from the 1964 World's Fair in New York.

"Tell me about this," he said, holding it up and glancing at the others. "Or any of these."

I didn't know if it was dumb luck on his part or if he had figured it out somehow. You see the World's Fair was my first. The first thing I stole for myself. The first time I really became a thief.

•••

"Stand up straight," my mother hissed as we stood at the Macy's perfume counter. "You look like a depressed crash test dummy."

"Is there any other kind?"

Shopping with Nadya Shaw had become the unofficial punishment for all of my shortcomings as a child—smart-aleck remarks, a Neanderthal posture, love of television. In short, it was the punishment for being me instead of the daughter she had hoped for.

Even at ten years old, I understood the curse of having a beautiful mother—the kind that turned heads and fit into any dress, the kind accustomed to male attention, the kind that moved through life expecting others to clean up her messes. I had seen enough of Mom's childhood pictures to know I would be a monumental disappointment. Charming smiles and movie-star poses, intriguing backdrops and sunny days. Mine catalogued skinned knees, tearful fits, and a dirt-smeared face. She used to joke that the hospital gave her the wrong baby in the exact way and with the exact tone you'd expect from someone who wasn't kidding.

No, I was the shorter, thicker, clumsier version of Nadya Shaw. I was my father's daughter. Jeff wandered through life with a half-puzzled look on his face, as if he was buying time until Nadya brought home a younger, hotter husband. Not that my father was ugly. He was just average—average height, average receding hairline, average potbelly—but he loved me in a way my mother couldn't. He loved me with the scruffy instincts of a kindred spirit. From him I learned to appreciate our uncanny ability to be fifteen minutes late to everything. Our color-blind fashion sense. Our visceral hatred of shopping.

The fact that these things drove my mother crazy just made the pudding sweeter, as he liked to say. Dad took pride in his ability to make up folksy expressions and to give me odd nicknames.

"Is there any other kind?" I repeated.

Nadya pulled back my shoulders with a yank and eyed the perfume counter lined with bottles in the shape of octagons, rectangles, and squares. Bottles with ribbons and diamond caps. Bottles colored pink, yellow, green, and purple. The assault of smells was suffocating.

"Perfume is made from whale poop," I added, happy to share my encyclopedic knowledge of all things annoying.

"With a mouth like that, you'll end up in a brothel."

"What's a brothel?"

My mother asked to try another scent. Over a dozen boxes were lined up on the countertop when the saleswoman stepped away to help another customer.

She reminded me of a deflated tire, sagging with each step.

"Her back is turned," my mother said in a low voice, her breath warm against my ear.

I had been wearing the camouflage backpack Dad gave me for my birthday. I wouldn't go anywhere without it, much to my mother's horror. She got her revenge by dressing me like a doll from American Girl. The contrast between my pink flare dress and military backpack made me look as if I suffered from a multiple personality disorder.

I hadn't noticed that she unzipped it. Even after I felt the weight of the perfume drop into the bag, I didn't know what she was doing. I just found myself being ushered away from the counter. We moved steadily toward the exit. My mother's green dress and peacock-patterned scarf flowed with each step. I plodded after her, trying to keep up.

Outside, the humid air hugged my body, and the sunlight made my eyes squint. I climbed into the backseat. Silent. I watched the other parked cars as we drove through the outdoor lot of the mall. Sun glistening off windshields and shiny metal surfaces. Mothers and daughters loading bags into trunks. We eased onto a broad four-lane street. With the windows down, the summer heat rushed inside and whipped against my face. Nadya didn't believe in air conditioning the way some people didn't believe in diet sodas or frozen yogurt.

"Why did you take the perfume, Mom?"

Her slender fingers tightened on the steering wheel, and she looked at me in the rear-view mirror, eyes hidden behind her aviator sunglasses with gold trim.

"It didn't feel like something I should pay for."

"Isn't that stealing?"

"It isn't stealing if you're owed something and there's no other way to collect."

I thought for a moment. "Like when Brendan Hunter ate my ice cream?"

Brendan Hunter was the boy in fourth grade who really knew how to burn my coffee beans (a vintage Dad-ism). He put boogers on my desk. He made pig sounds in the cafeteria. And at the school fair, he shoved my ice cream cone into his mouth after I specifically asked him to hold it for two seconds while I tied my shoe.

"In a way," my mother said with a nod. "He ate your ice cream, and you ended up without a dessert."

"Because you wouldn't buy me another one."

"Anastasia," she replied with a sigh, as if talking to me was a torment even the ancient Greeks couldn't fathom.

She pulled onto a street of one-story suburban houses with worn vinyl siding. She stopped the car and turned partway around, taking off her glasses before she spoke. Her green eyes were more emerald than mine, and freckles dotted her golden brown skin. I often wondered what my life would have been like if she had a kindness that matched her beauty.

"Everything costs, but someday ... someday you're going to realize that the price you paid was higher than you thought. You'll want to balance what you lost with what you have, and you'll come up short." She looked at the camouflaged backpack concealing the perfume. "That's something. At least for me it is."

She retreated, tortoise-like, behind her sunglasses, and started the car. "You'll be a woman one day. You'll see what I mean."

This was the start of Shopping Saturdays with Nadya Shaw. She bought some things and took others. At times, I played decoy—Misbehaving Brat, Hypersensitive Crier, or everyone's favorite, the Screamer. At times, I carried the goods in pockets, shopping bags, underpants, or socks. It was always small stuff. A tie from Barneys for Dad. A layered silver necklace from Anthropologie. A stainless steel garlic press from Williams and Sonoma. Nadya did have a few rules, though. Nothing from locally owned shops and garage sales. Nothing cheaper than ten dollars or more expensive than three hundred. And never from friends and family.

I tried to think of us as the Bonnie and Clyde of Long Island with guns blazing and cigars puffing. In truth, I was just a useless accessory like footed pajamas or nipple warmers. Being nothing more than a sidekick reminded me of the way I had always felt around my mother. Let's be honest. You can make a Batman movie without Robin, not the other way around. Without Batman, Robin is just a distant relative in green tights whom everyone in the family describes as "eccentric."

When Nadya died, I was sixteen. The Stage Four pancreatic cancer that ravaged her body only announced itself seven weeks before it took her. Just knowing about the disease broke whatever dam had been holding it back. Almost overnight, she had trouble getting out of bed. She lost weight in a way I didn't think possible, skin hanging like laundry from her clothesline bones. She had no strength, no appetite, no energy for anything outside herself. She preferred the darkness of closed window shades and dim lights. She didn't want anyone seeing her that way. Including me. We turned away neighbors and friends. She insisted that my father do everything for her. He gave her baths and wiped her ass. He washed sweat-stained sheets and cleaned up vomit. He didn't recoil at the stench of illness, the way I did. I tried to avoid the stomach acids on her breath and the stinging smell of urine in the room. I loved her. I needed her. But I couldn't watch her waste way.

She died on a Wednesday morning while I was learning about trans fats in my tenth grade nutrition class. By the time I came home, she was gone. The police and coroner had come and gone. The funeral parlor had begun readying her body for cremation. (She had made the arrangements herself, knowing Dad couldn't.) The vast infrastructure of the death industry had erased her in a way I resented. It took her body, the one thing I wanted to see and to touch one more time. It tried to make everything clean and orderly. Instead, it left the empty husk of my father and a shell-shocked daughter.

I don't remember walking out of the house that afternoon and driving my mother's sea-foam Toyota to the train station. I don't remember the train ride, the transfer at Jamaica Station, or the subway ride to Chinatown. But I must have done all these things, and without attracting attention. I only became aware of my body in a gift shop like a dozen other gift shops on

Mott Street. Shoulder-to-shoulder crowds moving through the streets. Chinese men chain-smoking to mask the miasma of freshly killed fish, garbage cans, sewers, vegetables, perfumes, and roasting cashews from street vendors. In my hand, I held a replica of the Unisphere from the 1964 New York World's Fair. The coolness of the silver globe felt like a damp rag on my fevered forehead. I slipped it into my purse and stepped back into the current of bodies on the sidewalk.

6
Moondude

Just like the night I grabbed the Unisphere from Brett and stormed out of the apartment, I am at the Haverton County Morgue. Again. If you don't notice the sign for the Office of the Chief Medical Examiner, you might mistake the building for the DMV—without the lines and the eyecharts. It is a sterile, colorless place with furniture that must have been discarded from a public high school. Cubicles with bulky wooden desks. Black pushbutton phones with no volume control. And a wall clock that clicks every minute. Here I process cremation fee waiver forms. I make sure death certificates get signed and filed with the Registrar of Vital Statistics. I fulfill release requests for autopsy reports. In short, this is where I do all the paperwork you need to be considered officially dead.

You're welcome.

The gray cubicles in the main office are empty at this time of night, but I still use my assigned desk—the one I share with Sherilynn. I've never met Sherilynn. She works days, but her name makes me picture a Paula Deen type with curly white hair and a cheerfulness not found elsewhere in nature. She has a Georgia accent peppered with "y'alls" and other Southernisms, and if we ever met, she'd offer me biscuits that would launch my cholesterol into the stratosphere. I'm not sure what time Sherilynn gets in. I have never seen her on my way out at six in the morning. She leaves nothing personal on the desk, no photographs or birthday cards or trinkets of any kind. Lucky for her, I guess. The only communication between us comes in the form of a paper-clipped stack of "TO DO" items.

Tonight, I have to prepare several insurance requests and finalize paperwork for the Golden Pastures Funeral Home. I also need to transcribe an autopsy report. Each audio transcription takes nearly two hours. It is without a doubt the most time-consuming part of the job, and I suspect Sherilynn leaves all of them for me. Bless her heart. At least Dr. McKelvey, the Chief Medical Examiner, tries to make them interesting. I've never met him either, but he peppers random facts about death throughout the reports. After three years of Sundays through Thursdays between 10 p.m. and 6 a.m. and hundreds of autopsy transcriptions, I can safely say I've become the Alex Trebek of death trivia.

Fun fact: Male corpses often get erections—since men apparently expect to get lucky in the afterlife.

Fun fact: More people die from dance parties than skydiving—which still doesn't make me feel better about missing my senior prom.

Fun fact: The human heart weighs less than a pound.

The last one still irks me. I had never thought about the heart weighing anything at all until mine went from helium light to shot-put heavy after Brett left. That's why I refuse to believe it weighs no more than a clenched fist.

I peel off my arctic parka, leave my iPod on the desk, and walk to the breakroom. I will need a coffee-induced miracle to stay awake through this shift. On the way, I realize that there is no paperwork on my desk for the dead man from the Humanities Department. I should leave it alone, of course. I should get my coffee and get to work. Instead, I take the elevator to the basement.

To tell you the truth, I thought morgues would be a lot creepier when I first started working here. Flickering fluorescent lights. Green walls. Zombies. Instead, the basement of the Haverton County Morgue resembles a hospital. Brightly lit with shiny floors. Nose twitching disinfectant. And a temperature five-to-seven degrees south of comfortable. At one end of the building is the underground loading dock for the delivery and removal of bodies. The other end has a reception desk where my manager, Vernon P. Smalls, deals with overnight intake.

Unlike the nondescript cubicles upstairs, Vernon's desk looks like someone vomited up a Grateful Dead gift shop. Bumper stickers crisscross the top with images of skulls and tie-dyed Volkswagen RVs. A sign reads "When in doubt, smoke out," and the broken alarm clock, painted purple and yellow, stays perpetually at 4:20. Even his computer has a Grateful Dead screensaver with the profile of a skull wearing a Native American headdress.

In an uncharacteristic stroke of good luck, Vernon isn't at his desk, so I can slip into the storage room to look through the personal effects of recent arrivals. The space feels stuffy and cramped from the ceiling-to-floor shelves crowded with cardboard boxes. "John Doe #5, Haverton University" is stacked on top of two other boxes by the door. It has the yellow sticker for new arrivals, which means the contents have not been catalogued yet. I open the box to find his rust-colored fedora, powder blue shirt, and pinstriped suit. There is a blue tie and white handkerchief. There are brown socks and bagged shoes. Gold cufflinks. But no wallet. Just a keychain with several keys, which I slip into my pocket.

I try on the fedora. It feels snug and soft against my brow.

As I hurry down the hallway, I enter uncharted territory. Vernon is still MIA but not for long. If he finds me snooping around the Body Storage Units, he will be pissed enough to toss some passive-aggressive "Hey, man" and "Uncool, dude" expressions my way.

I pass the autopsy bay. Through the observation window, you can see stainless steel tables and sinks with the kind of water hoses used to clean gutted fish at seafood retailers. There are trays with bone saws, scalpels, and rib shears. Scales hang overhead for weighing internal organs, and hand-operated lights, similar to those found in a dentist's office, perch hawk-like as if frozen in mid-flight.

The Body Storage Units are at the end of the corridor in the rear of the building. Unit 1 holds examined, identified, and soon-to-be claimed bodies. Unit 2 is the creepiest place here. It's for the unclaimed or unidentified. Sometimes next of kin cannot be reached or cannot afford funerals or cremation. Sometimes no record exists to identify a person. But even in death, the clock is ticking. Once a year, the morgue transports these bodies to a mass grave to make space for another batch of the abandoned and erased.

I enter BSU #2. New arrivals get stored here first, so this is where John Doe #5 should be. There are fourteen stainless steel lockers. Each one has a number and corresponding chart in wall mounts by the door. I grab Number Five's chart, but it does not have any of the standard paperwork. No intake form. No preliminary findings about cause of death. No formal request for an autopsy.

It is as if John Doe isn't here.

Before common sense kicks in, I step over to Storage Locker Five and grab the handle. This is exactly what stupid white people do in horror movies, I remind myself. They open closet doors or check out basements or have sex at Camp Crystal Lake. It is not like Doe has a driver's license or social security card in there. What do I hope to learn? Why this sudden compulsion to see him, to make sure he is here?

I tighten my grip on the cold, smooth surface and turn the handle.

The door swings open, and I find myself staring at a pair of feet. The rest of the body is covered by a sheet, but not his feet. Sprouts of white hair cling to his shins and above his ankles. The toe tag reads "John Doe #5."

I'm not sure what I was expecting—Jimmy Hoffa, David Blaine, the formula for New Coke? Anything but uncovered feet with bloodless, purple-white skin, shriveled toes, and callused heels.

I take a deep breath before placing the chart by the toe tag. I should go, I know. Doe's body is obviously here, but I've come this far. I want to see him. I need to. I take hold of the tray's handle and steady myself.

I pull. It doesn't budge, so I pull again, harder this time. The stainless steel table rockets forward before stopping with a jerk. The entire locker shakes, and Doe's right arm flops out from beneath the sheet. It has the purple-blue hue of a starfish, and it dangles over the edge.

"Crap!"

Now what? Sure, I've seen plenty of bodies over the years. In the autopsy bay. On gurneys in the hallway outside the Body Storage Units. But I've never touched one. I've never felt dead flesh against my fingers. I position my hands beneath his elbow and wrist. Before touching him, I'll count to three and lift.

One.

Two.

Fuck it.

Doe's arm is cold and dense. It has the rubbery texture of grilled octopus and the stiffness of a saddle. After lifting it, I struggle to get his arm back on the tray. It now hovers at a forty-five degree angle. I give it a strong, steady push until the arm clunks loudly against the metal. The sound echoes in the room.

As I reach for the sheet, I notice a small bruise above the crook of his elbow. The circular brown tissue radiates from a tiny circle in the middle.

"Dude!"

The chart falls to the floor with a loud "smack." The gravelly voice comes from behind me, not Doe, but it takes me a moment to be sure. I turn around to the shapeless tie-dye T-shirt, acid-washed jeans, and Birkenstocks of Vernon P. Smalls.

"Dammit, Vernon!"

He cringes at the sound of his first name. That's my revenge for the near heart attack. Vernon hates his name with the heat of a burning bong, so he insists that everyone call him "Moondude." On my first day, I assured him that was never going to happen: *"It's not personal. There are some words in the English language I've vowed never to say like 'Frappuccino' and 'woke,'" I explained. "'Moondude' just happens to be one of them."*

He claims "Moondude" captures his love of astronomy and hip mellow nature. I call it a thinly veiled cry for help. I figure Vernon is the kind of guy who gave himself a nickname because he never had many friends and never did anything to earn one. Not that I can blame him. With a handle like Vernon P. Smalls, I'd be looking for a life raft off that sinking ship. It's too easy to imagine the years of high school humiliation from jocks, cool girls, and nerds needing an edge over somebody. Maybe because of that, Vernon dresses like someone in the witness protection program—a thirty-eight-year-old guy disguised as a 1960s stoner cliché. Maybe he is in the witness protection program. I can't imagine a better place to hide.

So what's my excuse? At twenty-nine, I've descended to a ring of hell known as Moondude's Assistant.

"Tell me this is not some sick Edgar Allan Poe sex thing," Vernon continues with the mellow intensity of the recently baked. He shuffles over to the lockers and picks up the chart. "This a 'No Necrophilia Zone.' Okay, man? I mean, person."

(As part of the Haverton County Morgue's mandatory online sensitivity training, Vernon has been trying to use more gender-neutral words.)

"Gross," I mutter.

He grabs the handle of the tray.

"Did you notice that mark on his arm?" I ask.

Vernon looks at me with bloodshot eyes. All of a sudden, I remember I'm wearing John Doe's fedora. I hope he doesn't recognize it from the property room.

"Why the hell would I look at his arm? I'm not the coroner."

I grab the chart from him. "There is no paperwork on Number Five."

"So?"

"There is no intake form. Nothing to note that puncture wound. It could have come from a needle."

"You have no business being down here."

Vernon closes the storage locker and turns to me once again. His ragdoll limbs and Kenny G hair make me think of the Scarecrow from *The Wizard of Oz*, and I have to fend off a smile. He must sense that I am not taking him seriously, so he crosses his arms. The gesture only makes him look more like the Scarecrow.

"I was just checking …" I begin.

"To see if he wanted a blanket and some peanuts?"

"I'm not a flight attendant, Vernon."

"Exactly, person. We could get in big trouble."

He is right of course. I haven't thought about what might happen to him if I get caught opening storage lockers and lifting personal items off the dead. I've never considered the fact that Vernon doesn't just need this job the way I do. He wants it.

"I'm sorry." I glance over at the storage unit. "I'm … I'm the one who found him today," I continue. "I just need to know who he is. I need to know if that mark has anything to do with his death."

I am surprised by my honesty, by this desire to know his name and his story. Maybe I just want to convince myself that I won't end up an academic relic one day, forgotten and alone. That I won't end up "Jane Doe #5."

Vernon's posture loosens, and his arms fall to his sides. The tie-dye swirl on his shirt resembles a hurricane with the eye over his abdomen. "Dude, we can start an intake form, and I can find out if his fingerprints have been entered into the system."

"Really?"

"Yeah," he replies. "You just have to ask."

I hesitate. "Didn't I just do that?"

"You know what I mean."

A big smile shows his crooked, coffee-stained front teeth, and I know exactly what he means. For a moment, I consider letting him go for one of his signature kamikaze hugs that come in too fast and linger too long—but not long enough to mandate another sensitivity training. Instead, I swallow what is left of my Lilliputian-sized pride and clear my throat.

"Can you please check for me ... Moondude?"

"You see? That wasn't so hard."

7
Beethoven's Fifth

I didn't mean to sleep with a student. Not that I hadn't thought about it, especially since Brett left. Not that sleeping with someone could happen by accident like getting pink eye or watching a Keanu Reeves movie on television. Technically, he wasn't a student. Not *my* student. Not two months ago when I saw him at Tequila Mockinbird. I recognized him right away: the crooked smile, the chestnut hair stunted by a bad crewcut, the lean swimmer's limbs. The only thing missing was the white jacket and the nametag he wore while serving drinks at Tiffany Riggs's "soiree." Flannigan, the Flann Man. He sat at the bar sipping a frothy beer that matched his amber eyes. Blue jeans and a black collared shirt hung loosely on his body as if one size too big, and the mahogany countertop glistened with fragments of yellow light from overhead. The voice of Madeleine Peyroux swirled above his head like cigarette smoke.

I walked up to the empty stool next to him as if we had been planning to meet. I had just come from the department's holiday party on campus—an unbearable display of yuletide cheer and small talk—and if I hadn't had two glasses of cheap red wine sloshing in my empty stomach, I would have run away. The Flann Man had seen me drink enough to impress the Irish mob. He had gotten a glimpse of my final days with Brett. And he probably witnessed my theft of a wooden elephant.

"Hey," I squeaked out before realizing I had no idea what to say.

The Flann Man looked at me as if I were soliciting donations for charity.

"We met at Professor Riggs's party. I'm—"

"Oh, yeah …" He nodded, running his finger through the beaded moisture on his glass. "Rachel, right?"

"Ana … Ana Banana," I corrected as if everyone called me that.

I sat down next to him, and for the better part of an hour, I flirted with the Flann Man. It was the first time I seriously considered sleeping with someone since Brett left six weeks and three days earlier. In truth, Brett might as well have pulled up a barstool. I couldn't stop thinking about what he was doing at that moment, what he would say if he were here, what he would think of me and the Flann Man. Every time Brett interjected something in my head, I tried to power-flirt my way through it.

"He probably wears a MAGA hat during sex."

A coquettish laugh.

"Are you sure he's not a minor?"

A quick touch of his forearm.

"Gay?"

The lean-in whisper.

I had seen enough romantic comedies to be an understudy for Jennifer Anniston, so I could keep up the performance. I wasn't going to let Brett's ghost ruin my night with this hot, young, and, as it turned out, nice guy—the kind of nice-guy who remembered birthdays and cared about the environment.

The bartender interrupted with a pair of menus. Without looking, I ordered a burger with garlic cheesy fries. The Flann Man waved him off.

"Not hungry?"

"I don't eat that stuff," he replied the same way I would have if he had ordered a beet salad or a plate of raw vegetables.

"Are you vegetarian?" I asked. *Please, God. No.* I couldn't take another disappointment.

"Not exactly. I'm just vegan curious."

"Vegan curious?"

"Yep."

"I didn't know that was a thing."

"It is," he replied with the seriousness of a funeral director. As the Flann Man started to explain, I couldn't listen. The moment was slipping away. If he kept talking about the merits of vegetables and a healthy diet, I would never sleep with him. I had to do something.

"Let's get out of here," I blurted.

"What about your burger?"

"Leave it for the beef curious."

We gave it the college try in the parking lot of Tequila Mockingbird. Heater blasting in his SUV. The funky beat of Clarence Carter's "Back Door Santa" on the radio. Tinted windows moist from our breathing— not in a *Titanic* movie, car-sex way, though. Our dog-tired panting came from climbing into the backseat and trying to undress.

The Flann Man yanked off his jeans while I peeled off his shirt. As we got on our knees to face each other, I managed to slide my slacks halfway down my thighs. I needed to sit or get on my back to pull them off, but I couldn't move. The Flann Man was already unbuttoning my blouse like a dog digging for bones. When my bra clasp proved too much, he just squeezed my breasts through the fabric. He pressed himself close now. Both of our heads tilted against the roof, the pup-tent of his tighty whities almost touching my navel. He kissed me in staccato bursts. His breath smelled of beer and salty peanuts.

As he dropped into a sitting position, he tried to pull me on top of him, but my legs were still shackled by my pants. I was tugging at them with one hand, trying to keep my balance with the other, when I paused to look at him—to really look. It suddenly felt if someone just told me Justin Trudeau was gay. His narrow white chest had only a modest tuft of hair— nothing like Brett's broad, forested upper body. His face had none of the chiseled precision of Brett's. And his smell didn't remind me of a spring orchard. I had started this, though, so I would finish it.

I got one leg free—finally—and the Flann Man's body tensed. He reached for the floor and grabbed a condom from his wallet. We were exhaling short, hot breaths. Me wearing nothing but a bra, the Flann Man nothing but white gym socks. I straddled him.

"Do you like rolling it on?" he asked, thrusting the shiny purple package in my hand. His expression was earnest, as if every girl dreamed of unfurling a sticky piece of latex on some guy's joint in the backseat of a car.

"I'm allergic," I blurted.

What? Was that even possible? Can touching a condom give you hives or a runny nose or an irrational fear of gluten? I had no idea. In truth, I didn't want to think about birth control and STDs. I didn't want to tell him that I had finally decided to give the pill a chance two months before Brett left. I didn't want to admit that I was still on it, that part of me was taking that tablet every day in the hopes Brett would come back. I just wanted to feel better for a moment, not worse. I wanted a night of carefree fun. What was I expecting in the parking lot of a bar? Hell, I couldn't even remember if I changed my underwear that morning.

The Flann Man couldn't get much momentum sitting upright on the leather seat, so I did most of the cardio—pumping my thighs up and down and hoping nothing in my knees would pop. At times, it felt like having sex with a breadstick from Olive Garden.

A few minutes later he finished.

Exhausted, I lifted myself off him. We clumsily got dressed, trying not to look at each other or the used condom that lay on the floor like a beached jellyfish. As we climbed into the front, I hit my knee on the parking brake, hard. He banged his head on the overhead lamp. I guess that made us even. We settled into our seats, face-forward as if watching the road for traffic. The radio now hummed with Ella Fitzgerald's "Santa Claus Got Stuck in My Chimney."

"Is this one of those channels that plays Christmas music all the time?" I asked.

"Yep."

The Flann Man offered no further explanation, and his self-assurance reminded me of how little I knew about him. My stomach growled audibly.

"Hungry?" he asked with that sincere, crooked smile. He really was a nice guy. Just not the nice guy for me. Just not Brett.

I nodded. "I'm wondering if my burger is still warm."

The Flann Man laughed. "Let's find out," he said as he looked straight at me. "But only if I can have a bite."

"Now you're talking."

•••

A few weeks later, on the first day of spring semester, the Flann Man appeared in the front row of my Native American history class. He wore the same jeans and shirt from our night together. He had the same crooked haircut and sideways smile. He exuded the same subdued sexiness.

My first instinct, of course, was to pull the fire alarm. Neither of us had spoken, texted, or called since "the sex." It was as if we had both decided once was enough so why go to the trouble of talking about it— the fumbled excuses for not seeing each other, the awkward attempts not to hurt feelings. Seeing him in the front row brought that night back with a surprising vividness, though. Why *hadn't* we called? Why didn't we try again somewhere other than a parking lot? And what was stopping him from telling the class about my allergy to latex and penchant for dirty undies?

The Flann Man has proven to be a solid student who can keep a secret. He takes dutiful notes. He participates with a raised hand and respectful tone. And he always brings a book. What more can I ask? Passion for the subject matter? A natural aptitude for research? A history with me that does not include a backseat romp? Truth be told, he is the least of my problems in this class.

Enter Marcus "Clench" Duvall.

In the back row wearing a perpetual scowl, Marcus has made it his unofficial mission in life to torment me twice a week for eighty minutes. He arrives late most days. He has never taken notes or looked away from his phone for more than a minute—other than to scowl. He dons a black-and-white New York Yankees baseball cap that hides most of his face. In fact, he seems to own only one outfit: a black T-shirt with red lettering that reads "School Ruined My Life" and dark denim jeans that have probably never been washed. He also refuses to speak my name. Sometimes, he mutters "hey," but he has never addressed me as "Ms. Shaw" despite hearing it from his classmates countless times. Last week, he even showed up at the main office looking for "the chick who teaches that class about Indians."

Among the student body, Marcus's claim to fame rests on a singular talent. Rumor has it that he can fart the opening theme of Beethoven's Fifth Symphony. The football team enjoys an impromptu performance of this masterpiece at least once a week in the locker room, and they have rewarded him with the nickname "Clench"—an accomplishment any parent could be proud of. Today, after class, maestro Clench and I have a meeting to discuss his plagiarized homework.

Bodies shift restlessly in their seats, the unmistakable sign that class is almost over. I don't blame them today. I can hear myself droning on.

" ... As we discussed earlier this semester, the Pequot War culminated in the Mystic Massacre, the indiscriminate slaughter of over 600 Pequots by English colonists in 1637. Mostly women, children, and old men ..."

Sunlight spills into the room through the latticed windows, reaching about a dozen students. Their white faces appear divided in half: one plaster-white from the light, the other ruddy and flushed from the heated room.

"It's important to remember that the treaty ending the war demanded the end of the Pequot Tribe," I continued. "The surviving Pequot were either integrated into other tribes or sold as slaves to New England families. And they could no longer call themselves Pequot." I pause, most of their faces blank as the SMART Board behind me. "Think about that. The New England colonists erased the Pequot as a culture. They declared them extinct."

I dismiss class, and all of the students shuffle out except Clench. He lingers at his desk for a few moments before lumbering to the front of the room. That gives me just enough time to text Doug—"3 min"—and to leave my phone on the podium. Clench's chest presses against his shirt with impressive ferocity. His crooked nose makes his grey eyes appear slightly crossed, and a constellation of acne stretches across his neck.

Clench must be a foot taller than I, so talking to him requires either looking up or staring directly at his "School Ruined My Life" shirt.

"That's in the past tense," I begin, gesturing at his shirt.

Clench blinks.

"You're still in school," I continue. "Shouldn't it read, 'School *Is* Ruining My Life'"?

Clench stares at me as if I just asked him to decode the Rosetta Stone.

I take a deep breath and hand him his homework, a one-page analysis of George Caitlin's painting *Wi-jún-jon*. "We both know where this came from," I say. "Why don't you write your own thoughts about the painting for next class, and we'll forget about this one. Okay?"

"Where did it come from?" he asks roughly.

"You cut and pasted the Wikipedia entry about the painting."

"So?" His crossed eyes make it difficult to know if he is being sarcastic or serious.

"You didn't do the assignment."

"I did research," he replies as if using Google should be celebrated with a tickertape parade.

"No, you stole someone else's ideas and words. That is not research."

Clench doesn't move.

"Let's forget about the moral question of right and wrong. Let's even forget about the fact that you don't care about this class."

"Okay," he says eagerly as if I have finally said something worth his attention this semester.

"We cite sources because we should care about telling the truth. We should acknowledge what we owe to others."

He snorts.

"Take another swing at it," I add softly. "But if this happens again, you're finished here."

I have no idea what that means. It sounds good, though, like something a mobster might say in a movie, so I let it hang in the air between us. My phone brightens with an incoming call from Doug. Right on time. I have set the volume on high, and the ringtone pelts out the opening to Beethoven's Fifth Symphony.

Clench's lips fall open slightly, and his spotted neck turns a shade of red.

"I've got to take this, Marcus. I'll see you Monday."

I wait until Clench leaves the room and I am sure he has heard the tune a few times before answering. "Thanks, Doug."

"Did you get him?"

"Big time."

•••

My own words leave me shaken, though. Who am I to lecture on truth-telling? Anastasia Lightfeather Shaw, stealer of trinkets and Indigenous identity. I'm the living embodiment of plagiarism. But what about my teaching? I'm introducing students to historical truth. I'm challenging them to consider the past, as well as the present, from different perspectives? What can be more important?

In the hallway, a few students cluster by the water fountain. Their clothes have a mismatched sloppiness that makes me feel a little better about my own "uniform" for teaching: black slacks and a creamy blouse, the occasional scarf to add color. Today, it is Santa Fe turquoise with splotches of clay-red.

After rounding the corner, I see Professor Hinks talking with Professor Green near the man entrance of the office. Green resembles one of the guitar players from ZZ Top. His thick beard spills down his chest like a scraggly gray waterfall, and he wears sunglasses all the time, day and night. He also carries Charlemagne, his *Oxalis triangularis* plant. He takes Charlemagne wherever he goes—every class, every meeting, every social event.

Hinks catches sight of me first. Today, his curly hair has the unnatural stiffness of too much gel, but at least his black jeans appear firmly fastened.

"Congratulations on the interview," Green says. "When do you leave?"

"Tomorrow afternoon. I'm meeting several faculty members for dinner."

"Don't drink too much," Green adds solemnly. "They notice those things at an interview. Of course, once you're hired, you can drink as much as you want."

"Good to know," I reply.

Hinks clears his throat. "The building was buzzing with rumors this morning, so I sent an email to the department informing them about the man who died in the office. I also asked if anyone had any information." He hands me a small slip of paper with a handwritten name on it. "Someone left this in my box a few hours later."

"Who?"

"I don't know," Hinks replies. "I ran the name by payroll, and there is no record of Payton Wells ever working at this university. I am having the Registrar check student rosters. Can you find out if this is him? You know, at the morgue?"

"Why would someone give you this anonymously?"

"I assume not to get involved."

I look inside the office. The reception desk has been abandoned by the secretary whose claims of restless leg syndrome keep her perpetually walking the halls. Olive carpets. Yellow lighting. And of course the death chair by the faux ficus—empty without John Doe's body. I doubt anyone will ever sit there again.

"At some point, the police will want to know who wrote this," I say mostly to myself.

Hinks either doesn't hear or doesn't care. "Can you find out?"

"Sure. I'll ask Moondude."

"Who's Moondude?" Professor Green perks up, eyebrows lifting above the frames of his sunglasses.

"Nobody, just a walking defamation lawsuit for the Grateful Dead."

As I walk away, I can feel them watching me. I wonder what they are thinking. *How many people has she told about this morning? Isn't her boyfriend sleeping with Tiffany? Nice ass*—if only. The paper is getting moist from the sweat in my palm.

"Ana," Green calls out.

I turn.

"Why would that be necessary?"

"What?"

"Involving the police?"

His face remains unreadable, mostly swallowed by his beard and dark glasses, and I wonder if either of them has ever watched an episode of *Law and Order*.

"In case Payton Wells had help," I say.

"Help with what?"

"Killing himself."

8
Breaking and Entering

The brownstone-lined street reminds me of movies about the 1800s. Women in velvety Victorian gowns. Men with top hats and walking sticks. I imagine Keira Knightley and Daniel Day Lewis with tubercular coughs, strolling past these arabesque gates and moss-colored copper awnings. I pause in front of number Seventy-Four. The brown masonry, stained dark from the recent rain, seems to gaze down at my shabby modern clothing with disapproval.

The name "Payton Wells" appears neatly typed on the keypad for the top floor. I ring twice. No answer. As I search my purse for the keys I swiped from the morgue, Doug calls out from the bottom step. He wears a puffy winter coat and a brown scarf around this neck, but nothing over his head. Doug detests "hat hair" the way some people hate meditation instructors and parallel parking. The cold makes his ears burn red and his eyes water, which is hardly more attractive.

"Just us?" he asks.

"The girls couldn't make it," I say, registering the disappointment on his face. Without Yumi or Kavita within flirting distance, I am a poor consolation prize.

The key fits. We step inside the foyer, and the narrow staircase forces us to move single-file. Any hope of being stealthy gets dashed with each step. The stairs creak in agony, and the noise reverberates so loudly that we might as well be prying up floorboards with a crowbar. By the time we get to the fifth floor, the pounding in my chest makes me wonder if I'm having a heart attack.

"I'm so out of shape."

"I'd still do you," Doug replies with a cough, trying to conceal his own windedness.

"You're a class act," I say, still struggling to catch my breath. "No wonder everyone died so young in the nineteenth century."

"Yeah," Doug says with a nod. "It was the exercise that killed them."

Inside the apartment, sunlight spills through the bay windows. Radiated heat makes the air feel heavy and still, but everything else is exquisite: oak wainscoting that matches the living room floors, tightly packed bookcases, lavender tiles on the fireplace, and a high ceiling with elegant moldings. On the windowsill, there are several purple shamrock plants— the same kind as Professor Green's Charlemagne.

"Damn," Doug's voice booms with admiration.

"Volume."

"What?" he protests.

"We're not supposed to be here, remember?"

"This apartment is so much nicer than mine."

"You live above the Bodega Barn."

Doug shrugs. "It's convenient for a late-night snack."

"Come on," I reply. "We need to hurry. I can't miss my flight."

Without another word, we move through the house separately. I wonder if Doug is just as caught up in the pleasure of sifting through the details of someone else's life unseen. The unearned intimacy.

The surprising ease of imagining yourself in another life.

The rooms are pristine—a spotless kitchen countertop, bathroom faucets without water stains, trash bins with freshly-lined bags. Yet they all have the same peculiar feature. None of the picture frames have anything in them. Picture frames hanging in the hallway, sitting on shelves, resting on nightstands. All empty.

In the master bedroom, two suits have been laid out on the bed—a single-breasted, tan linen suit that reminds me of British colonial wear from the 1940s and a blue suit with a white shirt and red tie. The bodiless clothes make my stomach tighten. Payton must have been trying to decide which outfit to die in, I realize, but why leave these out? Maybe part of him hoped he wouldn't go through with it. Maybe he hoped leaving behind something unfinished, some mess to clean up, would bring him home again.

These elegant clothes make me think of my own colorless wardrobe with renewed despair. How does one choose a final outfit, a final song to listen to, a final person to kiss? What do you do with your last day? Maybe it is better to know—to put things in order and to say goodbye instead of being blindsided by the end of the world.

On the nightstand, there is a leather-bound journal. Blue ink flows across each page like running water. I turn to the final entry, dated the night before his death. The top reads: "The Morning Question. What Good shall I do this day?" A similar note appears at the bottom: "Evening Question. What Good have I done today?" The chart in-between lists each hour, blocking off times to eat, study, work, and read. I recognize it from Benjamin Franklin's autobiography. It is a handwritten copy of Franklin's daily schedule.

I flip through a few more pages. All of them appear to be passages from literature, poetry, and philosophy. There is nothing personal about Payton Wells here, nothing about who he is or why he chose to die in the main office of the Humanities Department. I slip the book into my coat pocket anyway.

Payton had wiped away all traces of himself, leaving nothing behind for scavengers like me. Just empty suits and picture frames. So did Brett in a sense. What did Brett do on the last day of our lives together? Before he wiped himself clean from our apartment and from my life? He knew the end was coming. I didn't. I still want to cry foul about that. I want to Pepto-Bismol the unfairness that continues to eat away at my insides. I want to stop resenting him like I resent the Electoral College and skinny jeans.

•••

Halloween. The Day of the Dead. Just two years and four months after Brett and I first met. Just two months shy of our second year living together. Just two-and-a-half weeks after Brett met Tiffany at the fall soiree. And just days before I learned the truth about him and Tiffany.

It was the day Brett left me for good.

Brett and I approached our annual Halloween costume contest with a fervor rivaled only by Red Sox fans and people who believe in alien abduction. We shopped in secret. We tried to throw each other off with false clues. We even wagered big to keep the pressure high. The Mockingbird Gang—Yumi, Kavita, and Doug—always decided the winner after we finished handing out candy. Last year, the loser had to clean the bathroom once a week for a month. I don't care how much you love someone, how intimately you know every crevice and curve of his body. Nobody, I mean nobody, likes cleaning toilets. Period.

As usual, Brett bought the hundred-piece candy fun pack with crunchy, peanut buttery, and caramel-filled chocolates. As usual, I worked my way through half of it before Halloween. I knew Brett would shake his head as he dumped the leftovers into a bowl for Trick-or-Treaters.

"You're going to save some for the kids, right?"

"We don't have kids," I'd reply, fishing out another piece.

More head shaking. Brett had never known anyone with my capacity for a high-sugar, high-sodium, high-fat, high-cholesterol diet.

I worked the nightshift before Halloween with two mini-Snickers in my pocket and a nagging feeling about my costume. If I had been hoping for inspiration at the morgue, I was sorely disappointed. There wasn't a toy skeleton, pumpkin, cardboard witch, or Rick Grimes outfit to be found. According to Moondude, the county considered it in poor taste to celebrate a holiday about death with so many actual dead bodies in the building. I viewed it as a missed opportunity.

I decided to go as an IKEA Assembly Technician. I sewed the name "OK-A" in big yellow letters on the back of a blue jumper, and my tool belt had an eggbeater and a spatula. I used safety pins to cover the rest of the jumper with random pages from different IKEA instructional manuals. In Swedish. Something was wrong, though. Instead of being funny or clever, the costume had an undercurrent of meanness to it. It was a dig at Brett—the guy who moved here and took this job for me. I loved him. I wanted him. But the part of me damaged from failed job searches and fruitless years, from protracted poverty and a stalled future, needed to look down on someone. Even him. Even for a night.

Because of a meeting on campus, I went directly from work to school, so I didn't get to our apartment until twilight stained the sky purple. Costumed kids scurried about sidewalks, screaming, laughing, and stuffing their faces. I assumed Brett would be giving out candy already, but the apartment was dark.

After I flipped on the lights, I could not figure out what was wrong. I was standing in our place, but it had changed. It was like a smile with missing teeth. Brett's DVD player next to the cable box was gone. So was the glass bowl his mother gave us for the coffee table.

We've been robbed.

Phone in hand, poised to dial 9-1-1, I moved quickly to the kitchen. The blender Brett used for his annoying sugar-free smoothies had been taken, but my Breville espresso machine (a college graduation gift from my father) sat there untouched.

What kind of thief leaves behind a $500 expresso machine? A tea drinker?

I started down the hall. That's when I noticed the empty picture frame on the wall. Someone had removed the photograph of Brett and his family—in a field of bright-yellow sunflowers, blossoms sagging with heaviness—from the frame. It was one of my favorite pictures of Brett, so I kept it in the spendy

Michael Aram frame my mother and I lifted from Neiman Marcus.

My legs started to buckle. I lurched toward the bedroom, using the doorframe for support. My chest tightened as if someone were pressing on it with both hands. I seemed to know everything at once. I knew half the clothes in the closet wouldn't be there. I knew his drawers in the *Hemnes* dresser would be empty. I knew half the contents of the *Lillången* bathroom cabinet would be gone.

No warning. No explanation. No chance to fix whatever had been broken. He took all of his belongings but the furniture. He knew he could replace that. Just like he could replace me.

I turned on the light and saw that he did leave a note of sorts—our Halloween costumes, laid side-by-side on the bedspread. Mine must have been easy enough to find in the closet while he was packing. I stared at his for a long time. Apparently, he had been planning to go as me, a history graduate student. The outfit was mostly a clichéd bag lady: a ratty coat, unflattering brown pants, and a mussy wig of curly hair. But on a white T-shirt, in black Sharpie, he had written: "History Graduate Student, Will Work 4 Food." On the floor, in-between the hobo shoes, were two bags—one with empty soda cans, the other with some books from my shelf on Native American history.

I felt a similar undercurrent of meanness, of lost respect, in both costumes, and I knew it was over. For good.

I collapsed to the floor and wept hard tears.

•••

One room in Payton's apartment appears to be an office. A few tightly packed bookshelves fill one wall, and a small desk faces the window with a clear view of the Haverton Zoo across the street. Doug stands there with a snow globe in his hand.

"I checked the laptop," he says, holding the alpine scene close to his face. "A nice machine. Pretty new."

"And?"

"Password protected."

"Shocker."

The glass sphere slips from his fingers, hitting the floor with a thud and rolling under the desk. As Doug gets on his hands and knees to retrieve it, I notice a mother and daughter at the zoo's entrance. The child can't be more than five, with wavy brown hair like mine and a similar taste for mismatched clothes. She clings to her mother's leg.

"Have you been to the zoo?" I ask Doug.

"No," he replies, his head and shoulders under the desk. "I don't like zoos."

"Everybody likes zoos."

"Not me."

"Why not?"

"Too much pent-up sexual frustration."

The Haverton Zoo specializes in junk food and extinction. Apart from vendors selling enough rainbow lollypops, cotton candy, and soda to take credit for diabetes, the zoo carries an air of wistful neglect and deflated aspirations. It stopped caring about appearances years ago like someone wearing sweatpants to a party or listening to Vanilla Ice in public. Broken water fountains. Closed bathrooms. Paths that lead nowhere. Only about halfway through the exhibits do you realize that everything behind the cages, roped-off marshes, and greenhouse glass is on the endangered species list. Plants from the western prairie and Georgia. An artificial swamp with mud turtles and northern cricket frogs. Even an American condor. It's a living record of life on the verge of erasure.

"What's this?"

Doug dislodges a plastic case—no larger than a smart phone—from underneath the desk. He hands it to me as he gets to his feet. Inside, there are four passports: one from Canada, one from Europe, and two from the United States. All have John Doe's picture but with different names and birthdates: Justin Patrick Wright, Jonathan Harden, Maxwell Peter Jenkins, and Payton Gregory Wells. The ages range between sixty-eight and seventy-five, and each name appears on separate credit cards and Social Security cards as well.

"What the hell?" Doug asks. "These credit cards are new."

"So are the passports," I add.

"Damn. This guy was the Jason Bourne of the early-bird special." Doug looks at me as I put the documents into the case and stash it in my pocket.

"I need to get to the airport," I say, lowering my eyes. I feel guilty for lying about my trip, for telling my friends I'm going to a conference instead of a job interview as Lightfeather. It's one thing to joke about making up an Indigenous identity over beer and bocce. It's another thing to do it. It's another thing to admit it to your best friends.

"So, what do we do about the Bourne identity?" Doug asks.

"Nothing right now, but I'll text Moondude."

"Who the hell is Moondude?"

"Nobody, just some extra from *Jesus Christ Superstar.*"

Part II

Climbing the Tower

9
Table Manners

The pilot's voice over the loudspeaker wakes me. I am convinced he just said, *"I've pulled a hamstring,"* but no one seems particularly concerned. My head has been pressed against the curved plastic wall of the window for over an hour, and my neck has the stiffness of new leather. I reek of recycled air and Doritos. My breasts are sore from the start of my period. And I can feel buds of acne sprouting on my neck.

The acrid stench of undigested almonds hits me before the sound of retching. The boy in the middle seat plunges his face into a barf bag while his mother rubs his back. He can't be older than nine or ten. His mussy blond hair probably looks the same now as it does when he wakes up in the morning, and his twig-like limbs make me think of a tiny, shivering bird. He glances at me with a baffled expression, as if he can't believe his body can let him down this way. He tenses and heaves again.

"Motion sickness," the mother explains, in case I am worried he has the bubonic plague or typhoid. "Some people do better with their feet on the ground."

"Tell me about it," I reply.

"Would you mind giving me your bag? I like to have a couple for the cab ride, just in case."

As I reach over, a roar comes from the boy's throat. Bile explodes from his mouth, splattering on my sleeve and hand. It has the color of cheap mustard and the heavy, sticky quality of snot.

To the boy's credit, some of it goes into his bag. To my credit, I don't scream.

The mother offers sheepish looks and muttered apologies as I hurry down the aisle to wash off the goop in the bathroom. The little boy makes it through the rest of the flight without incident, but the stench of vomit lingers on my clothes as I exit the plane and wait among the living dead at baggage claim. It is difficult to imagine a more joyless place than baggage claim. Solemn faces and swaying bodies. Wrinkled clothes and disheveled hair. The worst part, of course, is wondering if the conveyor belt will cough up your bags. I don't have to wonder for long. After all of the other passengers from American Airline's Flight 1890 get reunited with their luggage, I stare at the empty carousel until it sputters to a stop.

"Your luggage must not have made it on the plane," an agent with Customer Care informs me.

"I only had one bag," I plead. "On a direct flight."

"Then it must be here somewhere," she says flatly.

"Really?"

"No."

She plunks a clipboard on the countertop. The polish on her long, brown fingernails appears chipped and stripped away in spots. "Fill out the paperwork with your local address," she adds.

Only when I am standing outside in the gentle Southern air, breathing exhaust from idling curbside cars, do I remember that someone from the department was supposed to pick me up nearly forty-five minutes ago. I have no number to call, no back-up plan to follow. Less than an hour into the trip and I have already blown it.

"I've been waiting a dog's year for you," a man in a brown corduroy jacket and blue shirt grumbles as he approaches.

Somewhere in his late sixties, he is mostly bald with a few sunspots. Thin fields of gray hair cling to each side of his head, and he has long ears and a lanky frame that remind me of an elderly Ichabod Crane. "I'm parked over there," he says, pointing to a black Mercedes from the early 2000s.

"The airline lost my—"

"I'm Dante Wellington, Medievalist," he announces, lifting his eyebrows as if expecting recognition or genuflection.

"Anastasia Lightfeather Shaw, Job Applicant." I hold out my hand.

He doesn't take it, and I'm relieved. My blazer hides the water-soaked, vomit-stained sleeve, but I'm not sure if it will do much to mask the smell.

"Well, Anastasia Lightfeather Shaw, Job Applicant, we are late for dinner."

Dante keeps an iron grip on the steering wheel, eyes forward, and his concentration makes me leery about another attempt at small talk. My observations about the weather, airline customer service, and Southern food have gotten little more than a grunt. Who would have guessed that my aversion to grits and passion for anything deep-fried wouldn't be scintillating conversation? I crack the window.

"I've never understood it," Dante says as if responding to a question. "This need for Native American Studies, Asian American Studies, African American Studies. In my day, we had American

Studies, and even that was for kooks who didn't want to read the hard stuff."

The hum of highway traffic and the *click-click-click* of his turn signal fill the silence. He seems to be waiting for the ideal moment to change lanes. From the looks of it, that requires everyone else in the state of North Carolina to exit first. I imagine myself trapped for all eternity in the center lane with Dante Wellington, listening to him insult my fake ethnicity until he discovers I am just as white as he is.

"I think the beauty of these specializations is that they draw attention to lives that often get lost in broader discussions of American history," I say, not sure if he wants or expects an honest response.

Click-click-click.

"We're almost there," he says, "I'm from Washington, D.C. Big Redskins fan. Do you like football?"

"Not really."

Click-click-click.

"For decades Native Americans and politicians have been calling the name 'Redskins' racist. What about tradition and free speech? What are the fans supposed to yell? 'Go Indigenous Peoples!'"

Dante jerks the steering wheel and lays into the gas, whipping across two lanes and darting onto the exit. Several car horns scream past us on the highway. My heart races.

"So, what do you think about the name?" he asks calmly.

"I'm not good with sports. It drove my boyfriend crazy. My ex-boyfriend, actually. He likes sports—football, basketball, and that one with the ball and the stick—but he didn't watch much when I was around. Mostly I asked annoying questions to get him to turn off the TV—about uniforms, gum chewing, tattoos." I hear myself rambling, and I try to put on the breaks. "Have you noticed all the tattoos in the NBA? Barnum would have had a field day. Maybe that's why my boyfriend left. Maybe he needed to be a with a sports fan."

Dante pulls into the parking lot of Osteria Toscana and turns off the engine. "Do you always talk that way?"

"What way?"

"With a dizzying circularity about your personal life?"

"Only when nervous."

"Don't be nervous."

At the entrance of the restaurant, Dante reaches for the door and stops. "You didn't answer my question about the Redskins."

"Excuse me?"

"What do you think of the name?"

I exhale. "Of course it's racist, and of course it should be changed. Not just because it's politically correct. Not even because it's another example of historical amnesia about US efforts to eradicate Native Americans. But because it's an opportunity to admit wrongs and to treat people with dignity. We all deserve that."

For the first time, Dante breaks into a smile.

Game over, I figure. He can recognize a fraud when he sees one, a fraud with a sharp tongue and the whiff of a public restroom. He is going to drive me back to the airport. At least I can pick up my luggage on the tarmac when I get home.

"I'm going to like you," he says, holding open the door. "By the way, I despise American football."

"Good to know."

"And I'm not from Washington, D.C."

"I ... I don't understand."

"So many job applicants feel they have to pretend—to be something they're not, to be a version of what they think we want. Give us a chance to know the real you," he says as he gestures for me to step inside, "and we'll do the same."

I nod as if in agreement, but his words make me feel as if I'm being pulled under water by a strong current.

•••

The warm, dimly lit interior of the restaurant has maroon-painted walls, dark wooden tables, and flickering candlelight. It is perfect for the clandestine: illegal business deals, affairs, and, as it turns out, academic job interviews. Dante makes a quick round of introductions at the table.

"This is Delilah Morris," he says. "Our feminist."

Professor Morris, thin as cardboard, has blond-brown hair and pale skin befitting someone who spends countless hours in a library. Her handshake feels fragile as parchment.

"Women's history of the Victorian Era," she corrects. From the affectation in her voice, I think she must have spent time faking an English accent at some point in her life and still resurrects it for the occasional party. "I see you've met our dinosaur. You can ignore Dante. The rest of us do."

"Delightful as always, Delilah," Dante responses before turning to me. "She is single and has a three-legged cat named Bitsy."

She nods. "All true."

"And this is our fearless leader, Jensen Sharp. Or as we call him, 'El Jefe.'"

I have been corresponding with Professor Sharp, the history department chair, and I assumed he would be older. Instead, he resembles a cutout from a Banana Republic catalogue with his snappy black suit jacket. Unbuttoned. Gray shirt with rolled up cuffs over the sleeves and a Western bolo tie. I half-expect him to wear dress shoes without socks, but it is winter after all.

"He is a Latin Americanist," Dante adds as we sit. "A fine scholar, but his Spanish leaves a bit to be desired."

"Grassy-ass, Dante," El Jefe says with such a gringo flair that it must be parody. "We've ordered another bottle of wine."

"I really shouldn't," I protest, though who am I kidding.

"It's not every day we get free rein with the university expense account," Dante chimes in from across the table. "The first rule about academic life: never pass up free alcohol."

The bottle arrives as if on cue, and the waiter pours. Yellow candlelight flickers on the outside of each glass, and the wine has the color of rose petals. I inhale the earthy, cherry aroma before taking my first sip.

The conversation stays breezy as we order. The bickering has stopped, and I pick up undercurrents of deep affection—even if they drive each other crazy once in a while. Like family.

Another bottle arrives with the pasta course. The smells of different dinners—some with shaved truffles, some heavy with pepper, some thick with garlic and tomato sauce—complement the wine. No one grills me about my scholarship, my teaching, my career aspirations, my background. They will have plenty of chances for that over the next few days. This dinner is about something else. It is about seeing if I could be one of them, if they could tolerate me year after year at department meetings and holiday parties and job dinners. In truth, I'm doing the same. Could I call these people my colleagues, even my friends at some point?

I think so.

"What's this?" El Jefe asks lifting his finger toward the ceiling. "George Gershwin?"

No one speaks as we listen to the music humming through the restaurant's sound system.

"No," he corrects himself. "Jerome Kern."

"Cole Porter," I blurt out.

Dante's gray eyebrows raise, and Delightful Delilah suspends her fork of *cacio e pepe* midair.

"It's not 'All the Things You Are'?"

"'You'd Be So Nice to Come Home To' from Coleman Hawkins and Ben Webster's *Encounters* album."

El Jefe nods, but something has shifted at the table. The exchange quiets things. Dante grins from ear to ear.

"Did I say something wrong?" I ask.

"Not at all," Dante replies with a chuckle. "El Jefe thinks of himself as the name-that-tune guy in the department. Big source of pride." Dante downs the last gulp of his wine. "Looks like he has met his match."

"Don't be silly, Ah-me-go," El Jefe replies, and though his "amigo" sounds as white as his teeth, it has lost some of the friendly enthusiasm and warmth. He turns to me. "How did you know that?"

"My mother."

10
Old Records

"I didn't spend seventeen hours in labor for you to grow up feeling sorry for yourself," my mother announced as she stared down at me—my limbs spilling over the couch like pancake batter.

Reruns of *The Twilight Zone* started at noon. Just three minutes away. Everything else on daytime television featured nightmares of a different kind. Cheery discussions of home-care products. Cooking tips. Actors plugging films. And, of course, the weather. I never knew there was so much to say about a sunny day or light rain.

Rod Serling with his dapper suits and endless supply of cigarettes became my savior. From the moment he coolly teased a new, mind-bending mystery, I was hooked. Until the previous week, I had never seen *The Twilight Zone*. Pig-faced surgeons. Fevered dreams about the end-of-the-world. William Shatner. What more could a twelve-year-old girl who had been jailed by the chickenpox ask for?

I stayed perfectly still, hoping my mother would simply retreat into the other room, but when she didn't move, I knew she planned to ruin my afternoon with Rod. For Nadya Shaw, my illnesses fell into the same category as paying taxes or watching my school plays. They were ordeals to suffer through as quickly as possible.

"It smells like a raccoon died in here."

I coughed weakly, but even if blood were coming out of my ears, Nadya Shaw wouldn't take no for an answer.

"We're going out."

"I look gross," I said, pointing to the exploded minefield of red blisters on my face.

"Since when do you care about your appearance?" she asked, glancing at my army fatigue pajama top and pink sweats. "Get showered and dressed."

Thirty minutes later, we were in Sea Cliff, a Long Island town no larger than a postage stamp. We entered a two-story building with wood shingles and filthy windows. All manner of ancient junk—floor lamps, porcelain dolls, oak end tables, nineteenth-century fainting couches—crowded the dark, dimly-lit room. This wasn't the kind of place we typically swiped things from, so I couldn't figure out why we were here. In truth, I couldn't believe my mother stepped inside without a tetanus shot.

"Wait until you see the upstairs," she whispered.

"Is that where they keep the bodies?" I asked.

The claustrophobic staircase creaked with each step, and my eyes struggled to adjust to the dark. With so many episodes of *The Twilight Zone* spinning in my head, I half-expected to find talking puppets or the devil in a three-piece suit. I held onto my mother's hip with one hand as she led the way. The soft fabric of her white dress soothed me. Upstairs, we entered an enormous space that stretched the length of the building. There were aisles of boxes filled with vinyl records. All jazz. I had never touched a record before, never opened up sleeves or placed one on a turntable.

"Look around," she said. "Find something that intrigues you."

I did not know most of the names or faces on the records. But some of the covers were striking. Miles

Davis and his trumpet on *Kind of Blue*. Billie Holiday's face on *Lady Sings the Blues*. Nina Simone sitting on a bench in Central Park.

Against the back wall, there were three listening stations with turntables and earphones. Between the two of us, we had sampled dozens of records. My mother showed me how to place and remove the records, how to lower the needle. The large discs felt light in my hands. I marveled at how such flimsy things could contain so much aching beauty, so much gravelly lyricism. Charlie Parker. George Shearing. Oscar Peterson. Ella Fitzgerald. I paged through faded inserts that smelled of aged cigarette smoke. We listened for hours in these booths, side by side, separated by nothing more than a thin red curtain that fell to our waists. Looking down from my stool, I could see her long white dress, strapped shoes, and the silver anklet with tiny pearls that we had stolen from Nordstrom's.

When she tapped my shoulder, I was listening to Colman Hawkins and Ben Webster's *Encounters*. I could have any records I wanted, she told me, so I asked for all of them. She didn't sigh or shake her head or look to the heavens with exasperation. She smiled.

Nadya Shaw bargained with the owners—an old Russian couple who talked nostalgically about subzero temperatures in Saint Petersburg. The husband accompanied every declaration with a series of nods, and my mom nodded along with him. He eventually sold her the records at a discount. She even convinced him to part with a banged-up Crosby Turntable from the 1950s.

On the car ride home, she spoke to me as if I were an adult or someone other than her disappointing

86

daughter. She described the love of her life as a jazz pianist she met in college. It had never occurred to me that she loved someone other than Daddy. I could not imagine her life before me any more than I could imagine mine without her.

"People think of jazz as improvisation." Her voice sounded warm, and it reminded me of a purring cat. "But any musician will tell you that the trick is finding freedom within structure. As soon as you start, every song traps you in a rhythm and a harmonic structure. The genius is finding freedom within that."

On our block, we drove past trees with bright yellow leaves, and the crisp October air still had the lingering warmth of summer. My mother pulled into the driveway, her eyes hidden behind brown sunglasses.

"Life will box you in, Ana. The trick is finding enough freedom to hold onto yourself."

"But you love Daddy?" I asked, suddenly concerned about this smoky figure from her past whose music had been pulsing through her veins without the rest of us knowing.

"Your father is a good man. He loves me." Her voice flattened as she opened the car door and stepped outside.

I wanted her to say that they loved each other, that she loved him too. But it was a one-way street with him, like it was with me. She knew it, and so did we.

"Ana," she said as we walked to the front door. She carried two bags of records. I held the bulky turntable in my arms. "Don't slouch. It will make people think you've given up on life."

From that day forward, jazz became part of our family. After school. During dinner. Through the weekend. I chose the records. I placed them on the Crosby Turntable in the living room. I decided the soundtrack of our lives.

My mother and I went to that record store dozens of times before she died. Later, I would cram my iPod with these albums, relying on this music to get me through studying, researching, and even sitting at the morgue.

I miss the records, though. Touching them, breathing in the sleeves, flipping through inserts. Dad has them. He plays them at night when he misses her most.

I miss the days she and I sat side by side in those booths and listened to jazz, together and separately, at the same time.

11
Houdini

After Dante drops me at the motel and reminds me that I have a "light repast" with Delightful Delilah in the morning, I get my first piece of good news. The pimply, squeaky-voiced boy at the front desk tells me that the airline has delivered my bag. It is in my room. Hope pumps through my veins. Maybe I can sell myself as Lightfeather after all. Maybe I can pay off my student loans and get a subscription to Hulu.

As soon as I open the door, I slam into a hard, heavy piece of purple luggage. It is shiny and showroom ready. And, of course, I have never seen it before in my life. I dial American Airlines, and an automated voice puts me on hold. Fourteen minutes and thirty-two seconds of Andy Gibb on Muzak and helpful reminders about the American.com website break me. I hang up. I need a shower and a change of clothes. I need to rehearse my job talk. With no stores on the ground floor and no car, I decide to do some breaking and entering for the second time today. I roll the bag into the center of the room and open it.

Dior and Vuitton blouses. Gucci dresses and a Prada belt. A set of La Perla pajamas wrapped in tissue paper—a gift for someone else, no doubt. There is even a cellophane bag with individually wrapped Amedei chocolates and a note: "Good luck, Mabel. Knock 'em dead!"

Mabel? I don't imagine the Mabels of the world gliding down fashion runways, but she has the clothes for it. From what I can tell, Mabel is a few sizes larger and a few inches shorter than I, but that doesn't stop me from opening the pajamas after a quick shower. Against my skin, the cool silk tingles. I brush my teeth with her toothpaste on my finger. I dab my face with her Armani moisturizer. And I'm relieved to know that her deodorant will keep my underarms from smelling like a French subway tomorrow.

I pop another chocolate into my mouth as I spread the notes for my talk on the bed. My phone rings.

"This is Moondude," he announces as if I have been waiting for his call.

"What do you want?" The question comes out bitchy, but I don't mean to be. It just happens, the same way your leg moves when a doctor hits it with a rubber hammer. I don't backpedal, though. Moondude has never called before, and I need to steer him clear from asking me out or texting pictures of himself in his underwear.

"Doing you a favor, man. I mean, person."

"Sorry. I'm just stressed out, and I don't have any clothes."

"Want to FaceTime?"

"That's actually funny." I reply, somewhat surprised by his wit. I always assume stoners experience time too slowly for banter. "So, what did you find out? Is John Doe any of the names I texted you?"

"Yes and no. I checked his fingerprints statewide, but nothing came up. Not a single hit. So I plugged each name into the database for the Registrar of Vital Statistics. I found all of them, but something is strange." Moondude hesitates, his voice tight and unmellow.

"What?"

"Where did you get these names?"

"I'll explain later. Just tell me."

"According to their birth certificates, Payton Gregory Wells is 138 years old. Justin Patrick Wright is 126. Jonathan Harden is 111. And Maxwell Peter Jenkins tops the charts at 144." Moondude clears his throat. "What exactly have you gotten me into?"

"I'm not sure myself."

•••

The next morning, I wake to a mess of blood as my period has leaked through my only tampon, Mabel's pajama bottoms, and the sheets. I don't have time to do anything about the soiled sheets except yank them off the mattress. I wash everything else in the sink and hang them in the bathroom to dry.

In the side pocket of Mabel's toiletry bag, I am surprised to find a bottle of Tegretol. I recognize the anti-seizure medication right away. My father's brother, Uncle Sammy, had epilepsy, and he took these pills for most of his life. I never witnessed an episode firsthand, but I saw the aftermath once. Two summers before my mother died, he had a seizure in our living room after dinner. I was in the backyard, watching fireflies brighten and fade away like signals from a lighthouse. Then I heard a crash.

Inside, the glass vase from the coffee table had shattered. White, long-stemmed flowers stretched across the floor. Water darkened the overlapping diamond pattern on the rug. And Uncle Sammy laid on the couch, body spent. His skin was gray, and his eyes seemed unable to focus. Drool glistened on his chin.

I picture Mabel in a hotel room without medication. On the floor, writhing with a seizure that won't stop until it shakes the last breath out of her. I may not have been the one who misplaced her luggage or sent it to the wrong hotel, but I slept in her pajamas. I applied her makeup and ate her chocolates (all of them). And I am wearing her Sax Fifth Avenue blouse and La Perla medium briefs for today's interview— though both are too short and too wide for my body.

I repack the rest of Mabel's things while listening to some Muzak courtesy of American Airlines, Michael McDonald this time. I cannot get through to customer service, so I leave her bag with the front desk, asking the woman at reception to try the airline.

"Please mention the medication," I plead before hurrying to the car outside.

At 7:15 in the morning, Delightful Delilah bears all the signs of a hangover. Strained smiles. Whispered tones. Sunglasses on a cloudy day. Part of her must blame me because she takes us to a place called the Waffle Bistro. It reminds me of a Belgian beer garden with its half-timber interior and waiters wearing white shirts with suspenders. I get the Basic Bistro Breakfast to show my interest in all things local, even though the waffles come with grits. Delightful Delilah waits for me to order before asking for wheat toast and coffee. As the waiter leaves, she smirks, no doubt, with the thought of watching me stuff my face while she nibbles on crunchy bread.

"I'm usually at the pool now," she says. "Not today."

She shakes her head in dismay as if we are in the same boat, two athletes heartbroken about missing the morning triathlon. She chews without making a sound and blows sensibly on her coffee before taking a sip.

Not a crumb falls from her lips. Her porcelain skin comes straight out of Victorian novels and vampire films. She doesn't wear makeup because she knows she doesn't need it. We both have wavy hair, hers perfectly sculpted, mine crafted by Silly String. She wears a light winter coat and mustard-colored dress with the ease that thin women wear everything, confident it will fit. Perfectly.

Watching her, I am convinced she tacitly condones the bodily standards that have made every woman I know hate her own body since girlhood. I dislike her more with each syrup-soaked bite of waffle.

Delightful Delilah reviews the day's itinerary with me, reading steadily from an email on her phone, but I only half-listen. The skin under my armpits and around my crotch has started to itch, and I shift uncomfortably in the wooden booth. The syrup on my plate congeals, and I poke the grits with my fork. I'm not sure how long she has stopped speaking before she signals for the check. She wears the expression of a bored child at a petting zoo.

"We should get to campus," she announces. "I don't want to be blamed for making you late."

I am tempted to ask for a to-go bag just to see her reaction, but I check myself. I am trying to get a job, after all. She slides out of the booth with the agility of a young boy, and her lithe body makes the waffles feel stone-heavy in my stomach. As she puts on her coat, she glances at my plate.

"Hope that holds you till lunch."

Delightful.

•••

Devon University has an unsettling uniformity. The same limestone, neo-Gothic architecture characterizes each of the twenty or so structures on campus. From the rectangular quad, you cannot distinguish between dormitories and departments, art studios and auditoriums. Only the chapel, whose spires pierce the clouded sky, announces its function clearly. All of this sameness seems at odds with the promise of a university education—the cultivation of minds that critically assess and innovate, that use knowledge as a springboard for finding one's own path.

Delightful Delilah stays a few steps ahead of me the way my mother used to when she found my mismatched outfits and skinned knees distasteful. She stares at her phone without looking up, equally confident that everyone else will move around her. They do.

"Change of plans," Delightful Delilah announces, turning so abruptly that I almost run into her. For a moment, we are close enough to embrace. I have to admit there is something unmistakably seductive about the tightness of her lips and her yellow-brown eyes. "El Jefe needs to reschedule your meeting with him for later today. I am to take you to the library. Your talk is in an hour."

She leads me to a room that has been set up for the presentation—a podium, rows of chairs, and a screen for projecting slides. Two of the walls are made of glass, and they look out onto the ground floor of the library. Students burdened with heavy backpacks scurry back and forth.

"I'm off to educate," Delightful Delilah says with a cheerful smile—whether for the joys of teaching or ditching me, I can't tell. "I'll see you in an hour. Don't do anything I wouldn't!"

"Like eat?" I mutter once she is gone, scratching the itchiness beneath one of my armpits.

I am too nervous and waffle-sluggish to sit still. I am too self-conscious in this fishbowl of a room to rehearse my talk. So I decide to explore the most magical, most inspiring, and, oddly enough, most unattractive part of any library.

The stacks.

Here, you won't find soaring windows or grand entryways, gothic reading rooms or cozy alcoves. The stacks are all business. Metal shelves crammed with books. Low ceilings and dim lighting. Dust heavy in the air. But this is exactly why they are my go-to place. They are sanctuaries for hard work.

American history is in the basement, three floors below ground. I step off the elevator to the musty odor of wet socks, and the only sound is the light crunch of my footsteps on the carpet. I enter the first aisle, tracing my finger along spines and reading titles like some people relish a first sip of wine or the final bite of a Reese's Peanut Butter Egg.

I gravitate toward the newest books, those with the unbroken binding of neglect. I like to read a page from the middle to get a sense for the unfolding journey, to pick a place where the writer could have gotten stuck or abandoned the project altogether. Novelist Jeffrey Eugenides spent nine years writing *Middlesex*. I try to imagine what it was like for him in year four or five, not knowing how much longer it would take or if he could finish at all. Of course, every graduate student knows this feeling. We live in a perpetual state of uncertainty because every day feels like year five of a book with no end in sight. Coursework and comprehensive exams, dissertations and disgruntled students. When it is all over, instead of a best-selling book and a Pulitzer Prize, we adjunct at a community college for a salary that hovers somewhere between the poverty line and homelessness.

I take an uncreased biography of Harry Houdini off the shelf. The famous photograph of his chained, naked body is on the cover. Houdini, the Jewish boy who changed his name and spent his entire life trying to prove nothing could hold him—not straightjackets, handcuffs, jail cells, packing crates, bank vaults, or padlocked cans filled with milk. Not even his heritage. In truth, he seemed invincible until the day a stranger punched him in the abdomen, rupturing his appendix and killing him.

On a scale of salsas, my irritated skin has suddenly gone from mild to picante, so I hurry to the bathroom. I need to take off my clothes before Mabel's underwear gives me the clap. In the last stall, I stack Houdini and my phone on top of the tank. The door latch rattles but won't budge. My skin is on fire now, and I am practically hopping from one foot to the other like a cartoon character. I slam my palm against the latch. Once. Twice. On the third try, something gives, and the metal slide rockets into place.

I slip down my pants to assess the damage. The La Perla briefs are giving me an Irish-sunburn. My fingertips cool the rash on my inner thighs but only for a moment. It flares back angrily as soon as I let go. I find the same redness beneath my armpits. Something similar happened during a backpacking trip to Europe once—an allergic reaction to detergent from a public laundromat. Within hours, my skin burned as if stung by a jellyfish. Mabel's clothes are having the same effect.

As I touch my angry skin again, I notice the steady murmur of Phil Collins's "In the Air Tonight." It plays the way music does in department stores: hovering in the distance, nagging like something you can't quite remember but want to forget.

What kind of library bathroom plays easy listening?

Then something truly awful happens. "In the Air Tonight" ends—only to begin again.

Let me get something out of the way. I hate Phil Collins songs. Every single one. Phil Collins whose music is the unofficial soundtrack for teenage boys who can't get laid. Phil Collins who smiles like the guy who just pantsed you in the middle of a beach volleyball game. Sussudio Phil Collins. That fucking guy.

Of all the bad Phil Collins songs (a staggering list, I know), of all his blights on popular culture and good taste, "In the Air Tonight" might be the mother of bad songs. Until "In the Air Tonight," I did not know it was possible to write something that sounds like it is just about to begin and never going to end at the same time. The steady drumbeat. The synthesized chords. The nasal thin voice.

Snap.

The air around me cracks like a whip. Hinges squeal. And the stall door shifts to one side of the frame.

I flinch, heart thumping.

Everything gets still except for the drums from "In the Air Tonight." I listen for footsteps, running water, the rustling of clothes. Nothing. No one else seems to be in the room. I am suddenly self-conscious about my near nakedness. I zip my pants and button my blouse. My jacket still hangs on the door.

Phil whines about a pack of lies as I try the latch.

Nothing.

I try the latch again.

Stuck. Welded shut, more like it. I pound the door with my palm. I even try slamming my shoulder against it the way TV cops break into houses, but I don't have enough room to get much weight behind it. Each try only makes a dull thud. For the first time, I notice the stalls are particularly low to the ground, leaving little space between them and the floor. I don't think I can fit underneath.

Phil now promises not to help a drowning victim.

"Jesus Christ," I yell at the song. "Give it a rest!"

The acoustics in the room flatten my voice. No one knows I'm here, I think. No one will come looking for Anastasia Lightfeather Shaw, Job Candidate, in the bowels of the library. I check my phone. Thirty-five minutes until the talk. I can't call Delightful Delilah. I'd rather drown myself in a shallow puddle. What about the front desk upstairs? I'll just find the number online and—

No cell reception.

I drop the phone on top of Houdini and sit on the toilet. I get a vision of police dogs combing the library. Of headlines in the school newspaper: "Graduate Student Locks Self in Bathroom to Protest Student Debt, Groupons, and News Coverage of the Royal

Family." "Graduate Student Attempts Suicide After Listening to Six Hours of 'In the Air Tonight.'"

I have to do something.

With my back pressed against the tank, I grab both sides of the seat for balance and kick. First with one leg, then both. *Thud.* The stall door shakes. *Thud.* Metal groans. *Thud.* I imagine all of the walls falling away with the slapstick choreography of a Three Stooges movie.

Nothing. The door doesn't give. The latch remains firmly in place. I stand to adjust my underwear, and—

Plop.

Something heavy dislodges in my chest. I don't need to spin around to know that my phone rests at the bottom of the toilet. That water still undulates in the bowl and drops have splashed onto the seat. But I look anyway. There it is like sunken treasure. I can't help but think of the tens of thousands of students who have peed in this toilet over the years, who have, in effect, peed on my phone.

I grab it out of the tank and hold it with my fingertips as if the rest of my hand isn't already soaked. I dab the phone with paper. Pieces stick and tear. Finally, I swaddle it like baby Moses by the Nile, wrapping a few inches of paper around it. When I'm finished, it resembles a deflated football. I put it on top of Houdini who stares at me smugly. He, of course, remains unscathed.

"In the Air Tonight" starts again, and I seriously consider sticking my head in the toilet.

"Fuck off, Phil!"

"Excuse me?" a man's voice calls from outside the door. "Do you need any help?"

"Yes!" I blurt. "The latch won't budge."

99

"The Dungeon. Happens all the time with this stall." The door shakes as he tries to pull it open. "Yep, it's stuck all right."

The words come across so nonchalantly that I am worried he might leave.

"Do you have anything to pry it open?" I ask.

"Not really."

"A screwdriver? Backhoe?"

"Why would I have tools?"

"Don't you work here?"

"I'm Lawrence."

"Who?"

"I'm a junior sociology major."

"A sociology major?"

"My parents aren't thrilled."

"I'm sorry. ... You're a guy?"

I step back and look beneath the stall door. He wears white sneakers and stands somewhat pigeon-toed.

"Last time I checked."

"In the women's bathroom?"

"Not exactly."

"I'm having a bit of a day here, Larry," I say with forced calm, using as much of my teacher voice as possible. "So—"

"Lawrence," he corrects with a nervous laugh. "This isn't ... I'm not ... All the bathrooms on campus are unisex. It's a recent thing. They haven't gotten around to changing all the signs. I guess the basement of the library isn't a huge priority."

"You seriously expect me to believe that?"

"We live in a twenty-first century, gender-fluid world," Lawrence replies, a bit too pleased with himself for having the upper hand in a discussion about the patriarchal bias of ordinary restrooms.

"Can you get me out of here?"

"I'll let the front desk know—"

"This is time sensitive," I interrupt.

In truth, I don't really want someone on the library staff rescuing me if I can avoid it. The entire department will find out within the hour. I'll forever be the job candidate who got trapped in a unisex bathroom stall.

"Can you squeeze under?"

"I don't think so. Besides, it's smaller than an IKEA closet in here."

He pauses as if something important has occurred to him. "I love that store."

"Lawrence," I snap. "I need some focus here."

I take a closer look at the white-tiled floor. It has the yellowish stain of dried urine and the griminess of scuffed shoes, dirt, and neglect.

"Screw it," I say. "I need you to take these for me." I pass him my toilet-paper wrapped phone and my jacket beneath the door. "Careful with the jacket. These are my only clothes."

"Really?"

"Yes."

"Are you like homeless or something?"

"Just a graduate student."

The song accelerates, and I picture Lawrence air drumming along with it. Phil whines again about something in the air.

"What is with this fucking song?" I ask.

"Javier, the head of library maintenance, loves it."

"So it plays on a never ending loop?"

"Just in this bathroom."

"Lucky me," I say as I kneel in front of the toilet. "I mean who waits their entire life to be cheated on? This is supposed to be Phil Collins's signature song. Even Phil Collins admits that he doesn't know what the lyrics mean!"

I lie down on my side, getting into a near fetal position with the toilet bowl between my bent knees and my curled upper body. My face is inches away from the urine stain and the greased bolts fastening the toilet to the floor. I reach my right arm into the next stall as I roll onto my back. Then I do the same with my left.

With my knees bent and my feet flat on the ground, I start inching forward. I try not to think about the fact that I am using my body as a mop. After sliding a little more, I figure my chest is going to be a deal breaker. I can't suck it in the way I do my gut for group photos. Sore and irritable, my breasts make me wince as I squeeze through. One more push with my legs and I am halfway into the next stall. I press my palms against the interior wall and push.

That's when I notice Lawrence.

He stands by the open door in his white shoes, gray sweatpants, and a baggy sweatshirt with "Devon University" scrawled in gold. He cradles my jacket and the toilet-paper wrapped phone. His body has the shape of a pear with legs, and he has black, shoulder-length hair and dark-rimmed glasses.

"Some help would be nice," I say, holding out my hands.

He places my things gingerly on the floor and grabs my wrists. I am at an awkward angle, so he moves me in a zigzag motion. He grunts with each tug as he shuffles backward, bumping into the wall and cursing beneath his breath a few times before I'm clear.

I get to my feet and step to the mirror to assess the damage. My hair resembles a wet strip mop. Mabel's Saks Fifth Avenue silk blouse—wrinkled, baggy, and tight in all the wrong places—makes me look like a deranged circus clown. My armpits burn. My crotch itches, and I'm convinced I can feel millions of microbes smeared over my entire body.

Phil sings about not being a fool, and tears pool in my eyes, though I try to fight them. Lawrence stands at the adjacent sink, placing my phone and jacket on the counter. He watches me in the reflection. When he notices my exposed navel, he lowers his eyes.

"Stick your phone in a bag of rice," he says earnestly. "It'll absorb the moisture."

I laugh aloud, wiping my eyes with the back of my hand. "You don't happen to have some rice on you?"

He shakes his head. "Are you okay?"

"Not even close."

He lifts his eyes and looks at my reflection in the mirror once again. "That shirt doesn't fit."

"Tell me about it."

•••

"Naming is an act of power," I begin.

The roughly thirty seats have been filled. Delightful Delilah and Dante Wellington are in the front row. El Jefe sits toward the back in a lavender suit with matching shoes and the Western bolo tie from last night. Everyone else is a stranger. Administrators with suits. Faculty with buttoned dress shirts. Graduate students looking unkempt and a bit hungry. Through the glass walls, I can see the ebb and flow of undergraduates passing through the library.

"Naming is the first act of colonial aggression, of trying to erase a culture and a people."

At one point, I feel the weight of John Doe's diary and his fake IDs in my jacket pocket. I put them there before boarding the plane yesterday and forgot about them. I try not to think about it as I discuss the naming of newly baptized Chumash at the California missions. The Spanish chose names based on saints, long-lost friends, distant relatives, and even favorite pets back home. Imagine being renamed after a dog, I say. With each word, John Doe's book and the IDs feel heavier, almost to the point of knocking me off balance.

After the talk, Dante Wellington approaches the podium. His blue eyes have hints of gray, and his bald head shines beneath the lights. He wears the same corduroy jacket from last night.

"Well done, Lightfeather. I am curious, though." He pauses, and for the first time, I notice that I am about an inch or so taller than he. "How did you get interested in this aspect of Native American history? Simply from being Chumash yourself?"

There is a sincerity in his voice that I don't expect, but the question twists my insides into a corkscrew.

"Partly."

12
La Purísima Concepción

"It's a Danish village," I said.

"Why would that be fun for me?" Brett asked, hands tight on the steering wheel, eyes focused on the long stretch of highway.

Yellow-brown grasses, baked from the summer sun, clung to the rolling California hills. Gnarled olive groves. The splintered bark of eucalyptus trees. Dry desert spaces between lush green vineyards. And men in fields with skin the color of coffee-beans. All of it whizzed by my open window, crystal clear for a moment before vanishing into the dusty air.

"Because we're staying in a Danish village," I repeated as if no further explanation was necessary. "With a windmill."

In truth, I had no interest in replaying this argument. I was trying to imagine 1769 when the Spanish first started to colonize California on the cheap. Franciscan missionaries and leatherjacket soldiers—a hodgepodge of criminals and rapists—traveled between San Diego and San Francisco to establish missions. They offered natives glass beads and blankets, clothing and food. They believed mission life would civilize them. It would teach them Christian faith and farming, hard work and obedience. But most important, it gave the missionaries cheap, manual labor. Of the 81,000 natives baptized after 1769, 60,000 were dead within sixty years.

We were on a research trip to see as many of the famous California missions as we could cram into twelve days. After flying into San Jose and seeing the mission there and in Santa Clara, we stopped at Mission San Juan Bautista. That had been the highlight for Brett, because Alfred Hitchcock filmed parts of *Vertigo* there. Though he added a bell tower for the movie, which was later taken away, it was still easy to picture Kim Novak plunging to her fake death in a gray suit and black high heels.

We also visited San Carlos del Rio Carmelo, Soledad, San Antonio de Padua, and San Miguel Arcángel. The plan was to make our hotel in Solvang, the Danish Village of California, home base for visiting San Luis Obispo, *La Purísima Concepción,* and Santa Inés.

"I work full-time at IKEA—sometimes six days a week," Brett continued. Sweat beaded on his forehead above his sunglasses. "Why would I want to stay in a Danish village off the central coast of California? You know they have beaches here, right?"

"First of all, Danish and Swedish cultures are not the same thing," I corrected, eager to share the results of my cursory Google search. "The Danes aren't big on immigrants, but they like to drink, flirt, and shout at fellow cyclists."

"Sounds magical."

"The Swedes prefer gender-neutral terms and political correctness."

"Do they both eat pickled herring?"

"Yes."

"Case closed."

The car slowed as Brett turned into the parking lot for the Mission State Park of *La Purísima Concepción.* I had insisted on stopping at *Purísima* even before we checked in. As we paid our entrance fees, I recited some statistics. The original mission claimed over 300,000 acres of land when it was founded in 1787. You could still get a sense for its scope. Wide fields with cows, sheep, and horses. Rooms for candle-making and weaving. Tools for plowing fields and digging irrigation canals. Racks for tanning hides. Even the soldiers' quarters still had whips, swords, and muskets.

In the few minutes it took to get from the car to the mission buildings themselves, the bright sun pressed down hot and unforgiving. Brett and I ducked into the women's dormitory first. Wooden benches lined the walls, wide enough for rows of tightly woven mats and pillows to suggest the sleeping arrangements. A dark, grimy cross hung on the white plaster wall.

"What is a neophyte?" Brett asked as he looked at a sign describing the daily routine of the mission. He took off his sunglasses in the cool, shadowy room. With his shorts and Billabong T-shirt, he could pass for a surfer who got lost on the way to Pismo Beach.

"A Christian-in-training. That's what they called a native who joined the mission. It meant you couldn't leave without permission. Couldn't visit your tribe. Couldn't keep your name."

Something caught Brett's attention on one of the mats. "A doll."

The wooden figure was the length of a newborn. It had stiff, unyielding limbs, and the carvings on its face suggested eyes and a straight mouth.

"A punishment," I said. "Miscarriages were often treated as abortions. The women were whipped for two weeks and had to carry the wooden likeness of a baby to church and meals."

Brett reached for my hand again, but I wouldn't take it. He knew I was thinking about us. About our baby, our almost baby. I refused to cry again. Not on this trip. It had been over a month. I was fine.

For the briefest moment, though, I was tempted to pick up the doll.

•••

"Two lines mean yes," Yumi explained from the toilet seat.

She sat on the closed lid in a blinding white T-shirt and gray sweatpants. She fiddled with a silver necklace while studying the three pregnancy tests on the sink. A fourth was unopened next to them. Streaks of her summer red highlights cascaded down her hair. The room had faint traces of gardenia.

"Each has one line," I said from the doorway.

"I don't know why I bought four," Yumi added. "Who buys four? I can understand three in case the first and second are different, but four?"

"I'm not really a math person."

She looked at me with hazy, unfocused eyes. She sat perfectly still, as if she had no intention of leaving the bathroom, ever.

"You didn't call me over to read three identical pregnancy tests."

"Can you believe I have a client call in thirty minutes?"

"For Oriental Breeze?"

She nodded. When Yumi was not writing her dissertation, she worked for Oriental Breeze, a phone sex company specializing in Asian women. In some ways, the gig was a Godsend for her. Convinced that every white man had an Asian fetish, Yumi was always

108

looking for an excuse to prove it, and these calls did just the trick. She even sprinkled in the occasional Japanese word for "authenticity." Of course, she only knew a few phrases herself, so most of her vocabulary came from online dictionaries. Just a week earlier, she kept moaning the Japanese word for "dolphin" until a client exhausted himself.

"Every Saturday morning at 11:30," she continued. "He likes me to pretend that I get off while making dumpings for him. Because all Asian women make dumplings," she spat out the words.

The faint sound of Classical music came from the living room stereo, and it reminded me of light rain. I doubted Yumi listened to anything written after 1896. I figured I was not much different with my love of mid-century jazz and pop culture from the eighties and nineties. Not long after I told her about my mother and the jazz records, she took me to a practice room in the music department. She played something by Bach. I had never cried listening to Bach before.

"Who is the lucky guy?" I asked, glancing at the pregnancy tests.

"I don't even know. Not really. Jake something. I met him at Mockingbird." She shook her head and looked down at the floor. "Who does that?"

"Lots of people."

"One night stands and phone sex for hire? How did I get here?"

The tears came fast. Her body shook a little, but she didn't get up. All I could do was stand next to her and put my hand on her shoulder until it passed.

Fifteen minutes later, she was in the living room with a cup of tea, readying herself for the call. I was in the bathroom, sitting on the toilet, when I realized my period was late. Four days, maybe five. Not sure. Just a few days ago, Brett didn't pull out. There was also that time the week before when I wanted to feel him without a condom. Yumi's parade of pregnancy tests was still on the sink next to the unused one. I opened the box, and before giving it too much thought, I peed on the stick.

Three minutes.

What was three minutes? A pop song. An extended movie trailer. A bag of pre-buttered microwave popcorn (if you want to get all the kernels). I began counting the white rectangular tiles of her shower. First, by rows, then individually. I cradled the phone between my hands and glanced at the clock. The background picture of Brett and me brightened. We smiled at the camera, holding hands across a restaurant table. I checked the clock again. Over three minutes. I exhaled and looked at the test.

Two lines.

Later that afternoon, Brett and I were forced to cook. "Cooking for Couples," four classes through the continuing education program on campus, was my father's idea. A present to broker some kind of peace treaty between me and vegetables, I suspected. The instructor, Jessica Jarvis, Jr., called herself "Chef Three J's" for short. With a "Make Cake, Not War" apron, crisp khakis, and sporty sneakers, she pranced around the room checking our progress and being cheerfully optimistic about our failures. All of this motion exposed one odd detail about Chef Three J's. She wore only one sock.

Every week, I wanted to get to the bottom of that mystery. Brett wanted us to focus on cooking. I assured him I could do both. Each time I posed a theory, though, he became more convinced that I was hell-bent on not learning anything.

"Maybe she is mourning all the lost socks in her life?" I suggested toward the beginning. "Maybe she is hiding a scar from her days as a rodeo cowboy? Maybe it's from her stint in a hoosegow?"

"A hoosegow?" Brett asked, annoyed.

"You know. The Big House, the Slammer, the Pen. Don't they issue black-and-white striped socks with those orange jumpsuits?"

"I'm trying to separate egg whites here," he snapped.

A few days after each class, we tried to replicate Chef Three J's most recent recipes. Baby steps. That night, for Brett's birthday, we were making a selection of tapas from the previous week—empanadas, tortilla Espanola, albondigas. I had christened the meal "Fiesta Without Borders." Brett hardly cracked a smile.

My bigger problem was the gift. I didn't have one. I had been struggling to find something, which would explain why I ended up at Williams-Sonoma. Surrounded by salad spinners and garlic presses, fondue pots and pancake pans, Williams-Sonoma struck me as a place where passion came to die. Longing lovers and the desperate did not shop here. It was too cool, clean, and orderly. No, this was a place for the steady-handed and practical. Was that what Brett and I had become? Practical about love and cooking? A couple that could not manage without a stainless steel breadknife?

With a forty-dollar French whisk in one hand, wondering why someone couldn't just use a fork, I started noticing the people around me. A pregnant woman with a basketball-sized stomach. Two snot-nosed kids with filthy hands. Another mother with a stroller. I touched my stomach with one hand.

Did babies prefer eggs scrambled with French whisks?

I did not know.

I left without buying anything, and the next few hours had the hazy quality my eyes get after a long swim. Blurry around the edges. Other stores had similar cookware and utensils. They had variations of the same mothers, children, and baby bellies, too. Young families swarmed the streets of Haverton. How had I not noticed them before?

Six years of working, sweating, and struggling for a career. Six years of putting off any future but this one. Did a child shatter that? Did it make your work more or less meaningful? Did it demand too much to give yourself fully to anything else?

I did not know.

Brett's birthday dinner was a FEMA-level disaster. Not enough spices for the empanada. The tortilla Espanola resembled a fried egg in the shape of a beach sandal. The sangria had too much juice. And of course, I didn't have a present. I just couldn't bring our relationship to the stage of Williams-Sonoma cookware. I took another bite, and my meatball had the toughness of Clint Eastwood. I was tempted to suggest grabbing a burger at Tequila Mockingbird.

"I might be pregnant," I blurted out instead.

"What?"

112

"I took a test by accident."

"How do you take a pregnancy test by accident?"

"I'll go to the student health clinic Monday for some blood work."

He nodded before taking another bite. "Okay."

"Okay?"

"We'll know in a couple of days then."

The rest of the weekend had a strange hesitancy to it. We seemed worried about bumping into each other. We apologized for changing the channel or eating the last cracker. Like an amateur sleuth with an oversized magnifying glass, I was looking for clues to his state of mind. Proof that he didn't want a child with me. Ever. A packed bag. A one-way ticket. He didn't say anything negative, of course, but his silences left me hollow. There was no expression of joy. No hypothetical talk of raising a child together. Only wait and see.

The results came back negative.

"Pregnancy tests only work twelve to fourteen days after conception," the nurse on the phone reminded me. "You probably took it too soon."

She did not say "sorry" or ask if I was okay. She probably assumed a twenty-nine-year-old doctoral student with no job would feel nothing but relief.

I was relieved, but I also felt a distant sadness. For me and Brett. For our almost baby. And for knowing that Brett's relief eclipsed mine.

•••

Our rental car in the *Purísima* parking lot had a flat tire. I suggested calling AAA, which Brett considered an insult to his years as a mechanic in the family body shop. There were no trees within a few hundred yards. Sweat thickened on my neck.

"Let's wait in the shade," I pleaded, worried that my shoes would start sticking to the spongy asphalt.

"What shade?"

"Someone else can take care of it. That's the point of having AAA, right?"

"I can change a tire."

As he removed the spare from the trunk, I slipped away to explore the mission one more time. I passed beneath the pink bell tower and entered the cemetery. A dark wooden cross stood at one end of the barren yard, and a sign read: "One cross stands in memory of all the early Californians who are buried in this cemetery." No names. No reference to Indigenous tribes or people. All the dead were memorialized as "Californians," even though the mission was founded more than sixty years before California became a state.

I followed a dirt path for several yards before slipping beneath the long arcade of the main residence. Its overhanging roof, supported by white adobe columns, offered a much needed break from the sun. I soon reached the next building and stepped inside the mission church. In the cool quiet, I gazed at the painted ceiling beams and white walls with colorful wooden tassels, twisted vines, and bright flowers. The missionaries could not afford stained glass or marble altars, so they taught the natives to paint imitation marble and to draw niches, doorways, and balconies. They crafted wood carvings to decorate the otherwise barren churches and built false façades above the entryway to make the low roofline seem more imposing. All of these details to create the illusion of grandeur.

It made me think of the lack of grandeur in my own life. A Netflix subscription and a can of Pringles. Stolen trinkets and temporary Swedish furniture. An iPod crammed with jazz. I dreamt of writing books that would last. They might not last as long as a church, few historians get that, but long enough to carry some part of me when I was gone.

Like a child.

The tire had been replaced by the time I got back. Brett fumed quietly in the driver's seat. I should have stayed by his side, he likely thought. I should have offered to help. He was not a yeller or tantrum thrower or plate breaker. He never stormed off in the middle of a disagreement. He seethed, insides hardening like a slowly boiling egg. He would formulate a cool way to explain my shortcomings, but he would make me wait. Sometimes hours, sometimes days. That was my punishment between now and then.

In the meantime, I suggested a drive to the ocean. The town of Shell Beach, about an hour north of the mission, sat on a cliff overlooking a crescent-shaped alcove with large rock formations close to shore. They were worn and broken from the relentless Pacific and stained white from centuries of seagull poop. Sea lions sunbathed on a rock in the distance. In the 1770s and 1780s, runaways often came here from San Luis Obispo for food. The mission kept detailed records of escapees. They were pursued on horseback and punished without mercy. The whip and the rod, usually. Mission ledgers were filled with details about each crime and punishment: Otolón whipped because he did not care for his wife after she sinned with a cowboy. Tibúrico whipped for mourning the death of his wife and child. Liberato whipped for stealing rations to feed his starving parents.

Of course, their real names were lost to history. Only their Spanish names survived.

"This is the end of the road," Brett announced while staring at the ocean. The hard, square angle of his chin reminded me of a jagged cliff.

"What do you mean?"

"No more west," he said without turning toward me. "Remember that painting you showed me? The Indian chief watching the sunset over the Pacific. Just him and his family."

"And a dog."

"What?"

"Matteson's *The Last of the Race.*"

The breeze cooled my skin and thickened my hair with sand. Sun sparkled off the cresting waves, and a steady rumble accompanied the ocean's ebb and flow against the shore. I wanted to hold Brett's hand, but he kept a firm grip on the guard railing.

"We should go," he added.

"Let's take a swim. Our stuff is in the car."

"Maybe tomorrow," he said, turning to me, his eyes hidden behind sunglasses. "We should check into the hotel—the one with the windmill and the lederhosen."

"Lederhosen is German," I corrected, immediately wishing I could find a medication for keeping my mouth shut.

Brett forced a smile. "I know."

•••

Our hotel room in Solvang had a painting of the happiest Baby Jesus I had ever seen. Cradled in his

116

mother's arms, he had enough blonde hair to rival a five-year-old, and his raised hands made it look as if he was giving the viewer two thumbs up. He hung directly above the bed. The hotel manager, Lars, probably thought it would discourage sex of any kind. No doubt it worked. I just hoped Brett and I would try our luck later that night.

We had dinner reservations at the Viking Palace, and the décor did not disappoint. Inside a half-timbered house, the restaurant resembled a disassembled warship. A red and yellow striped sail covered much of the ceiling. Oars and colorful shields hung on the walls. Busts of Viking men appeared in random places—on the edge of the bar, by the restrooms, at the coat check. A dragon's head held up the hostess's podium.

I insisted on ordering the herring appetizer to share and bratwurst with sauerkraut. "And check this out," I said, leaning forward. "The Little Vikings Menu has Swedish meatballs."

The beer came in Solvang Steins with a sketch of main street and the windmill. I, of course, wondered if it could fit in my purse.

"*Skål!*" I said with a raised glass after Googling the proper way to toast in Denmark. "Isn't this place great?"

Brett's mug clanked loudly against mine. "I guess."

"What's wrong?"

He took a long sip, and the ocean waves on his shirt brought out the blue of his eyes. "Why aren't we happier?"

Something in my chest tightened, and I struggled to catch my breath. "What?"

"Why aren't we happier?"

"You're not happy?" The muscles in my neck tightened like guitar strings.

"I didn't say that." He folded his hands in front of his mouth, elbows on the table—his go-to pose when he knew I was not going to like what he had to say. "I said 'happier.'"

"It wasn't even a real baby." I plunked the stein on the table harder than I expected, and the silverware rattled. "You don't want kids with me. Fine. I'm not sure I want them myself, so forget about it."

"I never said that."

"I saw it in your face, in your everything, that weekend."

The waiter brought a platter of pickled herring with red onions and boiled potatoes sprinkled with dill. The stench of rotting fish made my stomach turn.

"I am not as smart as you," Brett said, seemingly unfazed by the herring. "I don't read like you. I don't live in my head like you."

I placed one hand on the table beside my plate, hoping he would grab it. My plaid sundress no longer struck me as flirty cute but as tablecloth not-so-chic.

"You fixed the tire. If it wasn't for you, I'd still be in that parking lot trying to prostitute myself for a ride."

"You would have called AAA."

"I'd be soliciting gentleman callers."

"Ana, you'll get bored with me." He shook his head. "You're already bored with me."

"Don't make this about me."

"Ana," he said, his voice calm and steady.

"What?"

118

I couldn't look at him. His eyes and lightning scar would tractor-beam me toward his mouth for a kiss. Instead, I gazed at the gelatinous fish.

"Ana," he repeated.

I looked up. This time he took my hand in his, and the warmth of it almost brought me to tears.

"Why aren't we happier?" he asked again.

"I don't know."

13
NASA

Delightful Delilah appears to be my official chaperone, lingering after the talk and tapping her silver wristwatch impatiently. Her body moves like a disaffected fashion model's, sashaying just ahead of me, close enough not to be rude but far enough away not to be mistaken for a friend or even a tolerable acquaintance. Students crisscross paths on the quad, and a web of gothic archways connects the limestone buildings on either side of us. Only when we get to the student center does she inform me that the job involves being faculty advisor for NASA. Their weekly meeting started ten minutes ago.

"NASA?"

"The Native American Student Association," she replies with a raised eyebrow.

"Of course," I mutter, though this is news to me.

The basement room has red, orange, and blue streamers that sag from the low ceiling and remind me of a deflated beach ball. Several folding tables have traces of party favors—paper plates and plastic utensils, an empty punch bowl and several cups. Yet the dim light gives everything an air of neglect as if the party were months ago and no one bothered to clean up.

Several chairs have been arranged in a circle in the center of the room, but only three students are here.

"I'm sure the low turnout has to do with midterms," Delightful Delilah says unconvincingly. "It's not you."

"Of course."

"That's the spirit," she replies before checking her watch and making a hasty retreat.

Delightful.

With armpits and inner thighs blazing, I join the circle. The students introduce themselves beginning with Inola, president of NASA and "aspiring documentary filmmaker." Her long legs stretch out with a liquid quality, and her face reminds me of a desert sky at twilight. Arched eyebrows and a constellation of light freckles. Hooped earrings and dark hair pulled into a braid that falls in front of her left shoulder.

"This is our Vice President, Onacona," she says, gesturing to the young man next to her.

He resembles a mailbox in sweats. A gray hoodie covers most of his head, and Bluetooth buds perch in his ears. I'm not sure if he can hear anything, but he nods after she speaks. A small mustache sprouts above his lips.

"Hello." The other student says with too much energy for the smallness of the group. He stretches out his arm for a formal handshake. "I am Satish."

"Obviously," Inola adds, "he is the wrong kind of Indian, but he keeps coming to the meetings anyway." Her smile has a Mona Lisa mischievousness to it.

I like her already.

"My parents are from Bombay," he continues without cracking a smile. He wears a formal, white dress shirt and brown slacks. "I am the treasurer for NASA and the Students of Color Club on campus. We organize meet-and-greets and other socials. Faculty are welcome, of course."

"Good to know," I reply.

"Most of us are from the Eastern Band of the Cherokee Indians," Inola says. "Onacona's parents still live in the Qualla Boundary."

"Word." Onacona lifts both hands in a raising-the-roof gesture before slumping back into his soft, shapeless clothes. Music hums faintly from his earbuds.

"That's the Reservation, right?"

"Most folks call it that, but it is land the Cherokee bought back from the US government. We are descendants of those who refused to relocate as part of the Trail of Tears. We could stay as long as we gave up Cherokee citizenship and assimilated."

I cannot quite read Inola's face, but her words carry the fatigue of being repeated many times.

"The Rez has painted fiberglass bears," Satish announces without moving. "You can 'hunt'"—he provides air quotes—"these bears throughout the town. Eagle Dance Bear is my favorite. Onacona prefers Out of Hibernation Bear."

"Don't forget about the casino," Onacona mutters.

"I prefer the interactive 1760s Cherokee Village," Satish replies with a thoughtful nod, and he turns to me once again. "We have an annual campus powwow in April, and we charter a bus for anyone interested in going to the Cherokee Indian Reservation Powwow in July. Faculty are welcome, of course."

"Word." Once again, the roof gets raised.

I lift my elbows to ease the burning sensation under my armpits, but the gesture makes it look as if I'm about to stand up and River Dance. I lower them.

"Are you working on a film right now?" I ask Inola.

"A documentary about my mother," she says. "She raised me in a RV. 'Life is not for standing still,' she'd say as if growing up without friends or a place to call home was normal. We drove from one protest to another, all around the country. Protests over pipelines, sacred sites, deforestation, commercial developments."

"You must have seen so much," I reply.

"Not really. If Mom didn't come back from a demonstration, the plan was always the same. Stay put in the RV. It could take days before someone posted bail."

"What did you do?"

She shrugs. "I lived on dry cereal and microwaved burritos. Listened to music and read. Watched videos. I waited until she knocked on the door or let herself back in. She always needed a shower and sleep. Sometimes, icepacks for her swollen wrists or bruises. I hated the ones on her face the most."

"I'm sorry."

"Don't be. She never apologized for being gone or for living life on the road. She was on a mission. There was always another protest that needed her."

Inola pauses. For a moment, her face seems older than twenty-something. Her freckles no longer remind me of stars but of ink stains on an old map.

"She still protests and speaks at powwows. I join her when I can. For the film. I interview other activists. But I still don't know how to tell her story without telling my own. That's the difficult part."

She shifts, pulling her legs beneath the chair.

"So what's your story?" she asks if we have been talking about nothing more significant than the weather or the most annoying Wahlberg.

This is the moment I've been afraid of. How do I tell my story as Lightfeather? I have been planning to go with a Chumash mother, born on the Santa Ynez Reservation, who left after falling in love with a white man she met at the Chumash Casino Resort. Very Hallmark Christmas Movie—minus the Native Americans, of course. Mabel's panties burn with the fury of sandpaper, and I slide to the edge of the hard chair.

Instead, I tell the truth.

"My mother was a kleptomaniac who thought stealing would make up for all the things she lost in life." It is strange to say it aloud, strange to realize that I have never said it aloud before, stranger still that I am choosing this group to do so. "I've learned to steal from her. I've learned to view stealing as nothing more than a vanishing act. It won't hurt anyone. It won't leave a mark or scar. I guess I'm learning that everything leaves a mark."

"Word."

14
Team Indian

After a meeting with the Vice Provost of Diversity, in a cushioned office, with cushioned chairs, for a cushioned conversation about "inclusivity," I have a break. One hour, sixty minutes, 3,600 seconds, 1/24th of a day to contain the brushfire on my skin. I need to submerge myself in a bath. I need to slather myself in calamine lotion or hydrocortisone or fire retardant. I need to put on my only pair of underwear, which has been hanging in my hotel bathroom to dry.

I take a taxi to the nearest pharmacy. The line for the only cashier is so long and everyone appears so patient that I figure he must be dealing OxyContin. Under glaring white lights, people move at the speed of grazing cows, and I want to tear the clothes off my body. Every minute here is one less minute in the bath. Every minute here is one minute closer to getting dressed for another meeting.

I could make a quick getaway, I tell myself as I let the Benadryl fall into my purse. I stay in line to fake-peruse the shelves beside me, picking up and replacing Pringles, Purell, and pink Post-it Notes. The lotion slides into the purse next. The bag of jasmine rice for my phone will be trickier. Bulky, but it might fit in my coat pocket. I shift the rice into my left hand and—

"Excuse me, Hon," a woman taps my arm. She has a thick Southern drawl and fire-engine red lipstick. Her store uniform—tan pants and a navy shirt—gives her body a rectangular shape. "We prefer you pay before putting anything in your bag. Thanks."

She shuffles away without so much as a glance, as if she has no doubt of my innocence. I wonder if that comes from my place in line or the color of my skin.

"Sorry," I call after her, but I am not sure she hears or cares.

•••

El Jefe's office reminds me of a travel agency. Artifacts from various trips to Central and South America compete for space. A Day of the Dead skeleton diorama. A miniature surfboard from San Juan del Sur. An alpaca poncho from Peru. The flag of Argentina. Pictures of Mayan and Incan ruins, of churches and museums, of bars and beaches.

"Oh-la," he says with the pronunciation of a Midwestern teenager working at Taco Bell. He gestures at the picture of himself in a wetsuit on a sun-soaked beach. "Have you been to Nicaragua?"

"No."

"Great surfing."

El Jefe's lavender suit makes me think of a groomsman at a gay wedding. He has a three-buttoned vest beneath the jacket and a navy shirt unbuttoned at the neck. I imagine him standing with one hand perpetually in his pocket, photoshoot ready. Yet there is something unreal about his youthful good looks— bushy brown hair, honey-colored eyes, the scruffiness on his jawline, and symmetrical eyes that make him both textbook attractive and forgettable at the same time.

Oscar Peterson's "Someday My Prince Will Come" plays from the speaker on his desktop computer.

"Is that Bill Evans?" I ask.

"Oscar Peterson," El Jefe corrects with a genuine smile.

I know at once that I have found my way back into his good graces. He can chalk up last night's name-that-tune lapse to beginner's luck on my part. I ease into the chair across from him. With enough calamine lotion on my body to grease a Slip 'n Slide, my skin is less angry, but my clothes feel as if I applied them with a glue-stick.

"How did you become interested in Latin American history?" I ask.

"Diving," he replies with a raised eyebrow, waiting for a look of surprise on my face. It is a staged moment, rehearsed dozens of times at parties, receptions, and fundraisers, no doubt. "What? Not a good enough reason?"

"That's like saying you did it for the tacos."

A deep laugh shakes his body. He leans back in his chair, arms behind his head with fingers interlocked, and I wonder how many more model poses he will strike before the end of our meeting.

"I do like tacos."

"I'm more of an enchilada girl myself."

"I don't mean to be flip ..."

Yes, you do.

"Actually, my first love was surfing, but after I got certified to dive in Roatán, I wanted to spend more and more time beneath the surface. I started feeling the same way about Latin America. The contrast between tourist towns and the surrounding poverty. Between popular elections and governments using the veneer of democracy to justify brutal oppression."

El Jefe speaks with the cool detachment of a scholar, but I hear an undercurrent of sincerity. He leans forward to strike another pose: elbow on the desk, chin in hand. He is Banana Republic's spin on *The Thinker*.

"I started looking on the job market and saw some opportunities in Latin American history. I decided to give it try. Of course, I'm not a native speaker," he continues without a hint of irony, "but I read flawlessly."

"So it was opportunistic?" I ask, unsticking Mabel's blouse from my chest. "I mean you looked for a niche in the market."

"I'd use the term 'strategic,' but yes, the job market shaped my decision."

"You weren't worried about not being Latino?" I ask before considering the risk of the question, the veiled implication that I could be talking about myself.

"Technically speaking, I'm Hispanic. My mother was born in Spain, but I've always believed that the quality of one's work should speak for itself."

"Of course."

Easy for him to say. He can check the Hispanic box at will. Promotions. Grants. Job applications. Cinco de Mayo. I never had a Chumash box to check. Until now. Is that all I am doing, though? Shaping myself into someone hirable? At least I'm not El Jefe, I tell myself. I want to challenge my students to rethink American history and to recognize their role in racial inequity. I don't want to turn Chumash culture into office decorations and entertaining anecdotes for university functions.

"So what about you?" El Jefe asks. "What inspired your focus on Native American history?"

"The enchiladas."

•••

The interior of McCarthy's resembles every other Irish pub in America—a dark oak bar with matching booths, pale waitresses, and the stale smell of beer. Its dim lighting tries to make you forget about time and daylight and other responsibilities. El Jefe leads me to a back table and makes a quick round of introductions before darting off with a "Grassy-ass."

I find out that Sunhawk directs the Learning Support Center on campus. It provides tutoring, counseling, and other resources to minority students and those with learning disabilities. His deeply-lined face has grooves running from forehead to chin. It reminds me of a wood carving.

"El Jefe never stays," he says with a shrug. "I think it's because I speak better Spanish."

"Who doesn't?" Bobby, the man next to him, adds. He works as an academic advisor, but unlike most of his twenty-something colleagues, he has skidded well into his forties. He has short gray hair and dark-rimmed glasses. He sips beer from a narrow glass, and his fingers, with cracked skin and thick knuckles, convince me that he is good with tools. "Do you know why we are having this dinner?"

"Come on," Sunhawk protests halfheartedly, as if he knows nothing can derail Bobby on a tirade.

"To eat burgers and learn more about student services?" I offer, mustering whatever charm can still be found beneath my lotion-soaked clothes and itchy skin.

"Because we are the only Native Americans on campus. That's right. We're Team Indian. Even with you, there aren't enough of us to play a game of bridge."

"Who plays bridge?" Sunhawk asks.

"My mother and her friends!" Bobby snaps. He raises his hand to catch the attention of a waitress who again breezes by our table without a glance. "So El Jefe decides to corral all the Indians he can find to make Lightfeather feel welcome."

"Well, you're doing a bang-up job with that," Sunhawk says before sipping from his seltzer with lime.

"No offence," Bobby says, scanning the room for our waitress. "You know I am only assigned students of color. Like I can't advise rich white kids how to take the easiest classes with the least amount of work."

"Don't pay too much attention to him," Sunhawk interrupts. "He gets this way when he's hungry."

"I'm always hungry."

"The Learning Support Center plays a crucial role on campus," Sunhawk begins, trying to shift gears. His dark eyes match his hair, and he speaks with the soothing calm of a psychologist or a Jehovah's Witness. "We help hundreds of students every semester. We have built a strong community among our staff, and more and more faculty rely on us—"

"But you're not tenured. Neither am I. We are part of the expendable labor force—like graduate students." Bobby turns to me. "No offense."

"I'm totally expendable. Just ask my ex," I add. "But you can't be fired for your ethnicity."

"So?" Bobby's dark eyes narrow, whether from my staggering ignorance or the waitress's talent for ignoring us, I can't tell. "What kind of role models are we? What kind of inspiration?"

"That is not fair," Sunhawk interrupts. "I am proud of my work here."

"Sure, students love you. Everyone loves you, Sunhawk. You're a nice fucking guy, and you don't rock the boat." Bobby takes a swing of beer. "How many Natives graduate from this place each year?"

"Less than 1% of the student body identify as Native American, but I'd say over twenty percent of that group graduates."

"Twenty percent of less than one percent? I'm not great with math, but it sounds like I have a better chance of being on the twenty-dollar bill. Waitress!" he barks, and several people at the next table look over. "And don't tell me our graduation rate is better than the national average of nine percent again."

"What's your point?" Sunhawk asks.

"You're not in front of a classroom. They don't call you 'sir' or 'doctor' or 'professor.' You don't get featured on the cover of the alumni magazine or on the university website. Some kid from the Rez won't take your class and think if Professor Sunhawk can do it so can I." Bobby finishes his beer. "Who the hell eats dinner at an Irish pub anyway?"

"People a lot less sober than us," I mutter.

"What about Lightfeather?" Sunhawk asks, a hint of irritation has crept into his hypnotic voice. "What if she gets to stand in front of the room and teach our history? Isn't that exactly what you're talking about?"

Bobby touches his empty beer glass before looking at me. "You tell me, Lightfeather. Is that enough? Are you our great Red hope?"

I'd rather do anything else right now—bungee jump, eat tofurky, or join a Matthew McConaughey Fan Club—than make a case for how I can inspire future generations of Indigenous people. Maybe I've taken this too far already. Maybe a desire to work and to do good in the classroom is not enough if I have to pretend to be Lightfeather. Dante Wellington, El Jefe, even the student union let me off the hook. Not Bobby. He understands the larger importance of this job. He understands that Native American identity is not a fashion accessory or something to package for tourists and Hollywood movies.

"No," I say as the rash in my armpits flares up. "Do I want to inspire students? Of course. Can I control how they respond to me or what they take away from a class? No. But I can confront all of them—regardless of ethnicity—with truths about Native American life in this country. I can challenge them to do something about it."

"Sorry," an impish, rosy-faced waitress with short black hair interrupts. Much to my surprise, she has a faint Irish lilt. "Are you ready to order?"

"Yes!" Bobby booms. "We just want to eat red meat and get the hell out of here."

Her smile does not waver. "Tell me about it."

As Bobby ravages his burger, Sunhawk enjoys a second seltzer water with a cobb salad. Salad strikes me as a particularly risky choice in an Irish pub. I stick with the deep-fried and grilled options, which is pretty much everything else on the menu. First, I slip off to the bathroom to inspect my rash. It has gotten redder and more irritated since this morning, but it has become bearable with the lotion. That seems to be my new bar in life. Bearable. Endurable. Perhaps there is an antihistamine for desperation and deception? For a broken heart?

As I make my way back to the table, the bartender is inspecting the licenses of two kids who can't be older than fourteen or fifteen. His muscular upper body is being strangled by a black T-shirt with "McCarthy's Pub" scrawled across the front.

"Y'all from Missouri?" he asks with a North Carolina accent thicker than humid summer air.

"Yes, sir," one of the boys chirps.

"What's the capital?"

"Excuse me?"

"What's the capital of Missouri?"

The boys' eyes widen as if he just asked them to recite π.

"Montana?" one offers.

"Come back when y'all grow some hair on your balls." The bartender smiles as he hands back the fake IDs. "And look at a map."

As I sit down to eat, Bobby's eyebrows raise. Nothing remains on his plate but discarded lettuce from the burger. My kind of eater.

"What's so funny?" he asks. "You're smiling."

"Oh, some kids with fake IDs were trying to pull a fast one at the bar, and ..."

"And what?"

"And I just thought of something for Moondude."

"Who is Moondude?"

"Nobody, just the president of *The Big Lebowski* fan club."

•••

"No civilized person is awake at this hour," Dante Wellington announces as I slide into his black Mercedes. He wears the same brown corduroy jacket from yesterday and the night before that, and his iron grip on the steering wheel bleaches his hands white. The car smells of citrus aftershave.

I am surprised how good it feels to wear my own clothes again. My limbs feel looser. Tension eases from my neck. And it doesn't look like my outfit has been put together by Salt-N-Pepa or Boy George.

Last night, when my luggage arrived at the hotel courtesy of American Airlines, I assumed it was a hallucination. The kind of hallucination common among desert explorers or fans of Nicolas Cage films. The squeaky-voiced teen at the front desk assured me that the bag was real and that they took Mabel's carryon. I still have her pajamas, though. I still ate her chocolates and used her moisturizer. I still wore her underwear. I wonder if she will be more puzzled than angry over what is missing. I hope so.

Once again, Dante appears impervious to small talk. His style of driving involves a curious mixture of fear and recklessness, and it demands most of his concentration. He chooses the center lane, driving just fast enough to annoy anyone trying to pass him and slow enough to make you want to try. I offered to take a cab to the airport, but he insisted on taking me. I suspect it involves one final test.

"There are so many trees in North Carolina," I say.

With these words, I have reached a new conversational low. After two days of talking and with no help from Dante, the tank is empty. I am out of small-talk material. I consider feigning sleep or throwing myself from the car when Dante clears his throat.

"I spoke with Inola yesterday," he says. "She is one of my students."

"Who?"

"The president of the Native American Student Association," he replies as if I forgot my birthday or the name of my firstborn child.

"Of course."

"She likes you," he continues, his eyes focused on the car ahead. "You talked about your mother. About 'actual you,' as she put it. Your honesty moved her." Dante pauses, and the word "honesty" knocks some of the wind out of me.

"You're a minority—and a woman," he adds quickly in case I forgot my vagina at the hotel. Dante seems to be teeing up for his special brand of misogynistic racism—the kind job candidates and graduate students have to chalk up to Fox News viewership or senility. "More importantly, Ana, you're a smart and talented. You do good work, and the academic job market needs more people like you. Jobs will be yours for the taking."

Years of rejection letters. Of frustration and failure. Of self-doubt and self-loathing. His belief that jobs are mine "for the taking" makes me want to laugh and weep at the same time. He may have said the same thing to the two other finalists, but I am still grateful. He has no idea how long I have waited to hear that. To feel wanted. To feel good at what I do.

"All of us—me, El Jefe, Delilah, the students—got glimpses of actual you. We like what we saw. You could have a place here."

135

"I think Delilah may have preferred a root canal to chaperoning me."

Dante laughs. "Delilah can hit you like a stiff drink, but she cares about people something fierce. You two have that in common, I suspect."

Dante has somehow gathered all of this from glimpses of actual me. My chest feels helium-light. I want to be the person he just described. I want to find a home for my career. But what about the rest of me? The liar, the hypocrite, the thief of Indigenous cultures and identity.

Dante yanks the car across two lanes of traffic to make the airport exit. I almost fall into him before the car changes directions and I slam against the passenger door. Car horns blare in the distance. Only when we get to the curb of the terminal do I fully exhale. I rub my shoulder, and its soreness makes me wonder if being Lightfeather is as reckless as Dante's driving.

Dante extends his hand to shake mine. "It has been a pleasure, Ana Lightfeather Shaw, Job Candidate," he says with a smirk. "And you're right about one thing."

"What's that?"

"North Carolina has a lot of trees."

Part III

In Memoriam

15
Bocce Balls

Ever since my phone deep-dived in a public toilet and I mummified it in a bag of rice, I have been going through withdrawal. Twitchy fingers. Irritability. A feeling of forgetfulness as if I lost my car keys or misplaced the family pet. I am home, or as home as I can be in half an apartment, but I don't know what is happening with my friends or with John Doe. After unpacking, I leave the rice-phone on the kitchen counter and head to Tequila Mockingbird.

The bar has a dense Saturday afternoon crowd. Loud with jostling bodies and buzzed cheerfulness. I don't recognize anyone at our table, but I catch sight of Doug's boxy shape at the bocce courts. Yumi stands close to him as he tosses the ball. She seems nearly half his size, her denim jumpsuit and blue-streaked hair striking against the backdrop of his white shirt. Nina Simone's "Love Me or Leave Me" swings in the distance, but most of it gets swallowed by the noise. I peel off my winter coat, already flushed from the heat in the room. Sweat makes my armpits prickly, and my breasts are still sore. I consider stopping at the bar when Kavita catches my attention. Her eyes widen, and she shakes her head as if to say "no." I can't figure out what she means until I see them. Brett and Tiffany. At the bocce courts. With the Mockingbird Gang.

It feels as if I have been turned into a pillar of salt. I can't move or breathe. I can't do anything but stare. Tiffany wears an obnoxiously playful green top with white jeans and open-toed heels. *(Who wears open-toed heels in winter?)* Her long body, undoubtedly rash free, perfectly sculpted blonde hair, and ample bosom make me feel like a hobbit. She stands close enough to nuzzle into Brett's armpit, and I have to admit that they look good together. Handsome, fit, red-carpet ready.

This cannot possibly be my new reality. The six of us sharing bocce and beer while they reminisce about their first kiss. How could Yumi, Doug, and Kavita do this to me? How could they substitute my Gollum for their Barbie and Ken? My Coors Light for their Guinness? I was only gone for two fucking days.

Brett waves at me, which means it's too late to feign a heart attack or claim amnesia. I have to join them. They cluster around a standing table at the midpoint of the court where Doug and Yumi are playing. Kavita wears a long-sleeve beige dress, and her dancer's posture only adds to my status as runt of the litter.

"So relieved you could make it," Tiffany says as she passes me a white envelope with light-blue trim. The color of her fingernails matches her green top. "I wanted to hand these out in person."

Three identical envelopes are on the table next to a pitcher of beer. All have been opened. Inside, I find an invitation to the baby shower of Tiffany Riggs and Brett Bergin. Four months from now. Some people at a nearby table explode into laughter.

"I've been texting you all day," Kavita blurts. "W—T—F?"

"My phone is in a bag of rice," I reply.

"That's curious," Tiffany says, but nothing about her tone suggests a desire to hear more.

The bocce balls next to us crack loudly, scattering in different directions. Doug gives himself a fist pump.

"Want to join me for a drink run?" Brett asks.

I nod even though the pitcher has plenty of beer and Briff (my new couple name for Brett and Tiffany) doesn't appear to be drinking. The noisy crowd forces us to stick close together. As I follow him, Brett's shoulders seem powerful enough to part the Red Sea. People give way until we find space at the corner of the bar.

"Is there any way you think I'm going to this fucking baby shower?" I unload, resenting the fact that he is wearing his sexy jeans and the blue-and-white checkered shirt I got him for his birthday last year.

"We don't want you to feel excluded," he says while signaling the bartender.

"'We'? You and *Tiff* are worried about my feelings? Don't treat me like the kid who wasn't picked for dodgeball."

"We're not saying that."

"'We' again? Jesus."

"I mean me."

"Screw you and dodgeball!"

The bartender comes over, and Brett orders margaritas on the rocks with salt. He asks if I want chips and guacamole. I do, but I say no. It feels too much like old times with him ordering for me. He asks for the food anyway.

"I have to tell you something," he begins, watching the bartender pour tequila into a mixer.

"That's never a good sign," I mutter.

"I've sublet the apartment."

"What apartment?"

"Our apartment."

"I live in our apartment."

The drinks and chips are placed in front of us. I scoop some guacamole and take a long swig of margarita to steel myself. The salted rim has the bite of seawater.

"It has been almost four months, and I can't afford to keep paying my share of the rent," he says.

The words have a practiced quality, and I wonder if he rehearsed his "talking points" with Tiff, if she gave him pointers on what to say if I proved difficult. A flash of anger tightens my jaw.

"Why the hell not? Is she charging you for sex?"

Brett doesn't take the bait, which makes me even angrier. "Technically, you're not on the lease."

"What?"

"I rented it for us, remember? You still had to run out the lease on your old place, so I ... You didn't have anything for the down payment."

The last words sting—a bitter reminder of the ongoing humiliations of graduate school and my failure to get a job. I didn't have any money. Of course, I didn't. I never do. I just forgot about the lease. We split the bills and the rent. We took turns grocery shopping and planning vacations. After a while, you get so intertwined with a person that you forget who does what. You forget that pulling one loose string can unravel everything. That seems to be what remains of Brett and me. Loose strings and unravelling.

That and a fucking baby shower.

"You're kicking me out?"

"No."

"Yes, you're throwing me to the wolves and the lions and the rabid squirrels. Why? To help pay for a crib? Just get one from IKEA."

"I don't live there anymore," he pleads.

"Whose fault is that?"

"I told the tenant he can't move in until April. That gives you six weeks to find a place. I can help with the move. Anything you need—"

"Anything I need? I need our life back!"

Crap. I finally said it. Out loud. In public. I have imagined this moment a thousand times. This moment where he takes my hand and touches the side of my face, where we confess our undying love followed by tearful apologies, impassioned kisses, and lovemaking with mutually satisfying orgasms. Instead, the world around me switches to a silent movie.

Brett's eyes drift toward Tiffany, and she glances over at the same moment. They smile at each other. The whiteness of her teeth reminds me of a magazine ad for toothpaste. It only lasts a second, this exchange, but it tells me more than I want to know. He is in love with her. They are in love with each other.

Briff.

I wonder why I need so many reminders of what is right in front of me. He left. He moved in with another woman and got her pregnant. He only speaks in the Royal We. And now he is evicting me. Shy of a few billboards with "It's over, Dumbass," what will it take for my useless heart to listen?

"Those tits are fake!" I yell before storming off with my drink.

I join Yumi and Doug at the bocce court, keeping a wary eye on Briff and Kavita at the midcourt table. Yumi gives me a hug as Doug launches the next ball.

Crack.

"Sorry," she begins. "They just showed up. We texted you like crazy."

"It's okay—as long as you're mean to them and don't go to the baby shower," I reply with a smirk. "Not to make you take sides or anything."

"Done." She hands me a blue-and-white striped bocce ball. "I need to pee. Can you take my turn?"

"Sure."

As Yumi snakes her way through the crowd, Kavita joins Doug and me. Briff stands side-by-side at the edge of the court. I wonder if they are waiting for me to throw the ball, but it doesn't take long to realize they are too busy flirty-talking to see anything outside of themselves. Let alone the Ex. I take another sip of my drink before handing it to Doug.

"How was the conference?" Doug asks, a bit too loud as usual.

"Fine," I say, my stomach tightening. "At least there was free food."

"Sweet."

Briff holds hands now. I've never seen them touch before. I have only imagined it— alongside my favorite scenes from *Hellraiser* and *The Texas Chainsaw Massacre*. She grips his hand at her side. He turns his head toward her, no doubt to say something down-to-earth charming, while the rest of his body remains at an angle facing the court.

"Seriously," Doug insists, "how did it go?"

"About as well as can be expected." I take aim at the pallino, wondering if Doug knows somehow, if he can see through the lie. "People seemed to enjoy my talk."

With the sour taste of these words in my mouth, I step forward. I don't realize how hard I am gripping the ball until I try to release it. I don't realize I haven't quite let go until Tiffany's laugh hits me like the chiming of a servant's bell. And I don't realize my arm has veered to the left until the ball takes flight.

Instead of grounding along the broken granite, the ball rockets waist-high toward Briff's table. I am not sure if I yell out a warning or if I just watch it sail through the air, quietly dumbfounded. But the blue-and-white striped sphere manages to smack Brett in the groin. Air explodes from his mouth, and he collapses onto the bocce court in a fetal position, scattering most of the balls.

The remarkable thing isn't that I just threw a bocce ball into my ex-boyfriend's crotch, without meaning to. It isn't that everything gets whisper-quiet in the bar as other guys cover their genitals. The remarkable thing is that the ball ricocheted off Brett's crotch and crashed directly onto Tiffany's open-toed shoe. She bends over so fast that her face slams into the tabletop. Both hands fly up to her nose as she drops into a sitting position. Only when she reaches for her toes do I see blood.

Somehow, I have managed to fell Briff with one bocce ball. I've never been much of a sports person, but if this were a bowling match, I would call that a touchdown.

"O—M—G!" Kavita yells.

"You just went nuclear." Doug pats me on the shoulder. "Nice knowing you."

A crowd gathers around the fallen until the bartender disperses them. Someone even calls an ambulance because Tiffany fractured her left middle toe and bloodied her nose. Fine—because *I* fractured her left middle toe and bloodied her nose. Yumi gets Tiffany ice from the bar. Kavita helps her to a booth where she can prop up her foot. And I stand there with a mound of napkins in my hands, useless. Tiffany won't look at me. She won't even touch my napkins. She grabs her own from the table and presses them against her nose.

"It looks like the bleeding stopped," I offer.

Kavita glares at me.

The paramedics, who eerily resemble two of the Jonas brothers, wrap Tiffany's third and fourth toes together with tape. The green nail polish has been scraped away on both, and her entire foot looks pinkish and swollen. Jonas One says it will heal in time, that she can wear a brace or a walking boot. Crutches can "do the trick" too, he adds with a music-video smile.

"Did you wish to file a police report?" Jonas Two asks, clearly the meaner of the brothers.

"Jesus," I blurt. "It was an accident."

Tiffany looks at me, eyes smoldering. "Really?"

"Yes, I suck at this game. Ask anyone."

"It's true. She is beyond terrible," Kavita offers in complete seriousness as if we were discussing global warming or the worst Jean-Claude Van Damme films.

"Let's not go overboard," I mutter.

Tiffany turns her attention back to Jonas Two. "No, I just want to get out of here. We both do."

Meanwhile, Doug has been sitting at a booth with Brett, who holds a cold beer bottle against his crotch. Doug later tells me that he convinced Brett it was an accident, using a similar argument about my staggering incompetence in all things athletic.

"We're lucky you didn't take up archery," Doug adds.

Brett waves off help from the Jonas brothers, and they leave for their next medical emergency or Comic Con appearance, not sure which. Briff leaves as well. Slowly. Gingerly. Tiffany, shoe in one hand, moves with the speed of a Macy's Day Parade float. She hobbles and winces with each step, gripping Brett's shoulder as she tries to keep her toes from touching the floor. Brett limps alongside her, occasionally wincing, occasionally touching his crotch until they open the front door.

•••

After the bocce ball-busting incident, none of my friends want to stay at Tequila Mockingbird or with me for that matter. Doug and Kavita have dinner plans for "date night," she calls it cheerfully. Doug hangs his head. Yumi nods, claiming to have some client calls. I too have plans, oddly enough. Before I left for the interview, I promised Moondude I would work Saturday night to make up my missed shift.

In truth, I have never been more grateful for the Haverton County Morgue. The quiet. The stillness. The absence of paramedics and pop singers. I unload my books and iPod at my cubicle. On top of the usual "To-Do" list from Bless-Her-Heart Sherilynn, I find a note from Moondude: *Been trying to reach you, person. On the roof.*

Part of me wonders if this is a euphemism for getting high, but Moondude sometimes takes his telescope to the top of the building. I know this

146

because he talks about stargazing at coma-inducing lengths. I have always turned down invitations to join him since he can get a bit handsy, but not tonight.

In the center of the roof, Moondude has set up a tripod and a blanket covered with enough astronomy equipment to rival a middle-school science teacher: star charts and a compass, pencils and a protractor. The air has a mild quality—one of those February nights with deceptive hints of spring. Moondude stands over the telescope, adjusting something with the eyepiece. I have never been up here. The roof is just high enough to block out light from the parking lot below, and the trees on all sides make the night seem darker. The sky teems with stars. In clusters and alone. Burning close and flickering like distant memories.

I recognize some of the constellations. Ursa Major and Ursa Minor—the bears nicknamed Big and Little Dipper for resembling ladles. The magical armor and winged sandals of Perseus, who beheaded Medusa and lies next to his wife Andromeda. Taurus with his horns appears ready for battle, and the Seven Sisters keep their distance, mostly huddled together. They will all bear children for the gods except poor Metrope—away from the others, outcast for marrying the doomed mortal Sisyphus.

"Person," Moondude says, kamikazing into a longer-than-appropriate hug. As he pulls me into him, there is no way to avoid a contact high from his weed-fumigated jacket.

"Any UFOs?" I ask, prying myself free.

"Just one sighting of Elvis." He gestures toward the telescope. "Take a look."

147

I peer into the magnifying lens. Instead of the King, four stars and a tail come into focus. "The Big Dipper."

"Not to the Skidi Pawnee tribe of central Nebraska. They called it 'The Star That Does Not Walk Around.' For them, the dippers were stretchers trailed by medicine men. They carried the gods exhausted from placing the heavens in order." Moondude pauses, putting his hands on his hips and looking skyward. "The Big Dipper has gone by lots of names in North America. The Ojibway called it the Great Fisher—a warrior who brought summer to the world and who sometimes appeared as a weasel-like animal with a long tail."

Moondude steps over to the blanket. A sudden gust of wind tussles his Kenny G hair, and his faded-orange coat reminds me of a discarded lifejacket. He opens a thermos steaming with warmth.

"Want some?" he asks. "Hot chocolate with marshmallows."

"Sure," I say with a shrug, mostly wondering where he hides the pot brownies. I could do with some cannabis and chocolate right now.

As he pours hot chocolate into a second thermos cup, the aroma reaches me. Sweet and inviting like a child's laugh. My tongue tingles with the first sip. It has been made with warmed milk, and the taste carries me back to childhood. Fall nights by the outdoor fire pit in my parents' backyard—my father and I close together in chairs, secretly happy to be sharing a blanket not big enough for three. My mother bringing us hot chocolate but lingering only a few moments to get a glimpse at our strange connectedness—so comfortable and cozy, so different from her way with me.

I watch Moondude as he adjusts the telescope. Jeans hang loosely on his toothpick legs, and he wears Birkenstocks without socks. His feet appear purplish in the dark.

"You must be cold," I say.

"Summer is a state of mind."

"Tell that to your frost bite."

"How about this one?" he asks, waving me over.

"Pleiades, the Seven Sisters," I reply. "That's one of my favorites."

He looks at me with raised eyebrows. "I thought you were Native American."

"What?" I can feel the breath stall in my chest. "What are you talking about?"

"I mean you specialize in Native American history, man." he adds. "I mean, person. Don't you know any tribal myths about the stars?"

"Not really. It is a part of Indigenous culture I never really considered," I say, realizing that Moondude has now shamed me both as a scholar and as a maker of hot chocolate.

"Well, the Arapaho called the Seven Sisters the Splinter Foot Girl. She was born from the leg of a male hunter and found herself so harassed by lusty men and animals that she and her family were turned into stars."

"So much for sensitivity training," I say before taking another sip.

"What?"

"I got your note," I reply. "You found out something about John Doe?"

He blinks several times as if I just woke him from a trance. A wave of disappointment crosses his face. He is reluctant to turn from celestial bodies to a dead one, from his rooftop view to cold storage. I can't blame him.

"The preliminary autopsy is in," he says. "We're still waiting for a few test results."

"And?"

"Good catch on the puncture wound in his arm," he begins. "You were right. That was the cause of death. Someone injected air into his pulmonary artery."

"Just air?"

"That's all it takes. Air enters the vein and travels to the right side of the heart causing a heart attack. Air embolisms are the most common cause of death for scuba divers. John Doe pretty much experienced the same thing. It's a quick, relatively painless way to die."

"So he definitely had help. There was nothing at the scene—no syringe, no tourniquet. Someone gave him an IV and cleaned up afterwards."

"Dr. McKelvey told me they would have needed a 20cc syringe."

"So?"

Moondude brushes aside his curls. "That is not a standard size. You need a prescription for it in most states, and any doctor would ask questions. The best alternative, McKelvey said, would be to swipe one from a hospital exam room. They're easy enough to find if you know where to look."

"McKelvey is a regular Nurse Jackie."

"Who's that?"

"Just a mobster's wife turned health professional." I finish my drink. It's almost cold now, and a thick layer of syrupy chocolate has pooled at the bottom of the cup. "Can you do one more favor for me?"

Moondude tightens the thermos cap and returns to the blanket. After folding the star chart, he starts gathering his compass and other stargazing equipment. "What?"

"You mentioned a friend at the State Police. Can you ask him to run Doe's fingerprints against a national criminal database?"

"This is already freaking me out. He had four identities—all names of dead people." Moondude folds the blanket and shoves it into a duffle bag. His shoulders are stiff with unmellowness.

"That means he wasn't an amateur. Maybe he got caught at some point." I step closer to Moondude. His brown eyes appear black and shiny, and his skin is white as starlight. "If this goes nowhere, I'll stop. I promise."

"This is the last one. I'm not built for this," he says. "Anxiety aggravates my eczema."

"Thanks." I hand him my empty cup. "For all of it," I add, glancing at the telescope. "I actually have to get to work, but you should really hang out a bit. There is so much to see."

"Yeah." He smiles. "There is."

16
Accounting

"Doug is breaking up with me because of my pubic hair," Kavita says as I enter the office and close the door. She stands by the window in a maroon blouse that deepens the flushed color of her cheeks.

"Wait a minute," Doug protests from his chair. Above the desk hangs a large poster of Alfred Hitchcock's *Rear Window* with Jimmy Stewart clinging to binoculars and Grace Kelly standing behind him. "I just said you've got a lot going on down there. It's distracting."

"Distracting?"

"Yeah," Doug replies as he fiddles with the top button on his shirt. "I shouldn't need celestial navigation to find my way around."

I clear my throat. "I think I should go—"

"No!" they both yell in unison.

"So what? You want me to shave it all off? You want my vagina to look like a pecan?"

"Gross." Doug shudders, his mouth twisting as if he just bit into a lime. "You have a lot of untamed bush. That's all. I don't want to feel like I have to comb my tongue every time—"

"Jesus!" I blurt.

"When was the last time you went down on me?" Kavita raises her voice, though she still speaks softer than the rest of us.

"That's kind of the point. Just a little maintenance—"

"O—M—G!"

"Seriously, guys," I interrupt. "I'm out of here."

"You shave down there, right?" Doug asks me in all seriousness.

"You are not bringing me into this."

"Why the hell not?"

"Because I'm not talking about my pubic hair. Or anyone else's for that matter," I say more emphatically than I expect. Students shuffle outside the door, waiting for classes to start. Some, no doubt, are listening.

"There is nothing wrong with my pubic hair," Kavita protests.

Doug stands up. His towering frame suddenly makes the office feel much smaller. He picks up a stack of papers and a book. "You said you just wanted to have fun, Kavi. Nothing serious. I took you at your word."

She holds her body still. Behind her, the branches of a dead tree claw at the window.

Doug goes on, "I was talking about some of the ways sex between us isn't working. I was suggesting we go back to being friends instead of part-time lovers. How can we break up when we're not even together?"

"I only said that casual stuff because of you," she pleads, the muscles in her face taut. "Your parents' messy divorce. Your dad's even messier second divorce. You're one of those guys who run from commitment."

"So now I'm supposed to run toward it?" Doug shakes his head as he opens the door. "What a relief to know that I'm just one of those guys. You think I walk around with chronic foot-in-mouth disease, that I always say the wrong thing at the wrong time. The truth

153

is I talk straight. I talk to you, to all the women, like I talk to men. No bullshit. No pedestals."

"Wait," Kavita pleads as she steps over and grabs his wrist.

Doug stiffens. "Their divorce didn't teach me to be afraid of commitment," he says. "It taught me not to say one thing and mean another."

He glares at me before slipping into the hallway of jostling, thick-coated, backpacked undergraduates. I follow. Doug's long strides force me into a trot, and we are at the door of my classroom before I catch up. I glance inside. Cheerleader Cliché, who has been hitting on the Flann Man all semester, flirty laughs at something he says. Clench sits in the back row with his Yankees cap and "School Ruined My Life" shirt, looking up from his phone just long enough to scowl.

Good times.

"Straight talk," I say. "Really?"

Doug clutches a thick stack of student papers to his chest with the one hand. Some of his handwriting is scrawled across the bottom, but I can only make out the words "try again."

"You're not sleeping with her anymore because of pubic hair," I scoff, both horrified that I'm discussing my friend's short-and-curlies and impressed by my ability to do so with a straight face.

"So?"

"How much of this is about Yumi? Did her name come up at all? The two of you are practically dry humping every time I see you."

He steps back as if I slapped him. His eyes narrow. "Nothing has happened between us," he says.

154

"Wanting to fuck someone and actually doing it are two different things. Just ask Brett."

There it is. The lowest of blows. The Tonya Harding of ice skating. The *Cats* of box office bombs. And in typical Doug fashion, it has been broadcast loud enough for all of my students and arguably the entire Humanities Department to hear.

Fortunately, my class begins with a quiz today, so I have some time to collect myself. They scribble answers but glance at me warily. They've had ringside seats for what looks like a lovers' spat or a bad breakup about my pubic hair. I'll be fodder for lunchtime gossip and dorm room speculation for the rest of the month, no doubt. Some will assume I have the Amazon Rainforest between my legs. I even detect a smile on Clench's face.

Good times.

My hands shake. Sure, I'm pained by the salt Doug ground into the festering wound of my heart, but it is more than that. I am angry—not because he lashed out. I deserved it. I am angry because the triangle of Doug's sex life jeopardizes all of our friendships. It risks making us choose sides. It risks afternoons at Tequila with bocce and beer, road trips, and movie marathons at Yumi's. I am angry because part of my life is about to become the collateral damage of someone else's choices. Again.

•••

When I get to the first floor of Humanities, Tiffany is teaching in the main amphitheater. Her voice spills into the empty hall, and it reminds me of a moist finger circling the rim of a wine glass. I can't leave the building without passing the open double doors. I can't

155

hide behind the potted plants for the next hour—though I consider it. Maybe she won't see me if I walk quickly and pretend to be zipping my coat.

"The novel begins with Ishmael assuming a false name and contemplating suicide. He describes himself as pausing in front of coffin warehouses and following funeral processions. Why does Melville present him comically here?" she asks from the stage at the bottom of the room.

Seats fan out on either side of her like ridges in a clamshell. She wears a tailored, navy-blue suit, flawless, and the whiteness of her blouse matches the whiteness of her teeth. Blond hair cascades to her shoulders, and her red lipstick has shades of purple. The only thing marring her stunning bearing is the walking boot. She limps across the dais with a few thuds, and the boxiness of her foot reminds me of Boris Karloff in *Frankenstein*.

"Why does it matter?"

Over a dozen students lower their glowing phones and turn around. The question comes from a gruff kid in the back row who resembles a bouncer-in-training at a nightclub. His boxer's face, baggy eyes, and mussy black hair appear to be earned from long, hard nights. I slip inside, staying close to the door for a quick getaway.

"Why does the comedy matter?" Tiffany asks with raised eyebrows.

"No. Why are we reading this book?" he asks, louder this time, emboldened by his staring classmates.

Tiffany pauses next to the podium, smile unbroken, and she looks directly at him with the curiosity of someone studying an exotic zoo animal.

"What do you recommend we study?"

"Something that doesn't suck." Though he gets a few chuckles, his voice wavers a bit. I imagine he has taken punches from guys a lot bigger than Tiffany, but he hesitates, unsure of the consequences of messing with a woman he'd rather have sex with than take notes from.

"Like accounting," the boy replies with little conviction.

I suspect this answer shocks the room more than his outburst. Nothing about him suggests even a rudimentary familiarity with math. He might be mistaken for a grunge band drummer or a panhandler, not an accountant.

"Accounting? Well, you certainly can take any number of accounting classes on campus. This just doesn't happen to be one of them—as has been abundantly clear since the start of the semester." She manages to say the words with the sweetness of a daycare worker.

He shrugs.

"Okay, let's talk about accounting. I've never known anyone whose life was utterly transformed by an accountant. I have known people who have been profoundly changed by seeing the *Pietà* or attending a performance of Brahms' *Requiem* or reading *One Hundred Years of Solitude*. We hire musicians to play at our weddings. We travel around the world to see art and architecture and nature. And we write poems when we fall in love."

She pauses, taking a few clunky steps toward the front of the stage. She still manages to move with a confidence I desire and despise.

"By all means, go to a good accountant, Jason. Pay your taxes. Get sound financial advice. Those things are important, as are accountants. But don't forget what connects us to our humanity. Don't forget what we turn to as the best reflection of who we are and who we strive to be. That is why we study these things."

Her ability to articulate what I care so much about, her way of explaining why I want this job, remind me of why I admire her. Still. They also remind me why her relationship with Brett has the power to re-shatter my insides day after day. I'll never measure up to her professionally or personally. I'll never even get the chance to compete because she has already beaten me in every aspect of life. Looking at her once again, I can't help thinking of him, of them, of Briff. I can't help thinking of the fucking baby shower. The scream inside my head could shatter windows.

Nearly fifty students turn around, startled. Tiffany stares at me with hands on her hips, and I realize something.

I actually screamed.

17
The Brett-Away

Kavita's apartment smells of a recently unwrapped McDonald's hamburger and fries. As with the rest of the Mockingbird Gang, she has an abundance of IKEA products. Brett hooked us up like a crack dealer in *The Wire,* and we all became Swedish furniture junkies. Kavita's living room sports a *knopparp* sofa, *flysta* shelves, and *nyboda* coffee table with reversible tabletop—the same one in my half-apartment without Brett. A print of the six-armed Dhana Lakshmi, Goddess of wealth, hangs on the wall above the television. Cloaked in red, her outstretched hands discard gold coins, and she holds a lotus flower by her shimmering face.

"Are you okay?" I ask as Kavita sits next to me on the couch. She crosses her legs and faces me. I do the same. Even her maroon sweatpants and gray sweatshirt can't detract from her exquisite posture. She smells of toothpaste.

"Doug's right, you know," she says, looking down at the tissues balled in her hands.

"About your Larry-Moe-and-Curly's?"

"No!" Kavita slaps my shoulder. "I wasn't honest with him about what I wanted."

"How honest is he being with you?" I ask. "All of a sudden he has a meltdown about your Hairy Potter?"

"What?"

"Your Dirty Cactus."

She shakes her head and smiles. "Enough with the euphemisms for pubic hair."

"But I have a whole list," I protest, taking a folded piece of paper from my pocket. "Southern Mullet, Bearded Lady, Hairy Garcia."

Kavita laughs.

"4 a.m. Shadow."

"Please."

"The internet is a beautiful thing."

Kavita wipes her nose with a tissue. She lifts a glass brimming with wine. Mine sits nearly empty on the table. "Did I ever tell you that we hooked up at that yoga retreat?"

"No way! It was like a quarantined prison there. How did you pull that off?"

"On a bench in the meditation garden."

"I will never see meditation the same way." I take hold of her hand. It is warm, soft, and lighter than I expect. "I am really sorry things didn't work out with Doug. Going back to the beginning won't help. Take my word for it."

"I know."

"Planning that retreat was really nice of you, by the way," I add. "To do that for me."

"You hated every second."

"True."

•••

The Mockingbird Gang pitched this road trip as a "Brett-Away"—a weekend in rural Massachusetts to clear my head from the breakup last month. Anything to shake me out of my languorous existence of Pringles, Coke, and reruns of *Criminal Minds*. But no one mentioned the Shanti Yoga Retreat. No one mentioned sweat and stretching and guys named Yuppie Joe. And no one mentioned all the rules.

160

At dinner on the first night, I muttered curse words until one of the cafeteria monitors hissed "shhh" as he passed our table. He folded his hands into a triangle in front of his chest and bowed his head. His nametag read: "Namaste Chet."

"Silent meals? Seriously?" I continued in a whisper.

"This does kind of blow, Kavi," Doug muttered. "No talking. No booze."

"It says here that they're assigning us roommates, too," Yumi added, looking up from a brochure and tugging at the neckline of her "I don't do math" T-shirt. "To build community."

"Fuck," Doug blurted.

"Shhh." Namaste Chet returned. His red-and-white crewneck sweater reminded me of a Christmas gift for retired dads. He wore thick glasses that made his blue eyes seem unusually wide and his nose too small. "Meals are for quiet contemplation. Please respect the energy of those around you."

"Excuse me?" I asked, just to see him flinch. "Is Namaste your first name?"

Namaste Chet eyed me suspiciously and explained in a hushed tone that "Namaste" was a respectful term for greeting someone.

"Has anyone ever been confused?" I added. "By the nametag?"

"No." He bowed and hurried away from the table, refusing to get sucked into any more unauthorized talking.

"Let's not torment the staff," Kavita pleaded. "This place isn't just yoga. There are meditation hours, cooking classes, afternoon hikes." She turned to me. "It will really help clear your head. Give it a chance."

161

We sighed, resigning ourselves to a weekend of captivity at the Shanti Yoga Retreat. We turned our attention to dinner. The evening's one and only option: Aloo Mater Gobi. I dug through the bowl of cauliflower and peas, hoping to find chicken or a shiv.

Doug took a sip from his copper cup. "The water is refreshing."

I snort-laughed. Namaste Chet glared from across the room. He was giving off some very negative energy, if you asked me.

We went to our room assignments to unpack. With only an hour until "Lights Out at Ten," we planned to meet in the Commons for a game of Monopoly. No electronics allowed, of course.

The room smelled of mildew and had the cinderblock charm of a federal prison. There was a desk and chair, both made of cheap pine, a sink, and, of course, a bunk bed. "To build community," no doubt. The top bunk had already been claimed by my roommate, "Carma with a C," who sat cross-legged on the mattress. She had twilight skin and braided hair that fell to her stomach. Without prompting, she explained that her main goal for the weekend was to focus on her prana.

"Is that a seafood allergy?"

"No, it's breathing, our universal life force," she explained with a cheeriness that verged on aggression. She sniffed loudly, blew her nose twice, and sniffed again.

"Oh."

"Why are you here?" she asked.

"I think I'm being punished." I replied while tossing my bag onto the bed. "To get out of my head, actually," I added. "I just went through a bad break up."

Carma with a C nodded as if I had uttered some great truth. "Don't let anyone steal your peace."

Was that what was wrong? Had I let Brett steal my peace? Or had I let Tiffany, who stole Brett, steal my peace? Either way, for a brief moment, I thought that I might actually learn something here, that I was supposed to meet Carma with a C and that she was meant to take me under her wing to teach me how to—

"Do you mind if I neti?" she asked as she climbed down the bed. Her thick legs moved hesitantly, and I could see that she was much older than I.

"What's neti?"

"A neti pot." She walked over to the sink to demonstrate. She grabbed a plastic container that resembled a flattened teapot. She filled it with water and added salt from a cafeteria saltshaker, stirring the mixture with a spoon. After tilting her head over the sink, she stuck the spout into one nostril and lifted her arm to pour. A moment later, water came out of her other nostril in a steady stream. The entire thing resembled an amateur magic trick.

"Ewww," I uttered.

"It really clears the sinuses," she said when it was over, offering me the pot. "Want to try?"

"No, thanks, I'm not even sure my nose can do that."

"You're missing out," Carma with a C replied. "I love Old Neti." She smiled at the pot like a proud parent.

"She's adorable."

•••

The following morning, I found myself attending a yoga class with Yuppie Joe. The studio smelled of sweaty socks and incense.

"How can I be doing Happy Baby Pose wrong?" I whined.

I was lying on my back, feet in the air and sweat pooling between my breasts. I resembled a floating sea otter.

Kativa stood over me. Her muscular legs and ridiculously flat abdomen reminded me of carved marble. Her clingy workout clothes left little to the imagination. After just fifteen minutes, she had been asked by Yuppie Joe to take on the role of assistant instructor. He wore khakis, buttoned shirts, and leather slip-on loafers around the compound. But in class, he went full strip-a-gram trainee. His workout shorts could make Speedo swimwear blush, and his tight T-shirts appeared stolen from Patrick Swayze's wardrobe in *Dirty Dancing*.

"Try to straighten your spine," Kavita said. "And stretch out your hips."

She placed her knees on the back of my thighs and slid onto me. As she spread her legs, her thighs pressed against mine until my knees were practically in my armpits. She grabbed my feet, and her crotch nuzzled against my own. She looked ready to ride a horse. It had been a while since anyone rubbed anything down there, and I was surprised by the tingling sensation. I glanced over at Doug, who was watching us. He licked his lips. Literally.

"Come here often?" I asked.

"Concentrate on your hips," Kavita replied.

"I'm a little distracted."

By the time Kavita finished with my crotch and Yuppie Joe dismissed us, I was ready to make a break for it.

"Just for lunch. Edith Wharton's estate is only ten minutes from here," I pleaded.

"We can't miss 'Indian Spice: Wasabi Pete's Caliente Cooking Class,'" Kavita said earnestly.

"There are so many things wrong with that sentence," Doug replied grimly.

I turned to Kativa. "I need a burger."

"I need a drink," Yumi added.

"Okay." Kavita nodded. What else could she do? She saw us foaming at the mouths. "As long as we are back for the Vinyasa class at 4:00."

I rolled down the window of Kavita's cranky SUV as far as it would let me. After hours of humid yoga studios, sweaty bodies, and steamed vegetables, the crisp November air smelled as clean and sweet as the top of a baby's head. Cotton ball clouds hugged the peaks of the Berkshire Mountains, and trees spilled over the hills in waves of orange, red, and yellow. The engine whined. The radio hummed something classical.

Edith Wharton's country house, the Mount, had a cool formality to it—white stucco and green shudders, arched ceilings and grand parlors. As you wandered past elegantly set dining tables and tapestries, the house gave way to more intimate spaces. Cozy bedrooms. Clawfoot tubs. A library teeming with books, inviting couches, and a desk—though Wharton preferred writing in bed every morning.

A path ran down the center of the terraced garden out back. Each level had grassy fields framed by hedges and identically manicured trees. At the far end, the path stopped at a wall of lime trees that hid the walkway to Wharton's secret gardens: one with stone walls and ivy-covered archways, the other with flowers and a dolphin fountain. Despite all of the straight lines and symmetry, the open spaces and sunlight, one could still find places to hide.

From the Mount Café and Bar on the porch, it felt warm enough to unbutton our jackets but not to take them off. Doug leaned far back in his chair, legs stretched out and eyes closed while the sun warmed his face. His gray sweatpants had drops of white paint from that Friday night we all drank beer and repainted the bookshelves in his office. Yumi munched on fries while Kavita and I finished our burgers. We all nursed a third round of margaritas.

"Which *Age of Innocence* character are you?" I asked, still chewing.

"I'm the dude," Doug chimed in without opening his eyes. "Daniel Day Lewis."

"I wasn't asking you."

"Countess Olenska," Yumi said, sipping her margarita. "The exotic rebel."

"Michelle Pfeiffer is so hot in that movie," Doug mumbled.

Yumi gave him a swift kick under the table. "She's also a talented actress, ass."

"I'm so Mary Welland," Kavita added with a touch of disappointment in her voice. "The less interesting cousin."

I kicked Kavita under the table. She smiled.

"I'm Daniel Day Lewis," Doug insisted again as he reached for his drink.

"We're talking about the novel, not the movie. His name is Newland Archer," I corrected.

"Daniel Day Lewis."

"Doug, stop stealing my peace."

He laughed loudly.

"So which one are you?" Kavita asked.

"Lily Bart."

At almost the same instant, Kavita and Yumi tossed fries at me. "Wrong novel!"

"I know, but I'm so *House of Mirth* right now. Alone. Poor. Suicidal."

"Hey," Kavita leaned forward and clasped my hand. "You're good, and we're here. Always."

I glanced at the garden. Gray clouds gathered in the distant sky. Beneath them, the colorful leaves reminded me of a dying fire, and I realized I hadn't thought about Brett for nearly a day. Strange that I could forget him for a minute, let alone hours. Strange there could come a time when I did not think of him at all. The idea filled me with sadness and hope in equal measure. I looked around the table at my friends, and my eyes burned with tears. Not with thoughts of Brett. With gratitude for them, for this ridiculous yoga retreat, and for Edith Wharton's back porch.

"We should probably head back soon," Kavita said.

"One more round first," Doug chimed.

"I'll drink to that," I replied, holding up my glass for a toast.

•••

The Lotus Flower Studio had the blinds drawn. Most of the lights were out, and it was hot enough for sweat to evaporate from the skin. As I waited for class to start, my head spun from tequila. I could still taste the saltiness of the margaritas, and my fingers smelled of lime juice.

Doug and Yumi stood on opposite sides of me. Doug swayed slightly, and Yumi tucked a strand of purple-black hair behind one ear. Kavita, once again the teacher's pet, walked around the room adjusting people's posture. She placed her hand on my lower back.

"Inhale," she said.

"It's one hundred fifty degrees in here," I whispered.

"This is a hot Vinyasa class," Kavita explained. "You don't have to push yourself on each posture. Just concentrate on flow."

"Flow?"

"The flow from one posture to another."

"Is passing out a flow?"

"Hey," Doug muttered. "I'm sweating like Paul Giamatti's ass."

"How would you know?" I asked.

"He likes it when we sixty-nine."

We both laughed, and I heard Yumi giggling on the other side of me.

"Guys," Kavita pleaded. "It's important to keep your inner focus."

Yuppie Joe walked in the room and gave everyone a Namaste shout out. Some combination of the heat and the alcohol was playing tricks with my vision because I couldn't stop starting at his shorts. I was convinced they had shrunk to a size outlawed in some countries and frowned upon in the uncircumcised male stripper community.

"Let us begin with Table Top," Yuppie Joe offered calmly as if nothing was cutting off circulation to his Tom and Jerrys. "Kneel onto the mat and press your hands flat against the earth, shoulder length apart. Remember to spread your fingers wide."

At least being on all fours required almost zero balance. The room no longer spun. Instead, it rocked back and forth as if I were on the deck of a ship. My forehead sweat dripped onto the mat with the steadiness of a leaky faucet. I moved my hand windshield-wiper fast to dry it, but I left behind a rainbow of sweat instead.

Yuppie Joe tiptoed around the room. Even in the dark, the front of his shorts resembled a jalapeno pepper wrapped in cellophane.

"Remember to align your neck and spine," he continued. "Just imagine I want to place something delicate on the back of your head. A crystal bowl or a tea cup."

"Or his junk," Doug muttered.

My Table Top wobbled from suppressed laughter. Yuppie Joe stepped between us to adjust something about Doug's posture. I glanced over. Big mistake. Yuppie Joe's ass cheeks were swallowing his shorts like quicksand.

"Let's return to the mat," he said. "Face down."

"That I can do," Yumi whispered.

Yuppie Joe walked cat-like to the back of the room as he talked us through downward dog. "Hips toward the ceiling everyone. Straighten your knees and elbows."

"I think I've gone blind," Doug muttered.

I could feel the blood rushing to my head. "You're telling me."

"It was like looking directly at a solar eclipse."

"Press down your heels," Yuppie Joe continued. "It's okay if they can't touch the floor. Don't be a hero."

A few people chuckled. I was not one of them.

"His junk has been branded onto my retinas," Doug said as he bent his knees, leaving him halfway between Downward Dog and collapsing in defeat.

Yuppie Joe's voice came from somewhere behind me. "If your wrists feel tense, you can drop onto your forearms into Dolphin Pose."

Sounded easy. I moved closer to the mat, but it was more difficult to hold myself up. The muscles in my arms began to wobble, and my sweat-soaked shirt clung heavily to my skin.

Kavita sidled up to me and cleared her throat. "You guys have to quiet down. Joe's already pissed."

"He burned my retinas," Doug moaned.

"Doug keeps stealing my peace," I protested. With these words, I collapsed onto the mat, my entire body hitting the ground at once with a thud.

"O—M—G," Kavita blurted. She squatted down and put her hand on my shoulder. "Are you okay?"

"I'm good. This is the perfect amount of flow for me."

Yuppie Joe hurried over and whispered something into Kavita's ear. Then he addressed Doug and me. "A word outside, please."

"Thank Christ."

As we stepped into the cool, brightly-lit hallway, Kavita's steady voice guided the class into Upward Dog.

"You are being disruptive to the energy of the group," Yuppie Joe began. The sweat stain on his Swayze shirt resembled a heavy necklace. He was shorter than I by a few inches, and his neck-length, curly brown hair reminded me of a hobbit from *Lord of the Rings*. "You are also making it difficult for others to maintain focus."

"My precious," I mumbled as I reached out to pat his head.

"What are you doing?" he asked, pulling back sharply.

"Sorry," Doug said as he took my arm with both hands and lowered it to my side. "She's just drunk."

"Jesus," I snapped.

"You've been drinking?" Yuppie Joe asked with genuine surprise. "Alcohol is not permitted on the grounds."

"We didn't drink here," Doug protested weakly.

"I'm afraid I'll have to inform the director. You won't be able to stay for the remainder of the weekend."

Yuppie Joe did an about face and marched down the hall, presumably to some office that could banish us from the Shanti Yoga Retreat. The dramatic gesture was undercut by the amount of ass cheek Doug and I had to witness in his wake.

"It's like watching two mangos tied together with a string," Doug said as he ran his hand through his wet, spiky-brown hair. "Do you think he's serious? Can we actually get kicked out of this place?"

"God, I hope so."

•••

Kavita and I finish the bottle of wine, though I do most of the heavy lifting. The six-armed Dhana Lakshmi watches me from across the room with a smirk. Kavita has stopped crying. Her nose no longer runs, and she pulls her shiny black hair into a ponytail. Maybe the storm has already begun to pass. I used to think that I could cry Brett out of my system, that you only have so many tears for each person in your life. But sorrow heals like a broken bone. It changes you. Parts reattach. The body goes on. But the experience leaves you a little weaker, a little less sure of yourself.

I turn to Kavita. We still sit cross-legged on the sea-green couch. Her face has a perpetual look of tiredness—something about the dark circles beneath her eyes—and there is a small cluster of acne on one cheek.

"I have to go to work pretty soon," I say. "Are you okay?"

Kavita leans forward at the same speed she speaks. Not fast, not slow, just steady. I have time to pull back or redirect her into a hug, but I let her move closer to my face. Part of me knows I will smell like bad decisions tomorrow, but a strange feeling seizes me by the throat. I want her to kiss me.

I want to be kissed someone who actually likes me.

Her lips are warm and moist. Her breath smells of ginger, and I can taste the red wine on her tongue. She touches the side of my face, her fingers cool and soft. The kiss is deep and long. It reminds me of a hug. Warm and comforting. But there is no fire beneath it.

172

No heaving chests or shortness of breath. No guttural sounds.

She pulls back as gently as she started. "I'm not gay. I just wanted to do that. Right now, I mean."

"Me too." I pause.

We are still close, knees touching and hands clasped together.

"I want to ask you something," Kavita says. "Whatever happened with that Lightfeather thing?"

"What do you mean?"

"Applying for jobs as if you were Native American?"

"Oh … nothing."

She studies my face for a moment and smiles. "That's good."

"Is it, though?" I let go of her hands and slide to the opposite end of the couch. "Remember Jasper Farms, the adjunct?"

"The cute guy from Iowa?"

"Well, I nicknamed him 'Jasper Farms' because of his wholesome Midwestern looks, and I probably said he was from Iowa, too."

"That was nice of you."

"I think he's from Queens. His real name is Robert something. Anyway, he slept in his car for two months last semester because he couldn't afford rent."

"O—M—G!"

"Yes, OMG." I glance down at the hole in my right sock. "Is that how we end up? How much longer are we supposed to live with cheap furniture and a stipend that qualifies us for food stamps? No job. Crappy health insurance. We deserve more than that."

"I know you're hurting," Kavita replies. "I know you're angry. About a lot of things. I am, too."

"I'm good at this job, Kavi. I'm a good teacher, a good scholar."

"I know." She leans against the armrest and nods. A few moments pass in silence before she speaks again. "It's funny. I eat like crap most of the time but not at home. My mom makes everything from scratch. Dal makhani. Shaag panner. She makes the most delicious mulligatawny soup—the onions and carrots, the peppery broth. The entire house smells of spices. When I was little, I loved sitting at the kitchen table while she cooked. The room warm from the heat of the stove."

She inhales deeply. "That food reminds me of who I am and where I come from. You can't fake that, Ana. You can't …" she pauses, her face drooping with fatigue. "It's something that shouldn't be defiled."

Defile. Is that what I've become? A defiler. One who spoils and debases. Or does she have a more hallowed meaning in mind? Does she think of Lightfeather as a desecration or violation of something sacred? If so, could she ever forgive me? Could any of my friends? The air in the room feels humid and heavy. I suddenly think I might vomit.

"I have to go," I say, getting off the couch and gathering my bags. I don't look at her as I slip into my shoes and open the front door. The cold air from outside makes me shiver. "Work," I mumble. "Moondude can't manage those dead bodies without me."

"Who is Moondude?"

174

"Nobody, just the bastard love child of Ben and Jerry and Cheech and Chong."

18
Charles Redstone Allard

With John Doe's fedora snugly on my head, I page through his diary at the desk I share with Sherilynn. The book smells faintly of smoke and well-worn leather. I have discovered a peculiar feature. The initials "BG" appear in the margins of several carefully copied passages, including the last two by Homer and Ben Franklin. John Coltrane's "Blue Train" swings through my earbuds, and I close my eyes. The trumpet swirls above the piano like a kite on a windy day. I picture John Doe in bed with the diary, blue pen gliding effortlessly across the page. I can almost hear the ink pressing into the paper—

"Dude," Moondude hollers from somewhere behind me.

I turn to see him walking toward me from the coffee room. His Kenny G hair bounces with each step, and his long limbs have a ragdoll quality. I peel the buds out of my ears and slide the diary under a stack of death certificates and funeral home paperwork.

"Pinky, my friend at the State Police, ran John Doe's fingerprints against a national criminal database," Moondude says as he places an open file on my desk. The freckles on his thin arms remind me of brown raindrops. His breath smells of weed and chocolate.

"Pinky?" I ask.

"His last name is Pinkerton, and his right pinky is as long as his fourth finger. What are the odds of that?" He pauses, shooting me a sideways glance in case I want to marvel over the statistical improbability of Pinky's digits. "Anyway, Pinky got a hit, so he talked to a friend at the Las Vegas Police Department. Doe's real name was Charles Redstone Allard. He spent almost two years in prison there for identity theft and fraud."

The mugshot shows a much younger man but unmistakably John Doe. The roundness of his eyes and high cheekbones. Clark Gable eyebrows. Nose shaped like a shark's fin.

"He was released twenty-seven years ago," Moondude adds. "Six months later, he stopped reporting to his parole officer. He just disappeared. No family. No bank accounts. No credit cards. The police figured he went to Mexico."

I lean back from the desk. The clutter suddenly irritates me. Sherilynn's To-Do List. The unfinished paperwork. John Doe's diary and his Haverton County Morgue file. A stack of books about the Chumash of California. Through my ear buds on the desk, the faint sounds of Coltrane's cheerful saxophone give way to the trumpet solo in "Moment's Notice." It races ahead, making you feel like a kid tagging along with an older brother.

"Is there anything else?" I ask.

"Not much. He was born in Tulsa, Oklahoma seventy-six years ago. His foster parents died when he was in his teens. No college degree. No record of marriage or kids." Moondude brushes aside some of his long, curly hair. "And he was a Gemini."

"Jesus."

"What?"

"Fucking astrology, really?"

177

"Don't mock the stars, person. Geminis are ruled by Mercury, the trickster planet. That makes them quick-witted and deceptive. John Doe was a trickster. False identities. The disappearing act. He had us fooled."

"What about the missing twenty-seven years?" I protest. "Charles Redstone Allard vanished for almost three decades. Doesn't that bother you?"

Moondude tugs at the collar of his Grateful Dead T-shirt. It features a skull wearing a garland of roses. "People change names all the time. They get married. They get nicknames. They try to find the right fit for who they are."

"Charles stole identities for a living and got caught. But as soon as he was free and clear, he did it again. Why? Why keep running?"

"Until Payton Wells."

"What?"

"He ran until Payton Wells." Moondude leafs through the file. "He bought that apartment twelve years ago, and he got his Connecticut Driver's License five years before that."

"So?"

"So he decided on Payton Wells seventeen years ago," Moondude replies. "Something made him feel he could stop running and be the person he wanted to be here."

I consider the two of us, Moondude and Lightfeather, working the late-shift at a morgue and pondering the fake identities of a dead man. Two white people with the luxury to assume names.

"What do we do now?"

Moondude looks at me as if I just replaced his weed with oregano. "The rest is up to the detectives in charge of Charles's suicide."

"The rest of what?"

"The criminal case against whoever helped him." Moondude pulls his earlobe. "I'm not sure how hard they'll try, though. The remaining tests on the autopsy came back."

"And?"

"He was dying. Late stage liver cancer."

Moondude places his hand on my shoulder. He means the gesture as comforting, but his bony fingers press awkwardly against my shirt.

"It's over," he says.

"I want to know why he stopped at Payton Wells, why he died in the Humanities Department. I want to know who helped him."

"You want too much," Moondude replies with a deflated sigh, as if he gave up wanting things a long time ago.

He picks up one of my books about the Chumash. The cover shows an unknown, nineteenth-century Chumash man in ceremonial garb. He wears a headdress of fur topped with feathers, a thick necklace of shells, and a grass apron. Black and white body paint runs across his arms and legs in horizontal lines.

"At least we know Charles's real name now. Some people don't even get that."

19
Lunch Date

Professor Green's office in the Humanities Department resembles a greenhouse. The thin, red-tipped leaves of a tall Madagasgar Dragon Plant, *Dracaena marginata,* hovers spider-like behind his desk chair. Peace Lilies, *Spathiphyllum,* rest on the windowsill next to a framed sketch of Thoreau's cabin at Walden Pond. The butterfly-shaped leaves of an areca palm, *Dypsis lutescens,* practically dance above my arm as I linger in the doorway. Other plants crowd the room as well, and I can only identify them because Green has labeled each species with a card. Charlemagne occupies the only uncluttered space on the desk. Mounds of books cover the rest.

"Hello," I announce.

Professor Green looks up from a book. The ZZ Top beard spills over his chest, and, as always, he dresses like a man who has just come from the frontier. Flannel shirt, blue jeans, brown boots.

"How was the campus interview?" he asks.

"It was the Hindenburg of interviews," I reply, unsure if I should step inside. "The Stephen Baldwin of Baldwins. The Mountain Dew of soft drinks. I can go on."

"That won't be necessary. I have no doubt you made an impression," he replies absently. He then points to the fedora. "May I?"

"Sure." I hand it to him. I've gotten into the habit of wearing Doe's hat in my office and at the morgue. It makes me feel closer to him, closer to solving the mystery of his shifting identities.

"My father used to wear hats like this," he says, tracing his fingers along the brim. "He was a salesman. He wore casual clothes around the house, of course, but I always picture him in his suits and hats. 'I have thirty suits,' he used to say as if the number were unfathomable to him."

Green checks his watch suddenly, as if someone just snapped him out of a trance. "I'm afraid I'm due at the hospital soon."

"Is everything okay?"

"Yes, I'm meeting my wife for lunch. She's a doctor of internal medicine."

"I didn't realize you were married."

"Twenty-seven years and two kids. The boys are older now. Both out of college. My wife and I have lunch together every Wednesday."

"A standing date. That's really sweet."

"It started as an act of desperation," Green replies with a chuckle. "Patricia, my wife, gets lost in her work. It's more than that, really. She gets lost in everything … *else*. On our anniversary once, years ago, she missed dinner because of a janitor. He struck up a conversation with her as she was leaving the hospital. She had never met him, never spoken to him before, but she spent the entire evening listening to stories about his family, his kids, his life back home. Honduras, I believe it was. I waited at the restaurant nearly two hours before giving up."

Green leans back and gazes up at the fern hanging from the ceiling.

"So I suggested lunch," he continues as if talking to himself. "Every week, the same day and time. I figured she couldn't possibly forget. We've stuck to it for almost twenty years now. At this point, we go more out of habit than anything else. It's funny how that happens."

"How what happens?"

"How habit makes you think everything is okay." The chair groans loudly as Green stands. "I'm afraid I must be going. Is there something I can help you with?"

"Yes," I say, swallowing the thick saliva in my throat. "I found out John Doe's real name last night."

"What do you mean?"

"Payton Wells was an assumed name," I explain. "He had several identities, actually. But his real name was Charles Redstone Allard."

Green stands perfectly still as I explain some of the other details about Allard's past, including his time in prison for identity theft and the illness leading up to his death. Amid so many plants, Green's beard reminds me of Spanish moss.

"Of course, only a spouse or family member can claim the body," I continue. "Otherwise, the morgue will transport him to a mass grave with the others."

"Others?" he asks.

"The other unclaimed or unidentified bodies."

Noise swells in the halls as students change classes. Shuffling feet. Staccato bursts of laughter. Complaints about quiz grades and homework, hangovers and hookups. And, of course, lots of profanity.

"Charles Redstone Allard," Green mumbles as he hands me the hat and gathers Charlemagne. Its purple leaves and white blossoms tremble as he nestles the pot into his arm. "So what happens now?"

"We sent our report to the police this morning. I assume they'll search the apartment in a couple of days."

"Why?"

"It's a murder case."

"But he was dying of cancer."

I shrug. "Someone killed him."

Green presses his teeth against his lower lips and nods stiffly. He gazes down at the plant. "Do you know why I carry this with me?"

Among the graduate students in the Humanities Department at Haverton University, Professor Green's *Oxalis triangularis* is the source of much drunken speculation. Kavita chalks it up to loneliness. Doug assumes Green was raised by a tribe of bearded horticulturists in the Yukon. And Yumi considers it another example of the crazy shit white people do. I have likened it to some of the greatest mysteries in American history: the Lindbergh baby's disappearance, Geraldo Rivera's deflated opening of Al Capone's vault, and the popularity of Ryan Seacrest.

"No," I say.

"I don't want to forget for one moment my responsibility to care for this planet and the people in it, even when it costs." He glances at the fedora. "Caring always costs."

We step into the crowded hall. I watch him walk away with Charlemagne in his arm, and I replay our conversation. About Doe's real name and the murder. About his father's clothes and lunch with his wife. Something nags at me, though. Something about the way Green looked at the hat and touched it. It's as if he recognized it—but not from his father's wardrobe.

183

There is something else I can't quite figure out either.

Why I just lied to him about John Doe?

20
Stakeouts

"I'm hungry," Doug complains as he plods behind me. His brown winter jacket and backpack straps remind me of someone wearing a barrel with suspenders. "We're supposed to grab lunch."

"I have a better idea," I reply as we follow Professor Green along the brick sidewalk.

"Does it involve eating or oral sex?" Doug asks.

"No, jackass."

"Then it is not a better idea."

The crisp February air makes my eyes water and dries my lips to the point of cracking. No warmth comes from the sun, but the white light makes the cold bearable. It adds clarity after so many hazy-gray days. It shines on cars filthy with rock salt and dirt. It reflects off storefront windows. And it makes an impassioned case for tanning salons.

Green keeps a brisk, steady pace. His jeans sag, and his boots clomp with the heaviness of horseshoes. Occasionally I get glimpses of purple Charlemagne. After a few blocks, I am winded and sweaty. Soon I realize I'm losing ground.

"Jesus," I puff. "I'm being body-shamed by a sexagenarian."

"Your aversion to exercise doesn't count as body shaming," Doug says with a grunt.

"Fine, I'm being fitness-shamed by a sexagenarian."

"There is a sexagenarian joke to be made here." Doug breathes hard at my side. "I just can't think of it."

"The state of Florida thanks you."

With its age-worn brick exterior and murky windows, Haverton County Hospital has the charm of a public high school. A sleepy-looking man in frayed scrubs finishes a cigarette by the revolving door. It moves steadily, making a suction noise with each rotation. When Green steps inside, it sounds as if he is being swallowed whole.

"Now what?" Doug asks.

"We wait."

"What the hell? It's cold. I'm hungry. And I can't think of anything that rhymes with sexagenarian."

I grab Doug's hand and lead him to the Soggy Frog—an old British pub turned trendy salad bar across the street. The dark wood, dim lighting, and stale beer have been replaced by a blinding whiteness. The shiny floors have the faint smell of cleaner, and perky employees wear green aprons. Even the old logo—a slightly depressed frog with a broken umbrella—has given way to a cartoon amphibian any toddler can coo over. Two long buffet counters take up most of the space in the center. Its stainless steel trays overflow with lettuce, tomatoes, onions, corn, carrot slivers, hard-boiled eggs, and artichoke hearts. I grab a table by the window.

"You realize this place has vegetables, right?" Doug asks.

"I'll find out what they can deep fry."

"Well, if you need an antihistamine or an EpiPen, let me know."

Doug lumbers off to fill a large bowl with green stuff. He rocks side to side as he studies the buffet, and his movements remind me of someone balancing buckets with a carrying pole. He comes back with a side of garlic bread for me and a dressing stain on his khaki pants.

"So," he begins, "why are we stalking Professor Green?" The crunch of hard lettuce and croutons nearly drowns out his voice. "It's not some weird sex thing, is it?"

"That's even more disgusting than your lunch."

"You know something kinky is going on with all that flannel."

The tall, unpadded barstools and tiny circular tables seem designed to give you just enough time to finish a salad without needing a chiropractor, but not a second longer. Doug chews steadily and loudly. He hasn't shaved today, and a thin band of scruffiness wraps around his rounded jawbone. In the sanitary light of the Soggy Frog, my signature teaching uniform of black slacks and a cream blouse appears particularly dour. I could be a cater-waiter.

"I lied about John Doe," I say.

"What?"

"I told Green the autopsy confirmed Doe's murder and that the police would be searching his apartment soon."

"So?"

"I haven't filed any paperwork with the police yet."

"I don't understand."

"I think Green will go to his apartment today while he still has the chance. I think he knew this guy. He might even know who helped kill him."

Doug takes a big slurp of Diet Coke. The logo on the paper cup shows a frog with an open-mouthed smile. "Why don't you just ask him?"

"Jesus, am I the only one who watches TV at this university?" I lean forward, lowering my voice. "We have to catch him in the act. We watch him, follow him to the apartment, and confront him there. I still have the keys."

"All I wanted was lunch," Doug protests. "Now, I'm in an episode of *Cagney and Lacey*."

"Don't worry. You get to be the hot one."

"Of course, I'm the hot one," he snaps, taking another sip of soda. "Which one is the hot one?"

"The one with the gun."

"They both have guns."

As he shoves another forkful of cucumber and onion in his mouth, Green steps out of the revolving door without his wife.

"Looks like he cancelled his date," I say. "We've got to go."

"I'm getting a refill first." He grabs the cup. "You know I've never been on a stakeout before."

"Oddly enough, I have," I reply. "Just a few months ago. With Yumi."

•••

"I'm all for expanding our dating pool, but the Golden Touch Retirement Home seems a bit desperate," I said to Yumi as we sat across the street from the main entrance. "It sounds like a rest home for convicted sex offenders."

Yumi stared out the window of the car. In the midmorning December light, her skin had the color of aged ivory. Blue highlights spilled from the midpoint of her hair, pooling at the tips, and she wore light blue lipstick. She had just made the transition from fall-purple to winter-blue highlights a few days ago. One spaghetti strap of her blue-and-white polka dot dress had fallen over her shoulder. I caught a hint of lily-scented perfume.

Yumi had discarded her tomboy aesthetic for girly-cute. I had never seen her in this outfit, and it revealed another side to her beauty—like looking at a diamond from a different angle or seeing Sarah Jessica Parker in casual clothes. Maybe I needed to start combing my hair again in the mornings. Maybe I should start losing weight and dressing provocatively. Brett moved out five weeks and three days ago. How long would it take to feel ready to move on? To want another man to look at me with desire?

"So, what are we doing here?" I asked.

She kept her hands firmly on the steering wheel even though we had been parked for over five minutes.

"Vincent," she replied without taking her eyes off the entrance.

"You're kidding."

"This is where he works."

"You're kidding!"

"Nope."

"Did you tell him your real name?"

"Yes."

"Jesus!" I yelled. "What's wrong with you? He could be a serial killer or a television weatherman."

For more than two months, Vincent had been a regular client of Yumi's through Oriental Breeze: "Thursday Nights at Ten." From the start, he was not like the others. He told interesting stories. He shared his thoughts on art, culture, and history. He asked questions about her. He wanted her opinion on current events and politics. He even sent a tasteful floral arrangement the next day, through the company of course.

Best of all—no sex stuff.

Slowly, she had been slipping in truths. About her family, her studies, her favorite novels. But a recent conversation made them realize that they were in the same Connecticut town. They both loved Elephant and the Dove, a Mexican restaurant decorated in the style of Frida Kahlo's paintings. He had already mentioned organizing a book club at the Golden Touch Retirement Home, so Yumi decided it was time to meet. Today.

"He knows you're coming?" I asked.

"Not exactly."

"You mean no."

She nodded.

"So, we're stalking him?"

Yumi turned to me. Her chocolate brown eyes glistened in the sunlight. "It's not stalking if we've been talking for months."

"Sitting outside his workplace, unannounced, when you've never met, is pretty much the definition of stalking."

As we entered the Golden Touch and peeled off our jackets, we approached the reception desk. A woman in a tan suit, roughly our age, talked on the phone. She had the well-practiced smile of someone in sales. If she found the contrast between Yumi's springy fashion sense and my soup-kitchen attire surprising, she did not let on.

"You talk to her," Yumi whispered.

"Why me?"

"You're a better liar."

"Thanks."

"Can I help you?" the woman asked as she hung up the phone.

"We're here to see Vincent Preston," I said.

"Sign in." She pointed to a clipboard. "He should be in Room 114."

The main residence hall reminded me of an unimaginative three-star hotel. Beige walls with brass ceiling lights. Brown carpet with a checkered pattern. Dark wooden doors. We passed a man with a walker. He had silver-white hair and parchment skin. His faded red T-shirt advertised a Turkey Trot, and gray sweatpants sagged over his orthopedic shoes. He did not look up. The effort of using the walker absorbed him completely.

The door to Room 114 was open. From the hall, we saw two men sitting at a desk. The younger one had neat, sandy-blonde hair, and he talked breezily about a recent summons for jury duty. His stylish gray suit had a crisp, newly worn quality, but it did not make him appear too formal. The older man held a deck of cards.

"Is that Vincent?" I whispered to Yumi.

She was too stunned to speak.

"He is soap-opera-doctor good looking," I added. "He is I'm-going-back-to-the-car-to-masturbate good looking. He's—"

Yumi elbowed my ribs.

"Ow!"

Both men turned. The older one resembled the judge from *My Cousin Vinny*. The rectangular face with a pronounced chin and neatly parted hair. Tufts of gray above his ears and a mole in the center of his forehead.

He wore an open, cheerful expression on his face. The deck of cards in his hands looked decades old.

"Come in," Soap Opera Doctor said. He shook our hands formally, with the same kind of sales smile that greeted us at reception. "No matter the card game, he beats the pants off me every time."

"I'd like to see that," I muttered.

Yumi elbowed me again. "Vincent?" she asked.

"Yes," Soap Opera Doctor replied with a nod, and he turned to the elderly man. "You should be working a table in Vegas. I'll leave you to your guests, Vincent. Thanks again for the game of war."

As Soap Opera Doctor left, I sucked in my gut and pushed out my chest, but he hurried past without a glance.

Bastard.

"The game should really be called 'Conquest,'" Vincent began. "The goal is to end up with all the cards in the deck, to leave your opponent with nothing. Wars end. Treaties get signed. That's not true with conquerors and colonizers. They want everything. Wouldn't you agree, Yumi?"

His voice reminded me of a cello, and his eyes resembled a mossy green pond. Yumi hadn't moved since Vincent started speaking. No doubt she was trying to reconcile the voice on the phone with the man living in the Golden Touch Retirement Home.

"How did you know?" she asked, her voice hoarse.

"Your face and the blue streaks in your hair," he added with a wink. "You mentioned them Thursday. Please, pull up chairs. You and ..."

"Ana."

192

He started dealing cards, two face down for each of us. His hands, each stained with dark sunspots, moved quickly and steadily. "I prefer Texas Hold'em. It's better with a few more people, but this will do. Have you ever played?"

We both shook our heads.

"Marvelous. I can cheat with impunity." His smile had a hint of mischievousness. He placed three cards face up in the center of the table. "Texas Hold'em is a bit like the Wild West—without the guns and the dysentery."

"I don't understand," Yumi said. She placed her hands flat on the desk and stared at them for a moment before looking up.

"I'll explain the rules—"

"Calls. Flowers. Oriental *Fucking* Breeze. A service that helps guys with Asian fetishes get off."

The middle button on Vincent's black shirt was missing, and his collar appeared somewhat frayed. He held the deck as if poised to deal.

"I have never spoken to you that way nor have I been interested in anything other than friendship. I was hoping we might play cards every once in a while. Perhaps become friends. You could visit with Ana or anyone you like. The more the merrier."

"Why Oriental Breeze?" Yumi stood abruptly, her voice tightening. "Because Asian women are compliant? Asian women will come over and play cards and cook food? You might even get a hand job out of it?"

Vincent did not flinch. Whether her words upset him or not, I couldn't tell. He had too much experience with poker to give away his hand. "I don't honestly remember how I came across the site. Probably from faces."

"What?"

"At night, I like to look at faces online—different ages and ethnicities, men and women. I try to read what they might be holding back, what small feature or expression gives something away about their personality. It's the gambler in me, I guess."

"What the hell does that have to do with Oriental Breeze?" Yumi blurted.

Vincent flexed the deck. As he released his thumb, the cards sailed from one hand to the other. He did this several times as if he were moving a stretched-out Slinky. Each exchange sounded like the fluttering of birds' wings.

"Sometimes, when I click to enlarge a picture, I get redirected to other sites. I will spare you the details. They are not always wholesome," he added somberly. "Maybe that is how I found you, Yumi. I don't remember. Honestly. But when I came across your face, you looked—you look—so much like my granddaughter—"

"You let them advertise with your face?" I gasped.

"I see." Yumi continued over me. "Your granddaughter dabbles in the phone sex industry?" She put her hands on her hips, and the gesture gave me a glimpse of what she must have looked like as a teenager, indignant about some parental complaint over boys or cigarettes or curfews. Her polka dot dress suddenly struck me as something a child would wear.

"So you paid an Asian fetish site to talk to me every week? To connect with your granddaughter. Do you hear how screwed up that is?"

Vincent maintained a steady expression. "I wanted the chance to get to know you."

"Bullshit! This isn't about me. Instead of talking to your granddaughter, you hired me to be her."

He lowered his eyes, the first break in his composure. "I can't talk to her anymore."

"I don't care." Yumi moved to the doorway. "Don't ever call again!"

"We're all lonely, Yumi." He stood unsteadily as he spoke. "Maybe in different ways, but we all are."

Vincent's words trailed us through the bland, brown halls, past the empty reception desk, and outside to the parked car across the street. The smell of burning wood hung heavy and thick in the air, but there was no sign of smoke. We drove in silence for a long time. The tires hummed against the pavement, and the engine sputtered.

"I never looked at my cards," I said. "The two face-down cards he dealt."

"What?"

"I wanted to look at them, even though I don't know anything about Texas Hold'em. Maybe that is the appeal of the game. Not knowing what you're going to get. Not knowing what you have but betting on it anyway."

Yumi kept a tight grip on the steering wheel. "So I bet blind and lost? Give me a break."

"What were you expecting?" I continued. "Someone younger, sure. But Soap Opera Doctor?"

"I expected ..." She hesitated. In the midday light, the blue in her hair reminded me of icicles. "I hoped for more."

"Like what? Vincent seems well-meaning."

"I'm sick of well-meaning racism, Ana," she scoffed. "I'm sick of the I-have-Asian-friends and I-like-sushi racism. I'm sick of racism no one has to take responsibility for."

Yumi slowed to a stop at the red light. No other cars were on the street.

"I want to be more than my ethnicity. I want real me to matter more than the way I was born."

21
The Exchange

"It's hard to imagine someone in this day and age not having a cheese grater," Doug says as he looks through the utensils in John Doe's kitchen.

"Isn't that the first line of *Pride and Prejudice?*" I ask.

"No," Doug replies, holding up a spatula with one hand. "It is a truth universally acknowledged that a single man in possession of a good fortune, must be in want of a cheese grater.'"

"A classic."

The kitchen is showroom ready. White marble counters and cabinets with a white tiled backsplash. Stainless steel appliances. Blonde-wooden floors and a matching island countertop. Yet there is no smell, no lingering aroma from a meal or rotting food. It is as if nothing has ever been cooked or eaten here.

"We should bake a strawberry rhubarb pie while we're waiting. I'd love a kitchen like this. The possibilities."

"You bake?"

"Not all of us live on a diet of fast food and free bar snacks."

"Cooking and baking are totally different things," I protest as if I were a judge on *The Great British Bake Off.*

I like to torment Doug's love of cooking aprons and cutlery, saucepans and steamers. Doug is the only guy I know who shops at Williams-Sonoma and watches the Food Network voluntarily. When Brett and I took "Cooking for Couples" with Chef Three J's,

Doug insisted on seeing every recipe and hearing all the details. He even offered to be Brett's plus one if I bailed.

Doug picks up a red pot with two handles. "A Le Creuset Dutch Oven. Top of the line."

"What do you use a Dutch Oven for?"

"Philistine." Doug sighs. "Soups. Stews. Risotto. Hell, you can bake bread in them. Personally, I find them amazing for braised short ribs. You can brown them on the stovetop then cook them in the oven. The meat stays juicy, slips right off the bone."

"You're freaking me out." I look at my watch. "What is taking so long? He should be here by now."

"Maybe, you're wrong. Maybe, Green isn't coming." Doug puts the Dutch Oven back on the stove. "I still can't believe we lost him."

"We lost him because you needed to refill your Diet Coke."

"We lost him because the man is track star."

"He's a sexagenarian."

"Stop saying that word!" Doug holds up his palms.

The bolt on the front door snaps loudly, and the hinges whine as it opens. Doug and I freeze. There is some snapping and rustling of clothes, along with heavy breathing. Then the floorboards moan as someone walks into the other room. A squeaking noise follows before everything gets quiet.

"What do we do now?" Doug asks in his best attempt at a whisper. "There is no place to hide."

"How the hell do I know?"

"This was your idea!"

"I can hear you," a voice says calmly. "Come on out."

Doug and I shuffle into the living room. Professor Green sits on the sage couch facing the fireplace, legs crossed. His green-checkered flannel shirt compliments the cool blend of lavender colors and wood in the room. Charlemagne has been placed on the windowsill with the other Purple Shamrocks. The four plants fill the space evenly. He does not look at us when we enter. Instead, he stares at the plants, sunglasses firmly on his nose, ZZ top beard clinging to his chin like stalactites.

"After you followed me to the hospital and waited at the Soggy Frog, I knew you'd be here. I saw you enter the building. I debated whether to come up. But I guess I want to find out what you're not telling me."

"So you knew him?" I say. "Charles Redstone Allard?"

"Not by that name. He was Payton to me. We met seventeen years ago in the Humanities Department. He asked if he could audit one of my classes." Green smiles, still gazing at the plants at the window. He crosses his leg, and the sofa cushion bends naturally under his weight. "He became close friends with me and my wife. We had him over for dinners. He knew the boys. They liked his old world charm, his sense of humor."

"If you were such good friends, why not say something sooner? Why give his name to Hinks anonymously?"

"I wasn't sure it was him." Green stands, but without Charlemagne in the crook of his arm, an essential part of him seems missing. "After I heard about the body, I came here. He always left a set of

199

spare keys with us. When I saw the suits on his bed, I knew."

"I don't understand." I want to move, but my legs feel anchored to the floor. "Why would you assume your friend died? Unless …"

A slight whistling noise comes from Green's nose as he exhales, and he lowers his chin to his chest. Some of the sunlight spilling into the room reflects off his dark glasses.

"Unless you knew he was dying," I continue. "You knew he was sick?"

"Yes," he replies in a whisper.

"Did you know he wanted to kill himself?"

"Yes."

"Did you help him?"

"For fuck sake!" Doug hisses.

Green gets to his feet, leaning heavily on the arm of the sofa. He steps over to the bay window and keeps his back to us for a moment, shoulders hunched and head down. "I could never hurt him. He was my dearest friend."

"You didn't answer my question," I say.

"Jesus," Doug whispers as he grabs my arm.

"No." Green turns partway around and takes off his glasses. His dusky green eyes pool with tears. "Payton asked for my help, but I refused. He saw it was too much for me, so he let me off the hook. That was his way."

Green gathers Charlemagne from the windowsill and carries him into the foyer. He places the plant on a shelf and takes his jacket from the coatrack.

"There is something else I don't understand," I continue despite another yank from Doug.

200

"What?"

"Why the office? Why not kill himself at home, in this beautiful place?" I ask.

"I assume he wanted to be found right away. He would have wanted me and my wife to know soon as possible. He wasn't close to many people in town— except us."

The air in the apartment feels heavy and hot again, and my blouse has gotten damp with sweat. Green finishes buttoning up, and he looks directly at me.

"Now, it's my turn," he says.

"Excuse me?"

"I have offered this confession of my private life at a price. I want something in return."

"I don't understand," I reply.

"I satisfied your curiosity. I gave you the story of our friendship and my failure to help him end his life. I did so in exchange for something."

"What?"

"His body."

"What?"

"I want you to release him to me. I want to hold a service, to bury him."

It feels as if the wind has been knocked out of me. Green has been playing a chess, while I showed up for a game of jacks. "I don't have the authority. I can't—"

"I need to do this for him, Ana. I need to say goodbye, and you need to help me."

22
Shiva

"You're not hunting elk," Nadya Shaw muttered as she hung her coat in the foyer.

I refused to give up my camouflage jacket—another Dad gift designed to drive my mother crazy. Like my backpack from last year, I wore it obsessively. We were both dressed in black gowns and stockings, and my stiff leather shoes hurt my feet. My mother's tall, thin figure reminded me of a palm tree in mourning. I resembled a New York City fire hydrant.

"Why are we here?" I asked.

Nadya shooed me with the wave of a hand, and I followed her inside. Everyone wore black and stood in clusters near food—a dining room table with sandwiches; a coffee table with cheeses and crudité, the most horrifying and uninspired invention of the catered food industry; and the kitchen with desserts. Everyone sipped wine from plastic cups. Two men lingered by the grand piano in the living room, talking quietly as they looked down at the keys. They seemed tempted to touch them. Other conversations happened in whispered tones. Of weather. Of politics. Of music.

"What's going on?"

My mother ignored me, so I gravitated toward the cookie platter in the kitchen.

"I didn't know you could serve wine at a shiva," an elderly woman uttered with a sneer. She resembled E.T. dressed as a girl, and she stood with a shabby man who nodded grimly. I imagined him as incapable of speech, moving his head up-and-down in eternal agreement with whatever she said.

"We're Jewish Light," the woman in front of the cookies replied before gliding out of the room. Thick blonde hair coiled to her shoulders, and she had blue eyes with flecks of gold.

Outside of parents and pedophiles, most adults didn't strike up conversations with children. They tolerated and kept a wary distance. Since I was the only twelve-year-old here, I got weak smiles, enough to pass for friendly but not enough to encourage conversation. Instead, I cruised for food and eavesdropped, picking up fragments here and there. Brad, dead at forty-three. Car accident. A gifted jazz pianist. Pictures of him and the blonde woman from the kitchen peppered the apartment. So did pictures of him at clubs, always wearing a black suit with a white handkerchief in his front pocket.

"Are you trying to feed a small country in Africa?" my mother hissed before taking the plate out of my hands and placing it on the table.

"Nadya?" asked an attractive bald man with an athletic build. His plate had so much food that I nudged my mom.

"See," I whispered.

"It has been ... since college, right?" he continued with a smile. "I didn't know you were still in touch with Brad."

"We reconnected about a year ago."

News to me. I gathered my plate and started with the turkey sandwich. I didn't understand what was happening at first. As they talked, something changed about my mother. She fidgeted. She twisted a strand of hair. She made a sound that resembled a giggle. That was when I realized that she was unsure of herself. He had taken her back to some awkwardness from her college days, and the thought of her giggling nervously around cute boys made me stop mid-chew. All of her efforts to iron out my clumsy insecurity. The endless catalogue of my shortcomings. The stern disappointment. And all this time she could giggle?

Of course, it did not occur to her to introduce me to Attractive Bald, nor did he appear to care. He inhaled a deep sip of red wine. I chewed quietly.

"I've been having this dream lately," Nadya said after a brief lull in the conversation.

First giggling, now dreams? I never considered whether my mother dreamt, let alone shared her dreams with others. She touched her white-gold necklace, and its blue sapphires made me think of Earth orbiting the sun.

"I'm in a theatre but can't find my seat. The lights are dimming. The show is about to start. I get to my row, but there aren't any seats with my number. An usher directs me to another section. I rush over there, but this time the entire row is missing. The rows skip from L, M, to O. Another usher leads me upstairs, but nothing is marked. No numbers or letters. It goes on until I realize I am in the wrong theatre."

She lifted a glass of wine to her lips. She seemed far away as if talking to herself. Attractive Bald glanced at me. I shrugged my shoulders.

"Do you ever feel like you're in the wrong theatre?" she asked.

He shook his head. "All I dream about is baseball."

The joke fell flat. Whatever hold he had on her was gone. Her body straightened, and she excused herself for the "powder room." Attractive Bald drifted effortlessly into another cluster of huddled adults. I grazed on chips and chocolate-chip cookies until E.T. and her companion settled next to my spot at the trough.

"Lays potato chips," she said to the nodding man as if someone defecated on the dining room table. "At a shiva?"

"Want some?" I asked, holding out my plate with scattered chips, bread crust, dip, and crumbs. Her face scrunched as if I just shoved a Dorito up her nose. "I think I saw some Cheetos by the piano."

A total lie, of course, but the thought of even more chips soiling a Shiva made her jaw drop in horror. The man stopped nodding. For an instant, I caught the hint of a smile.

"Stop tormenting these nice people," Nadya said, placing the weight of her hand on my shoulder. "Let's go."

Downstairs, my mom sat quietly in the driver's seat for a long time. It was cold inside the car, and I could see my breath. A dusky blue light came from a nearby streetlamp. Something about her stillness made me afraid to speak.

Slowly, she opened her purse and pulled out a white handkerchief. It shimmered in the colored light. It was Brad's. I recognized it from the pictures of his concerts. Nadya placed it over her nose and closed her eyes. She inhaled deeply and exhaled. Again.

And again.

And again.

Until she began to cry softly.

23
Saying Goodbye

The atrium for the Performing Arts Center at Haverton University resembles a greenhouse with its glass walls and pointed ceiling. An origami installation hangs from the rafters. Each bird is the size of a bowling pin, and together the red-orange-yellow flock ascends like flames from a dying campfire. At one end of the room is a large picture of John Doe wearing what appears to be Fred Astaire's outfit from the cover of *Mr. Top Hat.* His sly smile suggests a familiarity with the photographer, a shared a secret, and I wonder if Green took it. The sign beneath reads:

In memoriam,
student and friend,
Payton Gregory Wells

At the other end of the room, a mariachi band plays "Bésame Mucho." The three musicians wear black suits that have been embroidered with silver beads. Red bowties flare out from their necks, and a swirling pattern of silver thread decorates the massive orbits of their sombreros. Not far from the men is a table with quesadillas, taquitos topped with shredded cheese, and guacamole with chips. A makeshift bar serves sangria.

I hold a plastic cup with sangria, my second, and I am shoving a triangle of quesadilla into my mouth when Professor Hinks approaches. His signature black jeans, with belt fastened, match his buttoned shirt. Without any glasses, his silver-blue eyes seem dull and far away.

"I hear you did it," he begins. "You convinced the morgue to release the body to Bob."

I nod.

"That was kind of you."

The cheese tries to Gorilla Glue my teeth together, so I have to exaggerate my chewing to unhinge them. I swallow with an uncomfortable gulp.

"What's with the Mexican-themed memorial?" I ask, clearing my throat. "It's like a quinceañera in here."

Hinks shakes his head in irritation. "There was a mix-up with university catering. Our jazz trio and wine bar went to a Spanish department reception on the other side of campus. I tried to explain it to the band, but they don't speak English. I figured some music was better than nothing."

Two guitars strum louder, and the trumpet pleads as the men belt out, *"Bésame, bésame mucho."*

"Who's that?" I gesture to the woman next to Professor Green. She is thin with bobbed white hair and blue eyes. She wears the wide-rimmed glasses and stern expression of a retired librarian.

"His wife."

"I was expecting someone with more of an outdoorsy fashion sense."

Hinks smiles and takes a sip of his drink. "Excuse me," he says before stepping over to several faculty members grazing on chips and guacamole.

I look at Green. He wears a navy-blue suit with black leather shoes, and the clothes give his body an unnatural stiffness. Charlemagne nestles in his folded arm, and he stands close to the photograph of Payton. His wife continues a whispered conversation with him as he sips on sangria. Whether she is offering words of comfort or scolding him for overdue library fines, I can't tell.

I join Doug, Yumi, and Kavita in the corner.

"Do you think these guys take requests?" Doug asks, looking over at the band.

"That's kind of their thing," I reply.

"I'm so asking for 'El Mariachi Loco.'"

"Only you would know the names of mariachi songs," Yumi replies.

"Can we not turn this into a circus?" I plead.

"Have you looked around?" Doug asks with a smirk. "The only things missing are a piñata and a pickup truck."

"Jesus. Can you be any more racist?"

"Probably." Doug shrugs. "I could pretend to be Native American to get a job," he adds with an exaggerated wink.

My stomach drops as if in a freefall, and I wonder if he has figured out I went through with it after all. No one else says a thing.

Kavita just shakes her head. She wears a simple black dress with long sleeves. She keeps as much distance from Doug as possible, even though we stand in a circle. Her usual calm has been replaced by fidgety limbs and lowered eyes. She wants to get away from him, from here, and I wonder how many more times the four of us will be together like this.

Professor Green's wife makes her way to the taquitos while her husband lingers at Payton's photograph.

"I'm going to offer my condolences," I say to the Mockingbird Gang.

"Try not to call him a sexagenarian," Doug says too loudly.

As I walk across the sparse room, I count no more than fifteen people or so—mostly Humanities faculty and hungry graduate students. They huddle around small tables while snacking on Mexican food and sipping sangria. They talk about classes, poorly written papers, administrative irritations. I doubt any of them knew Payton. They're here for the same reason people slow down to gaze at traffic accidents. They want a glimpse of someone else's tragedy.

I approach Green, standing in the same spot as his wife just moments ago. He does not look away from the photograph. I catch a hint of lavender cologne, which seems out of place for his frontiersman aesthetic. Then I realize the scent wouldn't have been unusual for Payton. Perhaps it was a gift from him at some point.

"I'm sorry, Dr. Green."

"Call me Bob," he says with a weak smile. "I'm not about to perform open heart surgery."

The trumpet starts playing the theme to "La Bamba" before the other men start singing. *"Para bailar la bamba ..."*

Green sighs as he glances at the musicians. "Payton would have hated those suits."

"I can't imagine he'd have anything nice to say about their hats either."

"True."

I pull Payton's diary out of my jacket pocket. The leather binding feels soft against my fingers. "I took this from his apartment. I shouldn't have, I know. I was just trying to figure out who he was."

"His reading journal." Green puts Charlemagne on a nearby table and takes the book. The table has several empty cups, and I realize from Green's movements that he is a bit tipsy. "He marked all of my suggestions with the initials BG. Bob Green. Payton was a hell of a reader, with one hell of a memory. He probably could have recited this entire journal to you."

I study Green's profile. The pointed nose and perpetually perched glasses. The massive, greying facial hair and rounded stomach. What exactly drew Payton to this strange man with a plant named Charlemagne and a beard with its own ecosystem? His intellect? His view of him as a teacher? It seems they shared something deep, though.

Green turns to an entry two days before he died. The blue handwritten ink ripples evenly across the page.

"From Homer's *The Odyssey*. This excerpt is one of my favorites." Green pauses before reading the passage aloud. "'Any crewman who ate the lotus, the honey-sweet fruit, lost all desire to send a message back, much less return, their only wish to linger there with the Lotus-eaters, grazing on lotus, all memory of the journey home dissolved forever.'"

He places the journal on the table next to Charlemagne.

"I used to feel that way about my ex-boyfriend," I say. "It was like I became a Lotus-eater the moment we fell in love. I told Brett that once—that he became my addiction. In our apartment, in his arms, I lost all desire to return to real life. I felt he had to coax me back into the world every day. No wonder he lost patience with my love."

211

Green turns to me for the first time. "You have a curious way about you, Ana."

Unsure whether to take that as an insult or a compliment, I opt for the latter. "Thanks."

"You have a directness and an honesty that some must find exhausting. I like it."

As far as compliments go, this one is not improving with age.

"*Bamba, bamba,*" the band sings as the guitars strum. "*Bamba, bamba.*"

"This memorial is a disaster," Green mutters.

"It's like the Linsday Lohan of celebrities."

"I assume that's bad," he replies with a laugh. "Like the Hindenburg of interviews?"

"Exactly."

Green clears his throat. "So what do you think of the epitaph for Payton?"

I read the words beneath his picture again.

In memoriam,
student and friend,
Payton Gregory Wells

"Something about it saddens me," I reply.

"Why?"

"I hope that's not the only way I'm remembered."

"Well, there are worse things to be called, but you're right. He was loved like family. He deserved more."

I touch his arm where Charlemagne usually rests, and he looks at my hand. "Words on a sign don't change the truth," I say. "His life was better with you in it. What else matters?"

He nods.

"I'm curious," I begin. "Do you have any idea who killed him?"

"No." The word wavers, but Green offers nothing else. He continues to look at the picture.

"Do you think about it? About the last person to see him alive? What if you never know who is responsible?"

Something about the last question makes me queasy.

"Whoever did it," Green replies softly, "helped him die with dignity. In a place he wanted to be. In clothes he wanted to wear. Someone cared enough to do that for him. You're a historian. Think of all the people that don't get that."

Mrs. Green walks up to her husband's side and places her palm on his back. She eyes me warily.

"Bob, let's step outside for a moment," she says, but it is clearly not a request. Her tone has an I-don't-have-to-wait-in-line,   let-me-talk-to-the-manager quality, and she carries herself with a toughness her husband lacks. "The air will do you good."

I watch them leave, her hand still pressed between his shoulders. Leading. Green bows his head, and his arms swing heavily by his sides. For the first time in the more than six years that I've known him, he is not carrying Charlemagne. He has forgotten his charge, leaving the purple plant to stand guard over Payton's journal.

24
Chocolate Soufflé

"I was wondering when you'd show up."

That is all Brett says after he opens the front door of Tiffany Riggs's mansion. She is not home. I know because she teaches a graduate class on Thursday nights, dutifully lecturing on fucking other people's boyfriends, no doubt. I follow Brett into a kitchen readymade for the Food Network with its oak cabinets, black marble countertops, copper-trimmed stove, and pot rack hanging above an island wide enough to be a pool table.

Brett whips egg whites into a fluffy cream. The mixer buzzes and whines. Another large bowl contains melted chocolate, and a dusting of sugar and chocolate fragments—along with discarded eggshells—dirty the counter. Brett's apron reads, "I'm hot for teacher."

I hold back the urge to make barf noises.

He turns off the mixer, giving the room an abrupt quiet. The egg whites now have the texture of cotton candy. He pours them into the bowl of chocolate, and with a rubber spatula, he folds the two together, over and over, until they blend into a smooth, light brown paste. He transfers the mixture into a large ramekin. I watch each movement, taking in his alpine nose and lightning scar, the pointed knuckles and strong arms. Just seeing him makes my legs wobble. At first, I think I'm sweating from the burn I feel for his body, but I realize the warmth is coming from the oven.

I am about to say something playful about Chef Three J's cooking class when I notice a highchair next to the other stools at the island. Something inside my chest tightens. It all comes back with the power of a thunderclap. My immolating fury over Brett's affair. My self-loathing comparisons to Tiffany. My near suffocation at the news of her pregnancy.

"What the hell are you doing?" I snap.

"Baking," he replies as he slides the dish into the oven.

"What?"

"A chocolate soufflé."

"A chocolate soufflé? In an apron? Jesus, does she dress you now?"

Brett stays on the opposite side of the island. "Tiff and I cook dinner together most nights. Today, I thought I would surprise her with dessert. She likes chocolate."

"Everyone likes fucking chocolate!" I grip the edge of the marble countertop. "If you say 'Tiff' one more time, I'm going to break your nose with that spatula."

"This is what people do, Ana. They cook together. They have dinner together. They share their lives together."

"We shared a life together."

"Until we didn't."

"What the hell does that mean?"

"Working opposite shifts. Choosing to hang out with your friends at a bar instead of me. Sinking more and more of yourself into your work. I was disappearing right before your eyes, and you didn't even notice." Something cracks in his voice.

I grab a gooey eggshell and throw it at the word 'teacher' on his chest.

"Hey!" he protests.

"That gave you the right to humiliate me? I have to see her every day, Brett. I have to be nice to her every day, instead of screaming at the top of my lungs to relieve the pain. And the pregnancy—"

I pivot toward the highchair and kick as hard as I can. It topples over, dislodging the plastic tray table with the image of a blue bunny rabbit. Part of its ear breaks and skitters across the tiled floor. Brett comes around the island, and I expect him to snap into IKEA repairman mode. Instead, he stands in front of me. Arms at his sides. Only then do I realize that I am bawling. Tears and snot race down my face. I struggle to catch my breath.

"I am so sorry," Brett says, taking my hands. The warmth of him travels up my arms, and it almost caresses my neck. "You deserved better than that."

I pull free and slap him.

He doesn't move or defend himself.

I slap him again.

"I'm sorry," he says.

With these words, everything gets still. Then I push him against the island. This time I kiss him. Hard. He appears stunned, unable to move. I kiss him again, harder the second time until his mouth gives way to mine. I can feel his hands on my ass as I try to yank off that infuriating apron. Only when he unties the strings does it fall to the floor where I grind it with my shoe. I peel off his shirt. My hands rub against his hairy chest, and my fingers tingle from the sensation of touching his skin. I give him another push. This time he sits on the counter. I unbuckle his pants, and his erection presses against his cotton briefs. I stroke it with my fingernails.

At first, Brett glances anxiously at the stuff on the counter, but I start knocking everything off before he changes his mind. A rainbow of sugar flies in the air. Measuring spoons with egg yolk sail off the ledge. The bowl with melted chocolate clangs against the floor like a gong. I'm convinced the mixer shatters into a dozen pieces, but it comes to life, whining like a wounded animal. I lay Brett on the counter, slip off my pants, and climb on top of him, knocking over a stool on the way.

If revenge sex is a dish best served cold, a marble countertop is a good way to go. I feel the stinging icy surface almost immediately. I don't know how Brett can lay there on the cold slab, though he always did burn hot. My knees grind into sugar and eggshell, and the hard, unforgiving surface makes me feel as if I'm crawling across cobblestones. Pain shoots up my legs, but I don't stop. He unbuttons my blouse. As he reaches up to grab my breasts, I wonder if he notices how much weight I've gained since he left. I lean back, sucking in my gut—

Smack.

The back of my head slams into a copper pot hanging from the ceiling rack. Several other pots rain down on us. One hits my shoulder. Another bounces off my back. Two more plop onto Brett's chest. As they crash to the floor, it sounds as if we are overturning an entire drawer of silverware.

I feel a bit woozy, but a feral horniness powers me through the head injury. I guide Brett's erection inside me. It feels harder, larger than I remember. The firmness of his touch and the familiar rhythm of our bodies mitigate some of the awkwardness and discomfort of screwing on a marble countertop in the middle of his girlfriend's, my dissertation director's, kitchen. Soon he pulls me down on top of him, straightening out my body and slipping out of me.

I can tell he wants me on my stomach. I flatten out on the counter, and my breasts and stomach press against the cool surface, somewhat warmed by Brett's body moments ago. I can practically lap up some of the sugar with my tongue. Brett leans on his side, waiting for me to adjust my position, but I'm taking up more room than he expects.

Boom.

A crashing thud shakes the island.

I turn.

Brett is gone.

He slipped off the counter. In a fall that surely would have sent me to the emergency room and ruined my dreams of being an action movie stunt double, Brett hit the floor all at once, flat as a board. He grunts, trying to catch his breath.

"Are you okay?" I ask.

"Just a bruised ass," he mutters.

He gets back to his feet unsteadily and a bit winded. Fortunately, the fall does not dull his desire. He winces as he climbs back onto the island, and I get on my knees. Within moments, he slides inside me from behind. He moves slowly at first, in circles. He knows I like that motion best.

The mixer continues to whine, and from here, I can see one of the metal beaters wobbling. Brett takes his time, like he used to. The skin on my forearms feels grainy from sugar and chocolate fragments. He moves in and out faster now, his pelvis bumping hard against me. He finishes with a moan. His body shudders.

Without saying a word, I get onto my back, and he lies next to me. His body presses against my side, and he nuzzles his face in my neck, kissing and breathing hot. He sticks his fingers between my legs until I writhe and moan. Steady, small circles that gradually move faster and faster. Faster until I feel an electricity radiate from my groin to my toes.

I come with a scream that I hope Tiff can hear from campus.

Bitch.

We stare at the empty pot rack on the ceiling. Both of us on our backs, looking up. Breathing heavy. I hold his hand, fingers interlocked. I squeeze hard because I know this is the last time we will be naked—anywhere, let alone on a kitchen countertop. This is goodbye sex. A farewell fuck. We both know it.

"Why did you come over?" he asks.

"I'm sorry about the thing at the bocce court." I don't turn toward him when I speak. I find it comforting to look at the empty rack and the ceiling's smooth, cream-colored paint. "I didn't mean to hurt your man parts."

"Yeah, right."

"You know I can't aim worth shit." I pause. "It was pretty badass, though. A twofer."

"I knew you weren't sorry."

"Not really."

We both laugh, but a sinking feeling has already begun in my stomach. I don't want to let go of his hand.

"You said I would get bored with you because you didn't think you were as smart as me. Strange choice to hook up with one of my professors," I say, trying to sound objective as if talking about Briff does not make me want to moonlight as an arsonist or binge watch *The Jersey Shore*. "How is that not still an issue?"

"It's different somehow. I guess she doesn't feel the need to prove it."

The words take me back to our unworn Halloween costumes. His history student bag lady, my IKEA assembly technician. They take me back to a million dismissive comments I made about his opinions, his blind encouragement, his ignorance about what I was going through for this career.

My vision becomes cloudy. I can't tell if I'm going to cry again or if the pot did more damage than I realized. I blink several times to refocus. Then I smell something burning. The room is filling with smoke.

"My soufflé!" Brett yells as he hops off the counter.

He opens the oven door to a puff of smoke. Wearing nothing but two cartoonishly-large, green oven mitts, Brett removes the smoking ramekin and carries it to the sink. The soufflé has risen high above the rim. The surface is cracked and lopsided, and it resembles blackened wood after a fire. Smoke billows toward the ceiling. He turns on the faucet and douses it with water.

"So much for dessert," I mutter.

Brett gives me a weak smile. He stares at the watery brown goop for a few moments before turning off the oven and surveying the room. In the smoky haze, the kitchen resembles a warzone. Scattered pots and pans.

Discarded clothes. Dirty bowls and gooey spoons. A broken highchair.

The mixer still putters.

We begin the quiet awkwardness of redressing. It is my least favorite part of sex. Each article of clothing adds another barrier, another reminder of the real world—the world where we aren't lovers, where Tiff comes home to a surprise dessert, and where I sleep alone in an apartment that isn't mine anymore.

I pick up my satchel and take out a wooden, hand painted elephant with red lines and yellow dots. Underneath its stomach, the artist carved "Sri Lanka." I place it on the island as Brett starts cleaning up.

"This is the *other* reason I came over," I say.

"What?"

"Tiffany's elephant. I took it at the soiree where you two first met."

He runs his finger over the long trunk and spine. "I've never understood this about you. Your need to take things. When we lived together, you moved my Saint Anthony medal to that collection of yours on top of the dresser. Remember?"

I nod. My throat feels parched, my tongue thick.

"It was something my mom gave me years ago, and I got used to having it around," he continues. "I kept it in the drawer of my nightstand. One day, I noticed it was up there, so I moved it back. The next day, it was on the dresser again. I did that a few times until I just left it with your stuff. I figured you'd say something. You never did."

"Do you know what he is the patron saint of?"

Brett shakes his head. "Travelling?"

"That's Saint Christopher. Anthony of Padua is the patron saint of lost things."

As I talk, Brett continues to reassemble his new life with Tiffany. He rehangs pots. He puts the sugar and the vanilla in the cupboard. He picks up bowls, the highchair, and the broken bunny ear.

"The things I take—small things—make me feel connected to the people I love. Reassured, I guess. If I have something to hold onto, to touch, I can't lose them. At least that's what I tell myself. I can't lose what I feel for them, what I hope they feel for me."

"But we were living together. You didn't need to take anything from me."

"Didn't I? I felt you slipping away, too, and I was right. Look where we are now."

Most of the smoke has cleared, and not much more cleaning will be needed to restore the room to its pristine, pre-fucking perfection. Some sweeping, maybe a mop. Wiping the island countertop with disinfectant, I hope. And I have no doubt Brett can fix the broken bunny ear so it looks new. He'll always know a crack is there, though, the Ana Crack. I smile at the thought. It's a petty victory, but it is all I have.

"So, why return the elephant?" he asks.

"I don't want a connection with her anymore."

I reach into my bag one more time and take out the worn, silver medallion of Saint Anthony, dressed in the clothing of a Franciscan friar and holding a baby lovingly with his arms, as if he has cared for many children.

"I came to give this back to you, too."

Brett places the broken pieces of the mixer on the counter and takes Saint Anthony from me.

"So this is goodbye?"

I nod. "It is."

Brett walks me to the front door, in silence. We stand there a few moments, his hand on the doorknob, our bodies close. I wonder if he wants to kiss me. One last indiscretion before I go. I want to kiss him, desperately, and I hate myself for it.

"This never happened," Brett says. "Us. Today, I mean."

I'm surprised how much the words hurt, how much his desire to protect his new life hurts. Mostly, I'm surprised how much it hurts to be erased, to watch yourself disappear and not be able to do a damn thing about it.

Part IV

Reparations

25
Dining with Dante

Thaigasm is the last place on earth I'd expect to see Dante Wellington. The East Village restaurant has narrow white tables crammed with twenty-somethings. Pink neon signs decorate the walls—*Thai One On, I Believe I Can Thai, Thailicious*—and electronic dance music pulses steadily through the speakers. All of the servers—young, outrageously thin Asian women— wear skirts nearly short enough to expose their wax jobs. They smile as if they were watching their favorite cat videos on YouTube.

Oddly enough, I am here because Dante invited me. I keep replaying his email about dinner and bracing myself for the worst:

> *Dear Ana Lightfeather Shaw,*
>
> *I will be in Manhattan tomorrow for a conference. Can you join me for dinner? I have something to discuss regarding the job.*
>
> *Dante Wellington*

Why not offer me the job outright if the department already made a decision? Why meet in person just to reject me? Unless, Dante wants to talk about something else.

Unless, Dante has figured out that I've been lying.

A bamboo stick of a waitress takes me to his table. I am wearing a camel-colored, long-sleeve dress, in part to show him that I don't just own one pair of pants. A tassel hangs from my laced-up neckline, and silver studded beads wind around the wrists and waist. It hangs loose around the hips, which is the only reason it fits, and it gives me a tropical chic look. Or so I told myself at home.

Next to this waitress, I resemble a deflated hot air balloon.

The restaurant is dark except for the tea candles at each table and the neon puns. Dante's bald head shimmers in the glowing pink light. The strips of gray hair that form a "T" above his ears are newly trimmed, and he wears the same corduroy jacket from the interview. Even his Ichabod Crane body looks uncomfortable in the tiny chair.

"Lightfeather," he booms. "I would stand, but it took me fifteen minutes to squeeze in here."

Nearly a dozen tightly packed tables stretch out on either side us, and my seat appears to be the only empty one in the restaurant.

"Interesting choice," I say.

"The food is supposed to be Thaigastic," Dante replies wryly as he rolls his eyes. "It's my daughter's doing."

"How so?"

"She always recommends restaurants like this. For the hip, young, and loud. She went to NYU, so she knows the city well. She gets a kick out of trying to offend my professorly sensibilities."

"Does it?" I ask, while glancing at the pink menu. The two girls on our left share a mountain of fried rice with onions, red bell peppers, and chicken. My stomach growls. "Does it offend you?"

"Quite the opposite!" Dante laughs. "I love these claustrophobic New York spots. The energy and exuberance. The absurd music. She forgets when she was little. Our playful, silly games, our surprising adventures. Somewhere along the way, she started seeing me as a dusty academic. I guess that's what happens."

"What?"

"We project one part of ourselves to the world, and everyone starts to think there is nothing more to us."

Bamboo Waitress returns with waters and an incomprehensible cheerfulness about taking our order. Dante jumps in with the Thai Is Falling Spring Rolls and the Once Upon a Thai Special. I ask for the Thai Me Up, Thai Me Down Pad Thai. He selects a bottle of red wine that, thankfully, requires no pun. She writes everything down carefully on a small notepad before shuffling away.

"Does your daughter still live in New York?"

"No, she is in North Carolina. Not far from me. Her two boys are wonders. Six and eight, great ages. They're full of opinions and ingenious ways to torment each other." Dante smiles, no doubt at the thought of them.

I feel a flash of envy. I have viewed him through a single lens too—a curmudgeonly old academic who lives alone, annoys colleagues by mocking their politically correct pretentions, and drives a car as if he's in a *Mad Max* movie. I stand by the last one, but there is a richness to his life I never considered. He belongs—family, a place to call home, a professional identity to take pride in.

"So, Lightfeather," Dante begins, "the department has given me the privilege of telling you the news. We would like to offer you a job as an Assistant Professor of Native American History at Devon University. As you surely know, academics don't get paid well, but we make up for that with long hours and poor healthcare." He smirks. "Congratulations."

The words have an unreality to them. I am so grateful I want to hug him—but I won't risk overturning the table. My eyes burn to the point of crying—but I won't let myself. Not here. It is the end of a six-and-a-half-year quest for a PhD and a job. It is as if someone has lifted a UPS truck filled with pink neon puns off my chest. To be wanted and respected. To be given the chance to be Professor Shaw.

"Before talking specifics, I do have a question. To satisfy my own curiosity."

My heart seizes up. Here it comes. He suspects deception on my part. Something about Lightfeather does not add up, and he intends to Columbo the truth out of me. Is this why he wanted to meet in person? To see my face when he offered me the job? To hear what I might give away with the wrong word or phrase?

Bamboo Waitress interrupts with the wine, bottle already opened. The tulip-shaped glasses remind me of whisky snifters, and she fills both of them without letting us smell or taste it first. Dante nods his approval nonetheless. She beams like a child accustomed to compliments.

"Is there something you wanted to tell us about yourself?" Dante resumes, the glass poised in his hand. "Something at the interview that slipped your mind or you wish you said in retrospect?"

"Pretty much everything was a disaster, so it's hard to pick one."

But Dante Wellington, amateur sleuth, is not thrown off by an anemic wit and wan smile. He presses ahead. "Imagine if we had not offered you the job. Is there something else that might have swayed the committee in your favor?"

"Why?" I ask. "Do you still need convincing?"

"No, no. Forgive me," Dante says with a chuckle. "I like you, Lightfeather. The job is yours, and I sincerely hope you take it. I always find it illuminating to hear people reflect on what they would have done differently."

As Bamboo Waitress slides the Thai Is Falling Spring Rolls between us, I sip my wine and let the peppery overtones linger on my tongue for a moment before placing the glass on the table. I'm eager to shove a spring roll into my mouth, anything to avoid more talking, and I stab one with a fork. The motion is too fast, though. My beaded sleeve dips into the glass, and before I can react, it turns on its side. Wine gushes onto me.

I am so close to the table that my thighs slam into it when I stand. Silverware rattles, and my chair collapses to the floor behind me with a loud smack. My spring roll—with fork protruding like a spear—slips out of my hand and plops onto Dante's plate.

"Crap," I blurt as I grab a cloth napkin to pat the stain on my dress. "I'm sorry."

"Is there anything I can do?" Dante asks.

I shake my head. The electronic dance music moves faster now. Its steady drumbeat pounds, and I feel it throbbing inside my head. The singer's voice seems stuck repeating the name "Emperor Jones." It takes me a few moments to realize she is saying "Into the Zone" instead. A few people at nearby tables glance at me with expressions of amusement or sympathy, but they return to their own dinners almost immediately. No one makes an effort to help with my chair.

I make my way to the Thaiphoon Restrooms. Floor-to-ceiling mirrors make up the exterior walls. Once inside, you discover they are one-way mirrors, allowing you to see the clamor, bustle, and strange pink glow of the restaurant while safely hidden from view. The mirror above the sink has a question mark affixed to the glass, and the words inside the long, curved line read: "Do you like what you see?"

I am still holding the cloth napkin, thankfully, because there are no paper towels. Only hand dryers. I soak the napkin with water, but every attempt to wipe away the stain worsens the damage—smearing and widening the reddish-brown trail that descends from just below my chest to the hem of the dress. It looks like blood. It looks as if I were a serial killer or Victim Number Three in a slasher film.

When I return to the table, the Thai Me Up, Thai Me Down Pad Thai is waiting for me. Dante pours me another glass of wine. I shake my head, but he insists.

"I suspect you need this more than anyone else here."

We take a few bites in silence. The sweet, chewy noodles make me feel less lightheaded, less preoccupied with my bloodied clothes and the tireless beating music.

"Lightfeather," Dante begins. "Do you have any questions? El Jefe will contact you tomorrow with details about the offer, but is there anything you'd like to ask me about the department or the university?"

I take a deep swig of wine. "Would you have offered me the job if I wasn't Native American?"

It is a gift to be able to surprise yourself, I suppose. To speak without thinking. To knock yourself out without an opponent in the ring. I've done it throughout my entire life, mostly with my willingness to voice unpopular opinions. I like Roger Moore's James Bond more than Sean Connery's. I haven't read *Harry Potter,* and I'm not going to. Beyoncé is not all that. But now I am risking more than incredulity and ridicule. I am a moment away from admitting that I've been lying, from throwing away this job, this career, for good.

"No," he replies flatly.

"Doesn't that bother you? Don't you find the entire notion of Native American Studies and Asian American Studies preposterous?"

"Not at all," Dante says, placing his elbows on the table and folding his fingers together. "I wish the experiences and stories of these communities were better integrated into how we understand our national history. We need greater inclusivity and fairness. Sadly, we still live in an age where the best way for a university to hire a Native American is through a job explicitly for Native Americans."

He lowers his eye and reaches for the bottle to refill our glasses. For the first time, he seems unsure of himself. "I did not mean to offend you at the interview. I wanted to touch a nerve, to get a glimpse of your passion. And I did. That's why I'm here. That's why I look forward to calling you a colleague next fall, Ana Lightfeather Shaw."

He pauses after saying my full name. The words make my stomach feel as if it has been thrown into a blender. I fooled him, all of them. But I don't feel relief or glee or triumph. The muscles in my neck remain tight. My underarms dampen. And I struggle to breathe as if I'm descending from a high altitude too quickly.

"Me too," I reply.

We toast our glasses, which catch fragments of the pink neon light. As I lean back, I notice my dress again. Somehow, the blood-red, body-length stain appears fresh as if I just stabbed someone all over again.

26
Moving Day

After dinner, I learn that nothing can kill a buzz and your sense of self-worth faster than the Amtrak waiting area in Penn Station. With fluorescent lighting designed to make a vampire look peaked, everyone appears mortuary ready. Expressionless, slump-shouldered commuters gaze at the departure board for a track number. People with rollaway bags stare at their phones instead of looking up. Heavy-eyed travelers munch on fatty foods, and some sleep awkwardly on uncomfortable chairs while homeless people rummage through nearby trashcans.

It is a collection of the miserable and destitute.

After I take the escalator down to the train, I find an empty seat in an empty car. The window, which looks onto a dark tunnel, offers only a drab reflection of myself and the frayed, red-white-and-blue cloth seats around me. My hair falls messily to my shoulders, and my skin appears darker. Beads of sweat from the brisk walk through the station cool on my forehead. I don't take off my coat because of the stain on my dress, but I unbutton it.

A slender man with shortly cropped hair enters the car. He wears sunglasses and holds a white, red-tipped cane. It moves side to side like the pendulum of a metronome, smacking the base of the seats steadily until he gets to my row.

"May I?" he asks with a smile.

I am tempted to tell him every other seat is free, but I don't want to add insulting the disabled to my list of shortcomings.

"Sure."

He folds the cane expertly into six sections and lowers himself carefully onto the seat. He can't be much older than I, somewhere in his early thirties, and he smells of shaving cream and soap. At first I am self-conscious about the stain when I realize I could be flashing my boobs and it wouldn't matter. My purse is partway open at my side. I pull it closer to my body.

We sit in silence as the train ascends from the underworld of Penn Station. Soon we pass the burning lights of nearby buildings, the tentacles of utility poles, graffiti-stained walls, and the glowing brake lights of other trains.

"Have you heard of vegan mattresses?" he asks with the kind of playful warmth you might expect between old friends, not strangers.

"Excuse me?"

"Vegan mattresses. Have you heard of them?"

"Is that a real thing?"

"It is." He keeps his face forward, maintaining a friendly smile.

His pointed nose gives him a distinguished profile, and I realize for the first time how attractive he is. How did I not notice his good looks sooner? Is it because of his blindness? His cane?

"I didn't know about them until a few days ago," he continues. "Strange, right?"

"Well, I can't live without red meat and junk food, so yeah."

"I mean the concept of it. Did someone invent the vegan mattress because of a huge demand out there? Or was it designed to guilt vegans and environmentalists into buying them?"

"The latter."

"Bingo!" He laughs, easily, comfortably. He crosses his leg toward me, and his new Nike sneakers match the blue color of his jeans. He places his left hand on the seat between us.

"I assume vegans fill their mattresses with compost," I say.

"No, real vegans sleep on dirt floors." His smile widens as he turns toward me. His face does not line up with mine exactly. It is as if he is looking over my shoulder. "Actually, I did some research. The mattresses are made without animal products or byproducts. They have none of the chemicals used for fire retardants—only plant-based materials such as natural rubber and 100% organic cotton."

"Organic cotton? Is there any other kind?"

"Most cottons are treated with pesticides."

"Right." I nod, but the thought has never occurred to me.

"So they don't use wool," he adds.

"There is wool in my mattress?" For all I know, it could be stuffed with Twinkies and T-shirts for teams that lost the Super Bowl. "Should I be concerned?"

"Are you allergic to sheep?"

"No, they're just gross."

"How so?" he asks, leaning closer to me. He has soft, fleshy lips, ruddy cheeks, and a pronounced Adam's apple.

"They smell weird."

He nods. "Wet wool is the worst."

"Right after Celine Deon and movies with the Olsen Twins."

"And the Home Shopping Network," he adds.

"Bingo!"

We both laugh. The conductor announces the first stop, and the hum of the engine quiets as the train slows.

"This is where I get off," he says as he stands and shakes his cane into a long staff again. "It was nice meeting you ..."

"Ana."

I want to ask him to stay longer, to tell me about himself. I am always struck by the ability some people have to make you like them in an instant. Ana Shaw is more of an acquired taste, like competitive ping-pong and White Castle.

The swinging cane taps along the aisle as he makes his way to the doors. They slide open, but he hesitates. Cold air spills into the car. I wonder if he will change his mind, if he will decide to ride with me for a few more stops before getting back to his real life.

"For someone who doesn't like sheep," he says, "it looks like you've slaughtered a few lambs already, Clarice."

"Thanks, Hannibal," I throw back at him.

I pull my coat around me, embarrassed once again by the stain. He steps onto the platform, but only as the doors close do I realize that he has been able to see me the entire time. My mouth gapes. As the train pulled away, he waves.

I can't figure out why someone would pretend to be disabled, why someone would feign blindness. What was he up to? I grab my purse. The phone is there, so are the keys to my apartment.

But my wallet—driver's license, credit cards, cash, university ID. They are all gone.

Vegan mattresses, my ass.

•••

The following morning, the owner of Peaches Moving and Storage arrives at precisely 9:00. He resembles a human cinderblock with his Julius Cesar haircut, flat nose, and square head. On the upper-left corner of his black shirt, there is a drawing of two peaches and the abbreviation "PMS." I wonder if anyone has ever had the courage to ask about his menstrual cycle.

I doubt it.

He introduces himself as Peaches, no last name, and his thick Russian accent makes me think he has a side gig collecting protection money or selling human organs on the black market.

"That's an unusual name," I say.

"My parents like fruit," he replies with a disconcerting seriousness.

"Mine too."

Peaches nods as if I have passed the first of many tests to earn his approval. He glances around the living room, clipboard in hand. Neatly stacked boxes of books crowd much of the space. I have packed them with the care of someone shipping Faberge eggs. Each one is labeled "Books" with a few notes to help me find what I need to finish my dissertation: "First Encounters," "Pequot War," "King Philip War," "Native American History (California)," "Trail of Tears," "Manifest Destiny, Mexican-American War," "Reservation System."

Peaches points to the coffee table and couch. "IKEA," he mutters. "The Swedish. Very organized people."

"I still can't forgive them for Ace of Base."

"What is this Ace?"

"The nineties pop band? 'I Saw the Sign.' 'All That She Wants.'"

"Yes." Peaches' eyes widen, and he nods. "She wants the baby. Good song."

"No, Peaches, it's not a good song. It's about a lonely woman who tries to give her life meaning by getting knocked up in one-night stands." I pause. "Well, that is what I thought when I first heard it."

Peaches blinks.

"Some might argue that she just wants another lover, but I can't shake my first impression, even if it's too literal," I explain.

Peaches blinks again.

"Women are good for more than their reproductive organs and their ability to pick up men."

"You no like children?" he asks with the same seriousness he reserved for fruit.

"Children are fine. I mean they're walking Petri dishes, but that's not the point—"

A knock on the door spares Peaches the rest of my misplaced Ace of Base outrage. Kavita, in jeans and the same gray sweatshirt from the night we kissed, steps inside. Her tall, thin body has the shape of an obelisk, and she wears her silky black hair in a low ponytail that cascades down the left side of her chest.

"Thanks for coming," I say.

"I wouldn't miss it." She leans in for a hug, and I catch hints of nutmeg and coffee on her breath. "You're my first homeless friend."

Kavita has offered to let me stay with her while I find a new place. Brett's tenant wants to see the apartment, but I refuse to be here when he does.

Getting kicked out of your home is bad enough, but I can't bear the thought of watching someone parade through each room, taking measurements and sneering at my stuff. I don't want a front row seat to how easily my life can be replaced by his.

Peaches clears his throat. "I need picture ID and signature."

"I told you yesterday that a fake blind man stole my wallet. I don't have an ID."

"So strange, right?" Kavita chimes in, turning toward me. "I keep thinking about that story. Not about him, but about you."

"What do you mean?"

"You wanted so badly not to seem prejudiced against the disabled that you were duped by a phony."

Her words take me back to my dinner with Dante, and my throat gets tight. "I hadn't thought of it like that."

Peaches taps the clipboard with one finger. "Yes, this is strange story. But how do I know you are who you say?"

"Look at me," I begin, gesturing at my overalls and grubby white T-Shirt. "Look at this place. Who would pretend to live here with all of this junk? Goodwill wouldn't even take most of it."

"I am not Goodwill." His facial expression remains unchanged, lips tight together, dark eyes steady. "You be surprise. I have customer who come home to empty house. He is all day at work, and he come home to find everything gone. Furniture. Appliance. Wife. All gone."

"I don't have a wife," I reply. "Or appliances."

He sighs, tapping the clipboard once again. "Okay, I trust you this time. Sign here. I need down payment."

"Peaches, my wallet was stolen. I told you on the phone—"

"Yes, fake blind man."

"I am going to the bank today. I can pay you later."

"Must have payment before start job."

"Do I look like a criminal?" I ask.

"How do I know?"

Peaches' thick hands remind me of someone wearing oven mitts, and he blinks frequently as if communicating in Morse code. A strange thought crosses my mind. Nadya Shaw would have known how to charm him. She would have flirted and laughed. She would have worn something dazzling. After a few minutes with her, Peaches wouldn't have asked for IDs or signatures or down payments. Not me. I haven't said a kind word. I've just lectured him on the failings of Swedish pop music.

"How much?" Kavita asks.

"Four hundred dollar."

"I'll cover it," she says, taking a checkbook from her purse.

"Wait—"

"You can pay me back after the bank." Kavita starts writing out the name of the moving company using the abbreviation PMS.

"You carry around checks?" I ask. "Who carries checks?"

"Lucky for you, the person fronting your down payment," she says.

"Touché."

As Peaches gets "his guys" from the truck, Kavita follows me into the kitchen. Packing supplies and dishes have been scattered on the countertop. Empty wine boxes are stacked on the floor. The smell of coffee and buttered toast still lingers.

"You know this stuff has to go into boxes, right?" she asks, picking up some newspaper to wrap a plate.

"Good tip."

"Are those IKEA bowls?"

"Of course, they're IKEA bowls. Everything I own is from IKEA. They're from the *entusiasm* collection for adding *entusiasm* to my steady diet of cereal."

"*Entusiasm* bowls? Seriously?"

"The Swedish," I reply in my best Russian accent. "Very *entusiastic* peoples."

I retreat to the bedroom to finish with my "trinkets," as Brett used to call them. The Unisphere from the 1964 New York World's Fair. The Call Me Ishmael shot glass from Tequila Mockingbird. John Doe's passports. I am holding the letter "S" from a Scrabble game when Kavita knocks. She carries something silver that resembles a UFO.

"You own a vegetable steamer basket?"

"That's what that is?"

"O—M—G! You are a closet vegetarian."

"Yes, all the junk food is a smokescreen."

She looks around the bedroom. The empty white walls. The stripped bed. The opened suitcase with a messy pile of clothes and toiletries.

"Is it hard to say goodbye? I'm sure you'll miss this place."

"Technically, I'm being evicted, so I am not too nostalgic at the moment. But yeah." I pause, rubbing

241

the wooden tile between my thumb and forefinger. "I need to move on, and I can't do that if I'm still living here."

I don't tell her that I still catch glimpses of Brett everywhere. How he used to lean against the sidearm of the couch when we watched television. How he stood in the kitchen after a run, sweaty, shirtless, and breathing hard. How he watched me climb out of bed after sex, still hungry for my body. I can't keep seeing his ghost and expect a future of my own.

Kavita is about to leave when she notices the game piece in my hand. "Is that a Scrabble tile? Remember that night during the storm?"

"Yeah."

"Do you still play?"

"Just during natural disasters."

•••

"'Poxy'? What the hell does that mean?" I asked.

"It means rotten or lousy," Ayumi Kimoto replied with a laugh. She had long hair, black as squid ink, a sporty walk, and a baggy sweatshirt that looked two sizes too big. "I think it originally referred to someone who had smallpox or syphilis."

"Lovely."

Ayumi and I had seen each other in class, talked a bit on campus, but this was our first time hanging out. At the reception for new graduate students one week earlier, I discovered that we lived in the same crappy apartment complex. Along with Kavita Singh, our depressingly fit, depressingly tall, depressingly poised classmate. She remained distant, a bit wary of us, as if people had to earn their way into her life.

The hurricane winds made agonized sounds like a woman giving birth, and the rain fell steadily now. When my neighbors, Melanie and Matthew Barnes, invited me over for a hurricane party of vodka and board games, I asked if some friends could join. I used the term "friends" loosely because we were all new to Haverton University. Only six weeks into our new lives, we were all uprooted. Away from home. Thrust together by chance and a natural disaster.

Melanie and Matthew, a brother and sister duo from Michigan, moved in the day before classes started. Melanie to pursue a doctorate in economics, Matthew in chemistry. Ayumi arrived from San Francisco in August around the same time I drove up from Long Island, and Kavita referenced New Jersey a few times. From the sound of it, she drove back on weekends. Somehow, we all ended up at Oceanside Apartments. A place nowhere near a body of water. A place that looked onto an equally dismal apartment complex across the street. A place that specialized in providing substandard living accommodations to impoverished graduate students.

Melanie and Matthew—M&M as I dubbed them after my first shot of vodka—did not have much by way of living room furniture. A television rested on a cardboard moving box. The futon couch sagged as if suffering from chronic depression, and a disorganized, tightly packed bookcase did a decent impression of the Leaning Tower of Pisa. Since M&M only had Sorry and Parcheesi, Ayumi brought over Scrabble, a deluxe edition. We sat in a circle where a coffee table should have be, hunched over the board in jaundiced candlelight. The apartment smelled of wet fur, musk, and animal pee because of Cicero, Melanie's ferret. She held him in her arms.

"Is a ferret a rodent?" I asked.

"No, a member of the weasel family," Melanie explained.

"Weasels aren't rodents?"

"Nope. You're not a rodent. Are you, Cicero?" she asked in one of those sing-songy voices some people reserve for talking to animals and small children. "They're meat eaters."

"That's comforting."

Cicero bared his sharp teeth, in all likelihood sizing up my nose as an appetizer. She rubbed his belly, and his long, S-shaped body shivered.

Kavita moved with the sculpted fluidity of a yoga instructor and placed the word "chiaroscurist" on the cluttered board, adding letters to my previous contribution, "chi."

"What the fuck is a chiaroscurist?" I asked.

Kativa laughed, covering her mouth with her hand. "A painter who specializes in contrasting dark and light. Caravaggio pioneered it in sixteenth century."

"Nerd," Ayumi said playfully.

"Now, I remember," I replied. "Cicero famously said never to trust politicians, prostitutes, and chiaroscurists."

"That was Snoop Dogg," Ayumi corrected.

"Right."

"Cicero did say that 'silence is one of the great arts of conversation,'" Kavita added in a calm, steady voice, as if quoting Cicero was the most natural thing to do during a hurricane.

"Are you trying to tell me something?" I asked.

She snort laughed as Matthew refilled our shot glasses. M&M shared the same blue-green eyes and narrow bodies. Unlike Melanie's curly mess of blonde hair, Matthew had Matt Damon's haircut from the Jason Bourne films. He wore a similar expression of somber earnestness, as if he was on the cusp of remembering his real name.

"Cicero also said that 'the reward of friendship is friendship itself,'" he said, toasting. "To new friends."

We touched glasses before knocking back the shots. My throat burned, and the alcohol warmed my gut. The candlelight began getting a hazy quality.

"Now, can we please stop quoting Cicero?" I asked. "I feel bad enough. My first Scrabble word was 'nap.'"

"You were pacing yourself," Ayumi added. "Besides, I gave you a dignity parachute by turning it into 'napery.'"

"Thanks."

The rain pounded against the windows with the heaviness of car tires on gravel. At times, a gust of damp air slipped beneath the door and chilled me.

"I'm leaving graduate school," Matthew announced, his voice somber. "To be with my girlfriend. She's training to be a nurse in Ann Arbor."

"Why?" I asked. "Once she finishes, can't she get a job anywhere?"

"I feel her slipping away," he replied, studying his Scrabble rack and rearranging tiles. "She is getting more distant. If I don't go back soon, I'll lose her."

"You shouldn't have to give up your future to be with her," I said, my voice thick with judgement. I regretted the harshness of my tone, but an irrational anger bubbled in my chest. I didn't know him. This was the first time we exchanged more than a few sentences, but I could not understand choosing love over an avocation, over a chance to do something meaningful.

"I think it's brave," Ayumi said, wrapping her arms around her knees and pulling them close to her chest. "So many things in life are decided for us. Even being here. Haverton picked us before we picked it. A hurricane brought us together tonight. There is something powerful about choosing your own destiny."

"That's a nice way of seeing it." Matthew smiled, but I caught a hint of sadness in it. "I am not sacrificing. I'm choosing to be with her. That's the difference."

For the next couple of hours, we played Scrabble, drank, and told stories. Cicero yawned on occasion, and M&M sat together but apart from the rest of us. They seemed to be two halves of the same person, and it became difficult to picture Melanie staying after Matthew left. I couldn't stop thinking about his decision and wondered if I could do the same. I tried to imagine myself leaving for love only to watch that relationship fall apart years later, as I believed it inevitably would. Then what? Regret? Smoldering resentment? Still, I had to admit feeling a certain pang for not having the choice to make, for not having a love so magnetic I couldn't resist its pull.

Yumi (she insisted we drop the "A"), Kavita, and I joked easily. We talked as if we had known each other for years. And we lost track of time, even of M&M and Cicero after a while. Only as the last of the candles began to fizzle, shortly after two in the morning, did we thank M&M and head back to our separate apartments—drunk and happy in the glow of new friendships.

I was not outside for more than a minute before I got home. Still I found myself dripping wet. I began taking off my clothes when I felt it in my pocket: the "S" tile from Yumi's Scrabble game.

27
Moondude's Observatory

Throughout the morning, Peaches Moving and Storage grows increasingly impatient with my anecdotal approach to packing. Each item comes with a detail or story I share with Kavita. I linger over Quackers the Duck, my purple stuffy from childhood. I unearth the LP of Colman Hawkins and Ben Webster's *Encounters*, the only record I couldn't leave with Dad. I hold a book of Pablo Neruda's poetry—a gift from Brett on our first Valentine's Day. He read it, so he could underline parts that made him think of me.

Only my vibrator, a Pussycat Turbo 2000, gets shoved into the suitcase with a "no comment."

At a certain point, Peaches' two guys begin packing boxes quietly, efficiently. One has an uncanny resemblance to a brooding Christian Bale, and the other reminds me of an extra on *The Sopranos*. Neither speaks English nor smiles. Neither takes a break. I don't object to the help—not that they would understand why I want to slow down. To them, this is just another job on the way to another job. This isn't their half-life being boxed up. This isn't a new beginning.

Soon the apartment is empty and eerie in its stillness. Apart from scuff marks on the walls and chipped paint, dust and discolored carpets, no traces of my life with Brett remain. And even that will be wiped away with nothing more than a vacuum and a new paint job.

Most of my stuff goes to storage, but a few boxes make it to Kavita's place. After unpacking in her guestroom, which I dub the "Shaw Sanctuary," I head to the morgue. I swapped shifts this weekend because Kavita wants to have dinner tomorrow—to celebrate my move. In truth, I'm relieved for the distraction. I don't want to spend Saturday night staring at the walls of my new room and thinking about how much smaller my life has become.

Once again, the roof has been transformed into Moondude's observatory. Constellation maps, notebooks, measuring equipment, and pencils lie on a beach towel with the same image as his Grateful Dead screensaver: a skull wearing a Native American headdress. He stands next to the telescope, and there is a thermos of hot chocolate at his feet. As he peers into the eyepiece, his curly hair falls like strings of beads around his face.

I take in the night sky for myself. The crowded stars play hide-and-seek behind passing clouds, and a nearly full moon, with its pummeled, blasted surface, appears to sit a few clenched fists above the horizon. It glows pale white.

"How is the Star That Does Not Walk Around?" I ask. "Still there?"

He looks up with a smile. "See for yourself."

Moondude pours me a cup of hot chocolate as I look into the telescope. The stretchers for the gods and the trail of medicine men come into view. One story about the Skidi Pawnee's view of the Dippers—told to me by a man with the improbable name of Moondude—has changed the way I see the sky.

We have slipped into an easy rapport since discovering John Doe's real name. Of course, I still want police lineups and wisecracking detectives working around the clock. I want to solve the murder like Hercule Poirot or Sam Spade or Angela Lansbury. I want the truth. But every time I mention it, Moondude warns me about watching too many crime shows. *"They give easy answers, dude,"* he says. *"Caught and convicted. Case closed. Life doesn't work that way."*

I lean back from the telescope. "I got a job as a professor. In North Carolina."

"That is so cool, man. I mean, person. I'm really stoked for you."

Moondude kamikazes into a bear hug, which gives me the usual contact high, but I don't stiffen. Not this time. The hug has a warm sincerity to it. In truth, I'm oddly grateful for this spontaneous expression of happiness on my behalf. He picks up our cups of hot chocolate, and we toast.

"This means I won't be working here once the semester ends," I say.

"Right." Moondude nods as he sits in the folding chair next to the tripod. He fiddles with the eyepiece. "On to bigger and better things."

"I guess." I look at the constellation of Splinter Foot Girl, twinkling overhead as if she and her family were still on the run. Another new way of looking at the stars, courtesy of Moondude. "Can I ask you something?"

"With you, I assume that's a rhetorical question."

"It is," I reply. "How did you end up here? In this job? You could have been anything. An astronomer, a hot chocolate barista, a Grateful Dead hagiographer."

"There is still time," he says with a smile before gazing into the telescope.

"Seriously. Why work with the dead?"

"Isn't that what you do as a historian? Work with the dead?"

"In a way. But I want to tell their stories, like the stories you told me about the stars."

Moondude leans back, and his bony body moves with the stiffness of a marionette. He does not speak for a long time. We sip our hot chocolates, and the creamy texture blankets my tongue. In the distance, a dog howls.

"I'm sorry. I wasn't trying to be nosy," I say. "My mouth sometimes gets the better of me. Most of the time, actually, and—"

"I used to be someone else. Maybe that's why I got caught up in John Doe's story, why I let you drag me into it."

"What do you mean?"

"I used to wear a suit and tie to work."

"No way."

"Way." He nods. "I was a marketing guy for a medical device manufacturer in Arizona. Heart monitoring equipment. Pace-makers. That kind of thing. Had an average house in an average suburb in Tempe. Had a wife, too. She deserved a better-looking husband, but her loss, my gain. Right?"

"I didn't know you were married."

"Not anymore."

Moondude's face has a bluish hue in the white moonlight, and his eyes seem black. He unbuttons his lifejacket coat. The swirling, hurricane pattern on his tie-dye shirt consumes his torso.

"I was driving home from work one night," he continues. "Twilight. I was on our street, no more than ten houses away. I wasn't speeding. I hadn't been

251

drinking. A little distracted, maybe. Work stuff. That's all. He was on a scooter. He just shot out between two parked cars. I hit the brakes as soon as I saw him."

Moondude leans forward and grabs one knee with his hand. His jaw tightens.

"Nathan Jones. Five years old. Fractured skull and a brain hemorrhage. He died forty-seven minutes later at the hospital."

"Jesus."

"After that, I couldn't sleep. I couldn't concentrate at work. I couldn't even make love to Nina." Moondude sips his hot chocolate and stares into the cup. "We had been trying to have kids, but not after that. How could I? How could I take someone else's child and still have my own? I couldn't wrap my mind around the injustice of it. I started sleeping on the couch."

Moondude glances at me, still hunched forward as if he is about to stand. The thermos cup looks like it might drop from his fingers. "Misdemeanor vehicular manslaughter. Two years probation. That's what the judge decided. Can you believe it?"

"What?"

"Measuring how much a life is worth. That must be a tough job, being a judge. I wouldn't want it. I still don't understand the sentence, though. How can you repay what I did? How can you make it right?"

"It wasn't your fault."

"Whose fault was it? Nathan's? His mother's? The client who kept me at work later than usual that day? At a certain point, you have take responsibility for your role in the course of things. We all owe something to somebody."

Moondude gets out of the chair, awkwardly. The metal frame creaks. He begins packing up the telescope, and I help gather the equipment on the Grateful Dead towel. I take another sip of hot chocolate, and the sweetness warms my mouth. Instead of reminding me of my dad's fire pit, I think of the things Nathan didn't get to do. Kiss a girl. Fall in love. Go to college.

"Not wanting kids anymore pretty much ended my marriage," Moondude says as he folds the tripod. "Nina wasn't keen on the ganja at that point either. I quit my job and started getting high all the time. Once I finished probation, I moved here. I used to have a friend in Haverton, years ago. I visited once and remembered liking it. Small. Quiet. The rest just fell into place. I found this job almost immediately. It felt like the right kind of work for me—a way I could do right by the dead."

After Moondude tucks the rest of the astronomy equipment into a duffle bag, we enter the stairwell and walk to the first floor, our footsteps echoing loudly. We still carry the cups, and the chocolate aroma has a bitter quality to it. So, this is penance, I realize. To erase his name and become a cliché. To give up family and care for the dead. To study stars through the stories of forgotten people.

But will it ever end? Will he ever feel as if he has paid enough?

"I'm glad I worked here," I say, surprised by my sincerity. "I appreciate everything you've done. The stuff with John Doe, the stories about the stars—and the not firing me part."

"There's still time," he replies with a smile.

253

We both laugh.

"I am actually going to miss you," he says.

"Me too."

28
Potlatch

The smell of Kavita's apartment hits me as soon as I open the front door. Onions and garlic. Curry and cinnamon. The aromas carry a warmth, a coziness I don't expect. In the kitchen, Kativa chops ginger on a cutting board. Fresh cilantro and raisins are on the countertop. Yellow lentils simmer in a pot. She wears an orange pleated chiffon dress with a plunging neckline and a crisscrossed pattern that exposes the sides of her stomach and her lower back. Against her skin and obsidian hair, the dress resembles the last moments of a sunset.

"Unless that's a Big Mac, I am going to assume this is *Invasion of the Body Snatchers* and you've done something with the real Kavita."

"L—O—L."

I step over to the stove. "This smells amazing. I didn't think you owned a pot. I didn't think you could identify a pot in a police lineup."

"Is that something police do?"

"This is like real food."

"It's my mom's recipe." She lifts a wooden spoon to her mouth, blows on the creamy yellow mixture, and extends it to my lips. "Dahl with chickpeas."

"Isn't this technically a vegetable?"

"More than one. Try it."

The chickpeas thicken the smooth texture of the lentils and dissolve gently on my tongue. "This is *really* good."

Kavita tastes a spoonful and adds more ginger to the mixture. As I lean back against the counter, I notice the spotlessness of the kitchen—no dirty dishes, sticky surfaces, or spilled spices. Admittedly, my only attempts at cooking have resulted in near Armageddon conditions, but this level of neatness means that she has already cleaned up. That's when I notice the *ypperlig* dining room table with four place settings and a centerpiece of fresh daffodils.

"What's with the sex kitten dress and the table?" I ask.

"We're having a dinner party. Just the gang." She continues to stir the dahl with her back to me. "In honor of your move."

"The gang? Doug and Yumi are coming here? Tonight?"

The doorbell rings.

"That would be yes," she says. "Don't worry about me and Doug. It's a celebration for you. Your best friends should be here."

"This is a bad idea."

Kavita turns off the flame for the dahl, but a pot of rice continues to gurgle on the back burner. She wipes her hands on a dishtowel before gliding into the living room with long, fluid steps. I shuffle after her.

"I just got back from the library," I complain.

"So?"

"I'm dressed like an usher at a movie theater."

"You always look that way."

"Thanks."

Doug and Yumi stand together in the doorway, but not too close. Doug's coat is unbuttoned, and he has on jeans and a white dress shirt. His brown hair is mussy, smile sheepish, and he hunches his shoulders, as if Kavita might hit him with something. He holds out a bottle of Irish whiskey.

"Kavi said potluck, so we potlucked," Doug announces. "My mom comes from Irish stock, my dad's a Brit. I figured I'd bring something they could both agree on as a family tradition. Alcohol."

"Family tradition?" I ask.

"I thought it would be nice if we all brought something associated with family," Kavita explains. "Glad you put yourself out, Doug."

"Anytime," he says loudly before lumbering inside.

Yumi follows, carrying a heavy pot with mitts. Steam pushes out from beneath the lid, making her face a bit flushed and moist. Her blue-streaked hair falls shoulder length. Beneath an unbuttoned black suit jacket, her white blouse, more girly than her usual style, stops just above her bellybutton. She wears spray-paint tight blue jeans and black leather pumps with a slight heel. Seeing her and Kavita together makes me realize I am the only one here not dressed to give Doug a hard on. Why do these brilliant women feel the need to dress up to titillate a man, and a doughy man at that? Not that I don't love Doug. I do. I love all of them. But sometimes the imbalance of it, the unfairness, infuriates me. It makes me want to send everyone home to change into something as effortless as Doug's outfit.

After putting the pot on the dining room table, Yumi lifts the lid to reveal a brown broth simmering with thick noodles. A poached egg floats in the center, surrounded by pieces of chicken and green onions.

"It's a noodle soup that my grandmother used to make," Yumi explains. *"Miso Nikomi Udon.* It's from the region of her hometown."

"What are those things that look like mini pieces of toast?" I ask, pointing at the floating objects like a kid at a tide pool. "And that brown thing?"

"Fried tofu and shitake mushrooms."

"What's that white thing with the pink swirls?"

"Kamaboko, a fish cake."

"Are you trying to kill me?"

Yumi laughs. "No, I left the crudité at home."

"Thank Christ," I reply.

"Let me get some bowls," Kavita interjects.

Doug follows her. No wall separates the kitchen from the small dining room, so Yumi and I can see them side by side. Kavita taking bowls from the white cabinet. Doug knowing the exact drawer for the wine opener, grabbing a bottle from the counter, and uncorking it—each movement familiar from having done it countless times. I can feel Yumi stiffen.

"Wine before whiskey," Doug booms.

"I've got it." Kavita snatches the bottle from his hands. "Sit. Everyone."

Doug returns to the table and slumps in his chair, appearing both hangdog and annoyed. As Kavita pours the wine, Yumi scoops soup into each bowl. No one speaks. The room has the same tension as a Thanksgiving dinner with a racist uncle or a Scientologist. The tanginess of the soy sauce wafts up from the broth.

"Can I play some music?" I ask.

"Sure," Kavita replies as she finishes pouring herself a glass. "Just tell Alexa what you want."

"Not Alexa, for crying out loud," I whine. "She gets things wrong on purpose just to spite me."

"Yes," Kavita replies, "Alexa was designed for the sole purpose of tormenting you."

"Alexa," I call out. "Play 'My Funny Valentine' by Miles Davis—"

"Fuck that," Doug blurts out before I finish.

The scratching beat of N.W.A.'s "Fuck the Police" starts pounding through the speaker.

"No, Alexa!" I yell. "My Funny Valentine—"

"Come on," Doug complains again. "No old crap tonight."

The steady beat and synthesized chords of "In the Air Tonight" take over, teeing up the nasal whine of Phil Collins.

"Anything but Phil Fucking Collins!" I blurt.

"And turn it down," Doug barks.

"Jesus, stop talking while I'm talking. It gets confused."

The music pauses.

"Here's what I found on the web about Jesus," Alexa announces.

"You see?" I complain to Kavita. "Alexa is an asshole."

Yumi clears her throat. "The soup is getting cold."

"I should serve the dahl and rice." Kavita walks over to Alexa and lowers the volume manually. "Alexa, play my Indian classical music station."

Tabla drums begin tapping complex rhythms, and a violin weaves in and out of the beats. Soon a woman's voice takes over—stretching out words and vowels, sliding up and down scales. The violin joins her in a duet while the drums continue to change rhythms, controlling the speed and mood of the music. She is telling a story. I can't understand the words, but it seems to be about loss.

Kavita goes to the kitchen. Her molten iron dress draws attention to her long legs and elegant movements. Doug watches her. Yumi, jaw tight, watches both of them. When Kavita returns, the yellow dahl has been sprinkled with raisins and cilantro. Some of it mixes with the mound of white rice next to it. She serves Yumi and me first. Doug's plate gets slapped onto the table in front of him.

I try to eat equally, not to offend anyone. I sip the soup, tasting the saltiness of the miso and soy sauce. Then I try some dahl. The ginger, onions, and garlic give it a spicy kick. I pick up the spoon again.

"Delicious," I say with lentils still in my mouth.

"Which one?" Kavita asks.

"Both." I hesitate, looking back and forth between Yumi and Kavita. I reach for my wine. "You know most people think the term 'potluck' goes back to the Renaissance. The English expression 'luck of the pot' refers to an uninvited guest who arrives just in time to eat."

"A mooch?" Doug takes a large gulp of wine. He appears constipated, shifting uncomfortably in his chair.

"Yeah," I reply. "Only during the Great Depression did it start to mean a community meal where everyone brings a dish."

"I like the story about the mooch better," Doug says.

"Of course you do," Kavita mutters as she scoops another forkful of dahl. Her soup is untouched.

"What's that supposed to mean?"

"Most likely," I continue over Doug, "the tradition is Native American, practiced among some indigenous tribes on the West coast of the US and Canada. It was called 'potlatch'—a celebration on special occasions with feasting, speeches, gift-giving, and dancing."

"White people get credit for everything," Yumi mutters.

"Not Tyler Perry movies," Doug quips.

"The goal," I explain, "was for the host, typically a clan leader, to give away as many gifts as possible to friends and neighbors. In these communities, power and respect came from giving, not taking things."

Doug turns to Kavita. "How exactly am I a mooch?"

"You were practically living here." Kavita's voice gets tight, her words spilling out against the quick rhythm of the tabla drums. "Until you came up with some bullshit excuse to dump me after you started sleeping with her!"

"Not the pubic hair again," I say.

"Yes, the pubic hair," Kavita snaps.

"We were not sleeping together," Doug protests. "Yet."

"Jesus, Doug," I say.

"What?"

Kavita slams her fist on the table. "You knew something was going on between you. You knew it was wrong. You both knew it was wrong."

"I'm sorry," Yumi says softly, her eyes lowered. "I didn't mean to hurt you. It just happened, something clicked between us, but we never—"

"You lied to me! You made a fool of me, day after day." She looks around the table, tears welling in her eyes. "You're all liars."

"How the hell did I get pulled into this?" I ask.

"You know exactly how," Kavita spits out the words.

"What?"

"Forget it."

"What?"

"I saw the email," she replies sharply. "Your laptop was on the kitchen table with your inbox open. The email with your job offer from Devon."

"Fuck," I mutter.

"Wait a minute," Doug leans forward, his hair mussy as if he has just run his hand through it. "You got a job? You went on an interview?"

"Yeah," I reply, flat. My stomach knots up, and my hands feel shaky. "I went through with the Lightfeather thing."

"Holy shit," Doug says.

"You did what?" Yumi asks, her jaw tightening as she stares at me through the daffodil centerpiece.

"I applied as Lightfeather and got a campus interview. I only went for the experience. I never thought they'd offer me a job." The words start tumbling out of my mouth as panic rises in my chest. "Seriously, my interview could have been labeled a natural disaster."

"Holy shit," Doug echoes before taking a deep gulp of wine.

"You're going to turn it down, right?" Kavita asks, her voice soft. She does not look up from her plate.

"I don't know. I mean—"

"You don't know?" Yumi barks with thick disdain. "You don't know? Are you out of your mind? You sit here talking about fucking potlatch. You with your great Native sensibility. *Please.*"

"I was just trying to ease some tension. Excuse me for not playing Musical Fuck Chairs with Doug!"

"Wait a minute," Doug protests.

Kavita slaps his bicep. "Shut up!"

"It's not like he has the only dick in Haverton, Yumi," I continue. "We were best of friends. Now look us."

"Because you have so much integrity? Don't change the subject. You and your bullshit Native American name and your bullshit Native American job!" Her cheeks burns red.

"I fought for that job, six years and counting. I've earned it."

"Keep telling yourself that." She glares at me. "At least the rest of us don't have to wear blackface to go to work!"

Kavita's mouth drops partway open, and even Doug lowers his head into his hands.

"What?" Yumi asks. "We're all thinking it."

"I don't believe this," I say.

"To be fair," Doug replies, raising his hand like a student, "I'm thinking more Dustin Hoffman from *Tootsie* than blackface."

"That's because you're white," Yumi snaps. "You think you can screw over anybody and get away with it. Imperialist asshole."

"Imperialist asshole? Because I'm white and my father's parents were British?"

"Yes."

"My mother's Irish. That makes me half colonized."

"You're still a white, patriarchal …" Yumi pauses, struggling for the word. "Imperialist!"

"And the Japanese never colonized anybody?" he asks sarcastically. "Hello, Korea. And don't forget about that alliance with Hitler."

Yumi grabs a handful of lentils and pelts Doug with them. It resembles an exploded paintball on his chest. Everything in the room gets still for a moment except for the Indian woman singing a trill over staccato drumming.

The second cannonball of lentils comes from Kavita, landing squarely in Doug's face. I've armed myself, but I'm no match for Yumi's rapid-fire precision. I've been pummeled with two helpings of dahl on my face and my chest before I land a clump on the side of her blue-black hair.

The entire gang is on their feet now, throwing handful after handful of rice and dahl. Doug bumps the table getting up, knocking over the flowers and a glass of wine. Through the blizzard of Indian food, he manages to connect with Kavita's chest. I smack Doug with a clump of rice the size of baseball, and it explodes on his forehead. He gives me a look of betrayal just before sending two fistfuls of rice my way. The first slams into my forearm, raised to shield my face. The second misses, mostly because Kavita and Yumi have started double-teaming him with another barrage.

We empty our plates.

Breathing heavy. Backed away from the table. We stare at each other. The room looks as if someone detonated a dahl hand grenade. Yellow goo covers the floors and walls. It drips from our hair. It clings to our necks, arms, and hands. It has left marks on every article of clothing. Doug still has a glob of lentils on the tip of his nose.

We wait for someone to speak or do something. Only Yumi has enough rice in hand for one more assault, but she drops it on the table with a plop.

"Fuck," she says flatly. "Hardly anyone touched the soup."

•••

The laughter after that helps. We laugh until tears cloud our vision. Until our stomachs hurt. I even pee myself a bit. The laughter doesn't fix anything, though. Doug and Yumi leave. Together. Kavita looks deflated as we clean the dining room. We mop the floors and clear the countertops. I load the dishwasher.

"You throw one hell of a potlatch," I say as we sit on the couch sipping wine. "We should do this more often."

"I'll check my calendar," she replies.

Neither of us has changed outfits. I can still feel the sticky residue of dahl and rice on different parts of my body. Stains darken Kavita's molten dress like oil, and she has some dried lentils between her breasts. I don't say anything because she still manages to look gorgeous. I look like I lost a fight with a refrigerator. Across from us, the print of the six-armed Dhana Lakshmi, Goddess of wealth, stares at us. Her red sari unstained. Her outstretched hands dropping coins out of reach.

"Are you okay?"

"No even close." She holds her glass with both hands, and the circles beneath her brown eyes seem darker. "I thought I could see him. I thought I could see them, together."

"Doug is a total ass."

"True," she says with a smile. "He's not wrong, though."

"About?" I tuck my legs beneath me on the couch and face her. The yellow stains on my black pants resemble polka dots.

"He wanted a causal relationship. Nothing serious. I told him it was casual. I even convinced myself. But I see them together, and I know I was wrong on both counts."

"Both counts?"

"He wanted something serious. Just not with me."

She holds the glass to her lips but does not drink. The lights are dim. Alexa plays some string quartets by Haydn, softly—though I specifically asked for the Charlie Haden Quartet. Bitch.

"And the second thing?" I ask.

"What?"

"Both counts?"

"Oh." She nods. "I was lying. You can only lie to yourself for so long before it catches up with you."

My stomach growls with hunger. I take another sip of wine. It tastes thick and sweet with a hint of cherries.

"I have an idea. McDonald's run. My treat."

"That might be the best idea you've ever had."

We put on our coats, and I grab my purse and car keys.

At the door, Kavita hesitates. "I'm sorry I called you a liar."

"You don't have to apologize," I reply, reaching for the light switch. "I'm sorry I wasn't more honest with you. I'm still not sure what to do. I want this so bad. I've wanted it for so long."

Kavita nods. Her expression changes, though, as if a shadow were passing across her face, and it makes me wonder if I've already broken something irrevocably, if she will ever see me quite the same way again. "Can I ask you something?"

"What?"

"Do you think taking this job is like wearing blackface?"

"It doesn't matter what I think. It matters what you think." Kavita gets still. "Does it feel like that to you?"

I snap off the lights. "Maybe."

29
Oxalis triangularis

My office in the Humanities Department overlooks a library parking lot with Dumpsters, parked cars, and a loading dock. Until this view, I never realized libraries produced so much trash. Trucks come twice a week to clear away black garbage bags and plastic recycling, broken-down cardboard boxes and loose paper. One night last fall, someone approached the Dumpster. She had a voluptuous body with a fitted green coat and matching backpack. Her moon-white face and flowing red hair reminded me of a wistful Irish barkeep. After lifting the lid, she tossed three books inside—one at a time. Each landed with a reverberating thud.

Something about throwing them out at a library seemed particularly spiteful to me. What kind of books inspire such anger and resentment? Paris Hilton's *Confessions of an Heiress? The Da Vinci Code? Moby-Dick?*

Maybe it was more serious than that. Maybe she learned something she wish she hadn't. Truth can hit you that way.

Above my desk hangs a framed map of the California missions. Drawn in the style of eighteen-century cartography, each of the twenty-one missions from San Diego to San Francisco is represented by a cupola with a cross. The parchment-style paper—even behind glass—makes you want to run your finger along the mission trail, to trace the Herculean effort of building these church towns along the coast. The rest of California is nothing more than dry, empty spaces—without any hint of the people and cultures already there.

I am staring at this ant trail of missions when I realize the poster is crooked. I lean over the desk and push up the left corner of the frame. The opposite side dips too much. I readjust, but each touch leaves it more lopsided.

"Busy at work, I see."

Professor Green, in full Brawny Man attire, stands in the doorway. Beneath his waterfall beard, his stomach pushes hard against the buttons of his red-checkered flannel shirt. Today, he carries two Purple Shamrocks.

"Just trying to straighten things," I say.

"A lifelong process," he replies as he places both plants on my desk and adjusts his sunglasses.

"I didn't know Charlemagne had a brother."

"The much overlooked Carloman, yes. But this is not Charlemagne's brother. This is for you. A gift."

"You shouldn't have."

He smiles.

"Seriously, I'm like the Black Death. Plants. Goldfish. Even my Yoda Chia Pet didn't last more than a week."

"It's a thank you gift," he says. "For what you did for Payton."

"It was nothing."

"Not to me."

Green sits, scratching his chin and straightening his right leg. I drop into my own chair, still annoyed by the map. What if it has always been crooked and I only just noticed? Is that possible?

Green slides the plant toward me. "Take care of your *Oxalis triangularis*. Find a room in your apartment with plenty of sunlight."

"I'm kind of between homes right now," I mutter.

"Don't overwater it," he continues over me, "and remember that plants thrive with good conversation. I find it particularly helpful to give them names. It will encourage you to open up."

"Okay." I take hold of the cool, clay-colored pot and look at the delicate white flowers and purple leaves. "I think I'll name it Payton."

He nods. "Payton, it is."

"I'm curious. Why do you like this type of plant so much?"

"It goes by many names," he says. "Some call it the False or Purple Shamrock because its leaves resemble Irish clovers. Some call it the Love Plant because they see the leaves as heart-shaped. I love that fluidity. That seems so human to me."

"Fluidity?"

"The way we are different things to different people. Our partners and friends. Our coworkers and students."

I wonder if he is trying to tell me something about being Lightfeather, if he sees a kinship between me and Payton, the man of many names? Or if he is trying to tell me something about himself?

"Does it bother you?" I ask.

"What?"

"That you didn't know his real name. Until the end."

"We are different things to different people," he repeats, his voice softer and further away. "The way I knew him and the way he knew me—that's what matters."

I consider the journal and the hat, the keys to his apartment and the False Shamrocks. Something about the intimacy of these details suddenly brings Green's story into focus for me. It makes me realize why he is really here. It makes me realize what I should have suspected all along.

I take a deep breath, gathering my notes for class so that I don't have to look at him. "How long were you lovers?" I ask with forced calm.

"From the first time we met in that ugly office downstairs," Green replies without missing a beat. "Seventeen years ago. That's how the love of your life hits you. In an instant. But we became lovers slowly." He smiles and looks up from the plants. "It feels good to say it aloud. After all this time."

But all I want to do is slap the Hallmark moment out of him. The old Ana would have fallen for it. She would have sympathized with the sentimental story about love, chance encounters, and secret romances. But I know too much about being the wronged woman. I am the Mrs. Green in this story. Like Brett, Green got to live a double life that he could take or leave. At least, his wife still gets lunches on Wednesdays. I get nothing.

"Why didn't you leave your wife to be with him?" My words have a barbed quality to them. "You stayed in the closet and gave Payton scraps. Why? To protect a sham marriage? To spare the kids?"

Green stiffens, crossing his arms over his chest. "I offered to leave," he says. "I wanted to get married, but Payton refused. He never had a family. He didn't want to break mine apart. He didn't want his criminal past to 'stain' my life. His word, not mine."

"But he gave you exactly what you wanted," I protest. "A free pass. No fallout, no messes to clean up at home."

"I would have accepted those messes, Ana. Happily." Green gets up and collects Charlemagne. "When you get to my age, you think you're done with passion. That it has left you behind, the way much of the rest of the world has. People take you a little less seriously, see you as a burden, shudder at the thought of your sexual desires. You start to think that this is my life. This is all there will ever be. Payton taught me not to accept that."

Students hurry past the door. Loud voices and intermittent shouts push their way into the room.

"Why tell me?" I ask. "After all these years, why come clean now?"

"I feel like you're the only other person who can understand," he says as he pushes his sunglasses up the ridge of his nose.

"Understand what?"

"That memorial service. Payton's real story, even the parts I didn't know, deserved to be told. He deserved a moment of truth." Green nods to himself. "I memorialized a lie because it cost less than the truth. I am ashamed of that. Now I have to figure out how to live with it."

The idea makes my knees feel weak. Is this why he thinks I will understand? Because I know Payton's real name? Is he trying to warn me about the pitfalls of pilfered identities and living a lie?

"It seems we both have classes to teach." Green steps to the door and turns to me once again.

"Don't forget Payton," he says, gazing down at the plant one more time.

"Not at a chance."

•••

The Flann Man stretches out his long legs in the front row. Cheerleader Cliché flirts with him as always, thrusting out her bosom and tossing her hair from side to side as if there were a strong breeze in the room. My petty revenge this semester has been refusing to learn her name. I know it begins with a "B," so I toss out different B names every class. *That's a good point, Brittany. Yes, Buffy, this will be on the test. Would you mind putting away your phone, Brianna?*

Clench scowls from the back, clad in his "School Ruined My Life" shirt, black jeans, and Yankees baseball cap. I'm surprised he is on time. When I walk in the room, he eyes my Purple Shamrock warily, as if it might trick him into learning something. Ever since my Beethoven's Fifth incident, I keep expecting him to interrupt class with an impromptu performance in flatulence minor. No doubt, he has considered it.

"Any questions about the reading before we start?" I ask, expecting dead silence and an awkward shifting in seats.

Cheerleader Cliché raises her hand.

"Yes, Bambi?"

"Barbara," she corrects, completely unfazed, and she begins speaking at speeds that could break the sound barrier. "The Civil Liberties Act in 1988 apologized for the internment of Japanese Americans during World War II, and the US government paid restitution to over 80,000 people."

"Yes—"

"And the victims of the Tuskegee Experiment in 1973 were compensated $10 million and their families were given health care benefits."

"Only after a class-action lawsuit against the state of Alabama—"

"President Clinton offered an official apology for Tuskegee on behalf of the federal government in 1997."

"Yes—"

"And Congress created the Indian Claims Commission in 1946. The US paid $1.3 billion to 176 tribes, and those tribes either spent the money on tribal projects or distributed it to individuals. The government formally apologized for the mistreatment of Native Americans in 2009. So why are we still talking about Native American reparations in 2019?" She pauses to inhale.

The Flann Man clears his throat. "We hear a lot about reparations for slavery, but Native Americans are rarely mentioned in those discussions. Besides, individuals only received $1000 from the Indian Claims Commission. Not cool."

She bats her eyes, as if the idea of restitution is nothing more than a good excuse for flirting and showing off.

"In truth," he continues, "any real reparations to Native Americans would have to include land, land other people have now been living on for decades. Winona LaDuke talked about that in last week's reading. 'The only compensation for land is land.'"

Cheerleader Cliché licks her bottom lip, and I half expect her to shake some pompoms or push up her tits. I find myself surprised and oddly turned on by the Flann Man's ability to quote something from class.

"So I have to give up cash and my house?" Clench barks from the back of the room. "$1.3 billion wasn't enough. Now I have to pay more?"

Everyone, myself included, freezes, and the room gets pin-drop quiet. Clench has never spoken in class. He, as far as anyone can tell, has never paid attention or taken a note or done the reading.

"You make it sound like you're writing a personal check," the Flann Man says, turning partway around in his desk.

"Taxes are personal checks."

"Dude, you don't even have a job."

"Some tribes have refused money, like the Sooks," Clench insists.

"Sioux," I correct.

"This article says that the Sooks have turned down payments because they say their land isn't for sale," he adds, impassioned. "They don't even want the money. It's about restoring justice."

My mouth hangs open when Clench references the reading. This has to be one of the signs of the apocalypse. The sea turning red with blood. The *Fast and Furious* franchise. Clench doing the homework. Just to be sure, I look out the window for locust and frogs falling from the sky.

"How do we do that?" the Flann Man asks.

"I didn't do anything, you know, to Cherokee Bob or whoever," Clench protests. "Why do I have to pay?"

"What about your ancestors?" the Flann Man asks. "What about the land they took? Aren't you the beneficiary of that?"

"Maybe. Maybe not." Clench turns to me now, waiting for some kind of response. "Isn't that the whole problem? How do you prove that?"

"Marcus raises a good point," I admit, stunned to hear these words coming from my mouth. "Let's stay with your example of Cherokee Bob. What if Bob is only half or one-eighth Cherokee? What if he is middle class and living a good life? How does the government compensate him? Should it?"

The Flann Mann sits up, and Cheerleader Cliché flips her hair.

"Now, if I took Cherokee Bob's house and shot his horse, the law would make me pay reparations. If you commit a wrong now, you need to make it right. But what about history? How do you quantify historical suffering? Isn't most of history suffering?"

A few students, including the Flann Man, nod.

"If so," I continue, "once you start saying you owe 'X' for 'Y,' where does it stop?"

"So reparations don't make sense for the past?" Cheerleader Cliché asks with a look of surprise.

"Not exactly, Bambi."

"Barbara."

I glance at Payton's purple leaves, which resemble the pattern of a kaleidoscope. "Historical and personal wrongs are difficult, maybe impossible, to fix, but we need to acknowledge them in order not to repeat them. Apologies matter."

"But apologies and amends are different things," the Flann Man says. "How do we make amends?"

"The government's job is to improve things for everyone—to look out for the least fortunate and to equalize opportunity. This community needs our help, and we need to help them improve their lives and the lives of their children. That is our moral responsibility as a nation."

"*Pfffft.*" Clench makes a sound as if he is trying to blow his nose. "Do we pay them or not?"

"Money to improve conditions and resources on reservations, absolutely."

"But what do *we* do?" the Flann Man presses. "Not the government. You and me. What's our responsibility?"

"Well, it starts by looking at ourselves and our mistakes honestly. That is the first step in making things right—"

"But let's say we have already taken that step in this class," the Flann Man interjects. "It just seems as individuals we should do something more. Right?"

I feel a pang of betrayal. The Flann Man is siding with Clench in an argument—a student who, until today, could have been confused for a coma patient or a mime. Or a mime pretending to be a coma patient. Doesn't sex in the backseat of a car inspire any loyalty nowadays?

Everyone stares, waiting. No one is texting or whispering or reading for another class. They smell blood in the water. Cheerleader Cliché has her pen poised to take notes. The Flann Man adjusts his crotch. Even Clench, with a smirk, pays attention. They have me on the ropes, floundering for the right words. They want easy answers for messy, complex questions.

"What responsibility does each of us have for the wrongs of history? That's what you're asking?" I say.

"Yeah," Clench spits out the word with the fury of a fist.

I half-sit on the table in front of the room next to the podium and Payton. Clench doesn't care one way or another. He just wants to embarrass me. He wants to convince himself that he has been right all along, that this class and I have been frauds, that learning about the past is a waste of time. Better to hunker down in ignorance and anger. Better to believe that you have no responsibility for anything but yourself.

"I've had a terrible few months. Shitty, actually," I begin. "I lost my boyfriend and my apartment. Well, 'lost' isn't the right word. It's not like I misplaced them. My dissertation director started fucking my boyfriend, and he kicked me out of our apartment. She could do that because she is my boss. He could do that because I was never on the lease."

Cheerleader Cliché's mouth opens, forming a nearly perfect circle, and the Flann Man runs a hand through his crooked crewcut. Some of the other students move uncomfortably in their seats. Clench smiles.

"American Airlines lost my luggage, so I had to wear someone else's clothes for a job interview. I've been insulted and thrown up on and trapped in a bathroom stall where I dropped my phone in the toilet. A fake blind man stole my wallet. I have no money, which is why I work the night shift at a morgue. My friends don't want to talk to me anymore, and I'm the one who found a dead body in the office."

The room is still. No sound. No movement. It's not every day you get to see a person implode in real time.

"I keep wondering if this is the only way to make amends," I continue. "To trade places. To lose your

278

dignity and power. To watch someone strip you of your belongings and your identity, your place in the world."

"So you get dumped by your boyfriend and kicked out of your apartment, and that makes you Native American?" Clench asks venomously, savoring the fact that I just made my disastrous personal life fair game. "You've paid your dues?"

"For the second time today, Clench, you're right," I reply.

Someone snickers at the use of his nickname. Clench glares.

"I am not Native American, and I have not paid my dues." I pause as the weight of this admission hits me. "My losses aren't analogous. They never can be. They certainly don't change anything for anybody. But maybe that is the place I have to start from."

Cheerleader Cliché's mouth still hangs partway open, and I realize for the first time that she is chewing gum.

"For what?" she asks.

"For justice. Making amends is about restoring justice, and restoring justice demands sacrifice. What am I willing to sacrifice? What are you? What are you willing to give up to make other people's lives better? That is the question you have to ask yourselves, the question you have to act on. That's how we make amends."

Students shuffle about the halls, which means class is over, but no one moves. No one reaches for a backpack or checks a phone. They all continue to stare at me.

"Do you know?" the Flann Man asks. His voice has a kindness and honesty that reminds me of the night we met in the bar, of why I liked him.

"What?"

"Do you know what you're willing to sacrifice?"

I nod. "I think so."

•••

Professor Hinks makes a sound as if small, furry animal is stuck in his throat. "What?"

"I claimed to be Native American when I applied for the Devon job."

"What?"

"I said—"

"I heard you the first three times," Professor Hinks snaps before pressing his lips tightly together.

His curly hair has more salt than pepper today, and his forest green shirt is the same from the day I caught him with his hand in his red silk undies. He grabs a pen from the "Vegetarians Party Till the Cows Come Home" mug, holds it for a second, then shoves it back with the others. I place Payton on the desk near the phone. Hinks glances at it but says nothing.

"What exactly did you tell them?" he asks.

"I changed my middle name to Lightfeather."

"Lightfeather?"

"Yes."

"You gave yourself a Native American name. Did you actually say you were Native American?"

"I think so. On my mother's side."

"For the love of God." Hicks stands up and steps over to the window. He puts both hands around the frame. For a moment, I wonder if he wants to throw me through it.

"Do you know what this means?" he asks. "If someone finds out? Remember Rachel Dolezal? The public scrutiny. The lawsuits. You can kiss your career goodbye. You will never set foot on a college campus again."

"I've thought about that—"

"Really?" Hinks steps over to the desk. "I don't think you have. I don't think you've thought about anybody but yourself. Do you have any idea what this is going to do to the department?"

John Coltrane looks down at me from his *Blue Train* poster quizzically, finger across his mouth and hand behind his head.

"Does anyone else know about this?" he asks. "Were any faculty members involved? You need to tell me the truth."

"No. It was my idea."

"Un-fucking-believable!" Hinks puts both hands on his hips. "We are going to carry this Scarlet Letter around for years. We'll be a national laughingstock. We'll be known as the department that produces fake Indians!"

"Most tribes prefer 'Indigenous people,'" I mutter.

"Recommendation letters. Phone calls. We put our reputations on the line for you. We vouched not just for your abilities, Ana, but for your integrity. Do you get that? How could you be such a colossal ass?"

"Colossal ass?" I snap. "I compromised the integrity of this department?"

"Yes! Yes, you did."

"This department where dissertation directors fuck their students' boyfriends? Where people kill themselves in the lobby? Where someone can be unwittingly masturbated at?"

Hinks places on hand on his forehead as if he has developed a sudden migraine.

"I am turning thirty in two weeks," I say. "Two weeks! I have no money, no apartment. I have been here for six-and-a-half years and on the job market for three. Not a single look, not a single prospect until I typed 'Lightfeather' on my CV. How is that fair?"

"So you thought pretending to be Native American would even the score?"

My hands are shaking in my lap, and I feel nauseous. "At first, if I got an interview, I was going to publish something about the problems with hiring and diversity in academia, but—"

The phone rings, brash and horror-movie loud. He doesn't move. It rings again.

"But what?" he asks.

"But I started to want it. I started to want this career I have been working so hard for. What if this is my only chance? How do I walk away?"

He grabs the phone with irritation. "What? This really isn't a good time ... I understand, Dean Matthews ..."

I grab my *Oxalis triangularis* and leave before Hinks can stop me. It isn't the first time I've left him with unfinished business. I take the stairs to the stone courtyard and hurry through the quad, passing carefree students and ivory tower buildings. The brick walkways are wet and slippery in places. The tree branches still resemble knotted old fingers, and the cool, damp February afternoon has another hour before sunset. I pull my jacket tight around my body.

I won't go to Tequila. None of the gang will be there. I won't go to Kavita's. She has yoga tonight, and I forgot the spare key. With nowhere to go and no one to see, I decide to walk west—with Payton in my hands. I'll walk until I'm too tired to walk.

I'll walk until there is nowhere else to go.

30
Second Chances

Last night, I walked for hours, stopping for a bacon cheeseburger with onion rings and getting to the morgue just in time for my shift. My feet were blistered, and sweat dampened my forehead. As soon as I checked my email, I found a terse note from Hinks telling me to be in his office tomorrow at exactly "High Noon."

The words "high noon" gave me a sinking feeling in my stomach. Was he challenging me to a duel?

But here I am now. 12:04. Sleep-deprived and hungry. Half expecting to find Gary Cooper with a six-shooter. Instead, the room is empty. Hinks's desk, pristine and orderly with stacks of papers and personnel files, has a large manila envelope in the center with some papers on it. Legal documents, at a glance. Never a good sign. My punishment, perhaps? A rescinded teaching assistantship? Expulsion? A lifetime subscription to *In Touch Weekly?*

I glance over my shoulder. With no sign of Hinks, I grab the document for a quick look—his divorce papers. I flip to the last page. Signed and dated one month ago by two attorneys, himself, and his wife.

Hinks clears his throat.

"Jesus," I blurt, dropping the papers on the desk as he walks into the office. "I never learn."

"It's okay. I wanted you to see them. Please, sit."

He strides to the other side of the desk, his arms loose at his sides. He has a pleasant, wide-eyed expression on his face. This is not gun-slinging, fire-and-brimstone, call-me-a-colossal-ass Hinks from yesterday. This is classroom Hinks. And I'm not sure which to be more worried about.

"My wife, Rebecca, and I never cared about stuff," he begins, looking down at the papers. "Our first apartment in Alphabet City was a dump. Fourth floor walk-up, no air conditioning, no screens on the windows. The mosquitos ate us alive in the summer. The radiators burned so hot in winter that we left pots of water on them at night to humidify the air. Completely evaporated by morning. Not a drop left."

Hinks leans back and clasps his hands behind his head with a Tim Robbins-*Shawshank Redemption* smile on his face. The top button of his white shirt is unfastened, and his skin appears shiny, most likely from his morning swim.

"I remember we had this DVD player that only worked if you tilted it against the cable box at a forty-five degree angle. What a piece of junk. It always froze at the best parts of a movie. But you know something? I still have that damn thing in my garage. Can't bring myself to throw it out."

He laughs, moving forward and placing his forearms on the desk. His blue eyes shine like the unbroken surface of a pool.

"There was a time when my wife and I cared more about each other than stuff," he continues. "We were different people back then, I guess. Somewhere along the way, she changed. Stuff mattered more and more, and when you get divorced, that's all lawyers talk about. Stuff. Who gets this? Who gets that? She came over the other day when I wasn't there to pick up some things, and she took the dining room chandelier."

"I'm sorry."

"There is just a big hole in the ceiling with these dangling wires. What an odd thing to take. A light fixture. Something that was part of the house when we moved in." He pauses as if I might have some insight into taking things that don't belong to anyone. "What an odd thing to lay claim to."

"I don't mean to be rude," I begin, "but why are you telling me this?"

Hinks slides the divorce papers into the envelope. "I wanted you to know what I was thinking about that morning. I was thinking about our time in that apartment with a temperamental DVD player and a mattress without a frame. About a time when we just cared for each other. That's what was going through my mind when you walked in on me, when I was … you know."

"Yeah." I lift my hands up as if I were the victim of a hold up.

"I am sorry. I should have apologized weeks ago," he says, tugging at his neckline. "I was embarrassed. I had just gotten served with these papers the night before, and I was in a strange place. That's no excuse. And if you wish to file a complaint with Human Resources, I won't deny it."

"I don't want to do that."

"Well, whatever you decide, I hope you can forgive me. And this business with Professor Riggs. There is not much I can do, but I have expressed my concerns to her."

Tiffany Riggs. The reason I was here early enough to walk in on Hinks. The reason I found John Doe. The reason I lost Brett and my apartment. Just the mention of her name makes my ears burn hot and my jaw tighten. The room gets stuffy. It is difficult to breathe. Why is he talking to her now? He has known about Briff for months. The entire department has. I loosen my scarf.

"I don't understand," I say.

"What do you mean?"

"Why are you apologizing today? Just hours after you bitched me out for lying to the search committee? For claiming to be Lightfeather?"

He lowers his eyes for a moment and takes a pen from his vegetarian coffee mug, only to fiddle with it.

"I see now that the circumstances with Tiffany and the incident in my office may have been more upsetting than I realized. They may have pushed you into making some decisions you wouldn't normally have made."

"I see." I am on my feet, breathing hard. "So this is a bullshit apology. You just don't want me embarrassing the department and hurting your reputation."

"Wait a minute—"

"Was that story about your wife even true?"

I know at once I've gone too far. Hinks's face drains of color, and his lips fall partway open. He inhales deeply and holds his breath to steady himself.

"Sorry," I mutter. "That was uncool."

"I asked you here to apologize," he begins calmly, "and to offer you a second chance. If you turn down the job, the department will give you a postdoc next year. You can start over, develop a new scholarly path. I will take a more aggressive role in helping you find a job. We can make this right."

A few days ago, I would have jumped at the opportunity. A way out. A blank slate. A Get Out of

Jail Free card. But is Hinks really offering that? Is it a second chance or bribe? A bribe to keep my impersonation a secret, to keep the department out of hot water. And even if I want to take him at his word, I can't shake the feeling that it is shouldn't be in his power to bail me out and make this right.

"May I ask you a question?"

"Sure." He leans forward with that eager-to-help, classroom-teacher expression.

"You want me to start over?" I ask.

"Everyone deserves a second chance."

"You want to help me find a job?"

"Absolutely."

"And where exactly have you been for nearly seven years? What about all of the other students in the program not getting enough funding or finding jobs? What about this profession? What are you going to do about that?"

"You're right." He nods. "We have to do more to protect the most vulnerable among us. Here. In universities across the country. We have to treat adjuncts and graduate students better. We have to give them legitimate opportunities to thrive and to advance, not to dangle false promises that leave them demoralized and broke. But changing your name isn't the way to do that, Ana."

"It has done more than you."

"This isn't just about you anymore," he snaps. "You really care about the other students in this program? Damaging our reputation won't help. It's only going to make it that much harder for your friends to get jobs, that much harder for you. Think about it."

My arms feel taut with tension, and I realize I have been clenching my fists. I open my palms and exhale.

"You're right," I say. "This isn't just about me. It's about something much bigger."

31
Reflections

"Don't act like someone rained on your perm, Tootsie Roll," Jeffrey Shaw said as he sat at the kitchen table.

He wore drooping blue sweatpants with a Penn State emblem and a top that resembled a pirate shirt. A faint yellow nightlight glowed behind the sink, and the clock on the microwave read 1:32. Otherwise, it was dark. The refrigerator, with pictures of Mom, him, and me, hummed insistently. Boxes sat on the counter and the floor—some empty, some with varying degrees of fullness. Dad recently decided it was time to move, time to replace some old memories with new ones.

"Dad, your expressions don't make any sense," I protested.

"They're folksy."

"They're confusing and, in this case, vaguely sexist."

A half glass of milk sat on the table. I cringed at the thought of anyone drinking milk voluntarily, let alone my father, but white mucus was his go-to beverage in times of nostalgia—mostly from missing my mother. His thin white hair and shapeless clothes made him look worn out, like a photocopy of a photocopy. He held a document in his both hands.

"Okay," he said. "Why so soggy looking?"

"I'm half asleep and exhausted from packing. What are you doing?" I asked, grabbing a glass from the cupboard and taking a pitcher of water from the fridge.

"I could ask you the same."

"I wanted a Ding Dong," I said.

"Diet of champions."

"Kidding. Just thirsty," I replied, though the mention of a Ding Dong was tempting. "What's that?"

He slid it across the table as I sat opposite him. It read: "New York State, Department of Health, Certificate of Dissolution of Marriage."

"About four years before your mother died, I asked for a divorce."

My father, whose idea of excitement was treating himself to Milk Duds while watching *Caddyshack* on television, never stood up to Nadya Shaw a day in his life. He loved her the way a drowning man clings to a life raft. It was one of the things I loved about him— our shared need for her. An unexpected hug from Mom or a kiss on the forehead could keep me afloat for weeks, convincing me of her unspoken affection. My dad and I swam in the same shark-infested waters of Nadya's love. Even two years after her death, it still felt that way.

Sure, she needed things from us. Dad's goofy sense of humor, which she mocked. Our stunned admiration for her beauty, he as a beaming husband, me as a daughter pleading with the universe for a fraction of it. Our blind willingness to do her bidding. If she itched for a night of dancing, Dad took her, though he hated every second and mostly watched her glide around the floor with others. If she needed a partner in crime, I tagged along, learning how to steal to please her, to feel close to her.

The idea of saying "no" to Nadya was both unthinkable and untested in the Shaw house. Yet Jeffrey Shaw handed her the biggest "no" of all. He decided to end their life together, to deprive himself of oxygen fifty meters beneath the surface of the ocean.

291

"I don't understand," I said.

"She was having an affair with a boyfriend from college. I found some emails, by accident. There was no doubt. She admitted it as soon as I confronted her." He stared at the papers in front of me, avoiding my eyes. "For days, I couldn't eat or sleep. There were times I couldn't breathe. It felt like a horse kicked me in the chest."

"I'm sorry."

"I didn't think about him, which is kind of strange now that I look back on it. I never once imagined them together. I didn't even care who he was." He took a long sip of milk, and it left a thick residue on his upper lip. "I knew men looked at her and wondered how the hell she ended up with me. I knew she wondered too, sometimes. But for whatever reason, I believed she loved me. Until those emails."

I reached across the table to hold his hands. The sleeves of my striped pajama top covered the papers.

"This love, which started before your mother and I met, was there the entire time we were together. It hadn't gone away. It was just dormant. That hurt more than the affair. To know she had this secret part of her, this history that made her wonder if she made the right choice with me."

He bit his lower lip and withdrew his hands.

"I never doubted my choice," he continued. "I never imagined a different life with a different person. I never imagined a different me. I had a lawyer draw up the papers for divorce, and I gave them to her a week later."

"But you stayed together," I said.

"She asked for a second chance," he replied. "She didn't plead or cry. That wasn't her style," he added with a slight smile. "She promised never to see him, never to speak to him again."

"So you said yes?"

"Who doesn't deserve a second chance?"

I glanced at the unfinished boxes, and I wondered how many secrets were still buried in closets and desk drawers throughout the house, how many wounds would be reopened before we left for good. Just today, I found Nadya's book of fairytales and her favorite anklet. She used to read fairytales to me at bedtime. Not the watered-down Disney versions, though. Only the best for her Ana. Only the Grimm brothers, the Stephen Kings of the nineteenth century. A stepsister cutting off part of her foot to fit into a golden slipper. A hunter performing a half-assed C-section on the belly of a wolf. Parents abandoning their children in the forest to starve to death. And, of course, hypersensitive, pissed-off witches.

"Rapunzel" was my mother's favorite, probably because it was about thieves—first a henpecked husband, then a horny prince. She would sit down on my bed, legs stretched out and crossed in front of her. Sometimes she wore sculpted jeans, sometimes flowing dresses of green, burgundy, mustard yellow, or blue. No matter the outfit, her silver anklet with tiny pearls, which I later learned she stole from Nordstrom's, sparkled in the low light. With her back against the headboard and a book in her lap, I snuggled as close as I could with her body above the covers and mine beneath. Her brown hair fell in coils to her pointed collarbone, and I dreamed of climbing up to close the distance between us.

"Don't expect a happy ending, Ana," she'd say before snapping off the lights, even though the carnage in most of these stories set the bar for happiness somewhere between temporary blindness and witch burning. "That way you won't be disappointed."

Dad got up and carried the empty glass to the sink. His rounded belly filled out part of the loose shirt. He kept his back to me as he turned on the tap, but I could see part of his reflection in the window. Head bowed, face sagging in the yellow glow of the nightlight.

"But first I asked her a strange question. One that hadn't occurred to me until the moment she said she wanted to stay."

"What?"

"'If I had cheated on you,' I said. 'If I had this secret love, this secret life, would you do the same for me?'"

He placed his hands on the edge of the sink and looked at the window. The darkness of the backyard was absolute, and I suspected he could see only his own reflection.

"She didn't hesitate. 'No,' she said. 'But you are better person than I am. That's why I married you.'"

I walked over to the sink, the slick tiles on the floor made my feet cold. I stood next to him, both of us reflected in the window. Boxes cluttered the counter.

"I think he died," I said in a whisper. "The college boyfriend. She took me to his wake."

Dad did not move. He just watched his own face in the dark glass pane and nodded slightly. "It doesn't matter. The last few years, before her cancer, were some of the best we had. All of us."

"Yeah," I said, though I didn't remember it that way. I remembered being absorbed in my own teenage world. I remembered finding my mother even more remote than ever. And by the time she got sick, I remembered being utterly terrified by it.

Dad turned for a hug, called me Pumpkin Spice, and shuffled out of the room, his slippers making scratchy sounds with each step. I touched one of the empty boxes and was tempted to start filling it with plates and silverware. Then I gazed at the window again, studying my reflection. I was looking for traces of my mother, some hint of her somewhere, but all I saw was my hurt, wounded father.

32
The Swap

The Swap is a Union Square coffee shop that, according to its website, prides itself on having a European sensibility and a book exchange for wayward travelers. It has a grim, colorless interior with faded gray walls and dark ceiling beams. Until I get there, I don't realize that "European sensibility" means no chairs. Everyone stands, sipping coffee at the bar or at one of the high, circular tables scattered throughout the room. Until I get there, I don't realize that "book exchange" means a few dilapidated shelves with the kind of reads you'd expect to find at a yard sale.

The shelves cling precariously to the rear wall, and a sign above them reads: "Free Books: Take One, Replace One." A woman, with her back to me, browses the titles. She wears a red hooded raincoat that drips water steadily on the floor. The rest of the Swap has the quiet hum of low-voiced conversations and the periodic hiss of steam from an espresso machine. All of the customers appear soggy from the cold, steady rain outside.

At a table in the center, Dante Wellington holds a cup of coffee with both hands. I expect him to be wearing his signature corduroy jacket, but instead he has gone Urban Outfitters casual with an unzipped tan raincoat and blue jeans. His bald head beads with moisture, but whether from the rain or perspiration I cannot tell.

"Thanks for meeting me," I say, hooking my umbrella on the edge of the tabletop and fiddling with the thick, black buttons on my coat. I keep my eyes lowered, afraid one penetrating look from Dante might crumble my resolve.

"Not at all. I was happy to get your email. Coffee?"

I shake my head, trying to steady my breathing and calm my thundering heart. "Are you sure I'm not keeping you from anything more important?"

Thai food? *Hamilton* tickets? A Toyotathon?

"My flight doesn't leave for several hours," he replies with a smile. "Your visit comes as a welcome distraction. I was planning to spend the morning walking around the city, until I realized it would require an ark."

Someone opens the front door, sending a gust of chilly air through the room. Dante sips his coffee. His reading glasses magnify his eyes, and their color reminds me of the sky on a gray fall day. A copy of *The Great Gatsby* lies on the table.

"Is that from the Swap?" I ask, gesturing toward the book.

"Indeed. Something to pass the time," he says breezily. "The great novel about imposters and our capacity for self-deception."

My tongue gets thick and dry as if I just swallowed sand.

"So what can I do for you?" he asks.

I can still pull the fire alarm, I tell myself. I can still claim a sudden case of laryngitis or feign a multiple personality disorder. The Chumash are a small tribe from a small stretch of California. They have fewer than 5,000 members. Who will ever find out the truth?

But that is exactly the point. That is exactly why I'm here.

"I can't take the job."

I actually say the words. I'm not sure what I'm expecting next. Air raid sirens. Explosions. Godzilla's foot crashing through the ceiling. Instead, Dante smiles and takes a slow sip of coffee.

"So you have another offer?" he asks.

I'm so shocked that I can't speak for a moment. "What? No, I—"

"We can increase your base salary by $5000 and get you an additional $5000 for annual travel and research funds."

My jaw drops wide open. This man, who offered me my dream job several days ago, is now offering me more money to take it. Have I lost my mind? I try to speak again, but nothing comes out. My lips move like a fish trying to gather food at the surface of a pond.

"We can beat any offer," Dante adds with a nod. "Being at a Research One institution will give you all sorts of advantages. Fewer classes to teach. Paid sabbaticals. Your own—"

"I can't take the job." I push the words out as if through a strainer. My stomach tightens, and I feel tears pooling in my eyes.

"I don't understand," Dante replies.

"I'm not Lightfeather."

"Excuse me?"

"I gave myself an Indigenous sounding name to have a shot at the job." My words have a speedy, breathless quality, and they make me think of a car driving off a cliff.

Dante does not speak or move. In fact, the entire Swap gets unnervingly still.

I've read that outer space is absolutely quiet. The absence of molecules creates a vacuum that prevents sound waves from traveling. The sudden silence in the room feels that way, as if I've been sucked out of an airlock or into a black hole.

If only.

"Is this some kind of joke?" Dante asks, his voice steady and low. He removes his glasses and places them in his shirt pocket.

"No. I lied about being Chumash."

"So you are not Native American?"

"No."

A loud *thwack* startles me. I look over Dante's shoulder, and the red hooded woman has dropped a hardbound book. She quickly gathers it from the floor.

Dante remains still, breathing loudly through his nose. With an abrupt motion, he zips up his coat and grabs the umbrella at his feet. He seems tempted to pick up *Gatsby,* but he stops himself. He then stares at me with the sternness of a middle school principal, and I wonder if he might whack the back of my hand with a ruler or send me to detention.

"Obviously, we are withdrawing our offer," he says.

"I'm really sorry."

"For what exactly?" he asks, eyebrows arching. "For wasting our time? For playing us as fools? Or for being a hypocrite?"

His calm, matter-of-fact tone gives the words a more pointed, searing quality. At the same time, I find his indignation infuriating. He can dish out racist and misogynistic commentary with impunity. His age, gender, and tenured position protect him. I don't have that luxury. I never will.

"Yes, I was desperate—desperate for a job, desperate for a damn interview. Nearly seven years of disillusionment and poverty can do that to a person," I snap. "And yes, I did a stupid thing, but—"

"I have no interest in excuses, Ms. Shaw." Dante holds up his palm as if stopping traffic. "I liked you … I like you, but I won't be able to keep a lid on this. The department will know what you did. Word will get around." Dante shakes his head. "You'll be a punchline at conferences and a cautionary tale for search committees across the country. This will end your career."

"I've been thinking a lot about that," I say, "about this profession."

Dante, with his long, bony limbs, seems poised to sprint from the room, but he lingers—out of curiosity, no doubt, as one would at a car accident, a hot dog eating contest, or a Kanye West interview. He wants one last look at the spectacle I have made of myself.

"And?" he asks.

"I've been thinking about exclusion. I got into this field because I fell in love with stories," I begin. I can feel a chill settling in from the dampness of my raincoat. "I started reading Louise Erdrich in college. Her books shifted something in me, something that transcended my background. I felt her speaking to universal truths—truths that made me want to learn more about Native American life."

"So you became Lightfeather?" Dante scoffs.

"Without Native American blood, I'm shut out of this field of knowledge in higher education," I protest.

"At a time when we need *everyone* to study the various cultures that make up American-ness, universities have become more siloed and insulated. How did we get it so wrong? How did we reduce diversity to political correctness?"

Dante steps away from his side of the table and exhales audibly. "Perhaps it is a question of balance," he replies, and his voice has a sudden warmth to it. "How long do you or I get to keep telling the stories of others? And what type of perspective is lost when we do? When white society, white academia, fails to view Native Americans as sufficient to be at the center of their own stories, what is the cost of that? Perhaps, with more balance, with more opportunity for marginalized groups to step up to the microphone, we can achieve the inclusivity you speak of. But we're not there yet."

I feel as if I'm sagging like a punctured bicycle tire. I came here to do the right thing, yet I'm still resisting, still thrashing against it.

"I wish you luck," Dante says, extending his hand.

We shake, and with that, Dante strides out of the Swap and out of my life forever. Even the red hooded woman is gone now. The murmur of the café continues. The steam of the espresso machine hisses.

Only *Gatsby* remains on the table, but I decide to leave his story for someone else.

33
Help Wanted

One week after the hurricane, Yumi, Kavita, and I walked to Tequila Mockingbird from campus. The first two years of the graduate program, as we were informed at orientation, required fulltime coursework. With only a couple of months under our belts, we had already learned this meant countless hours of lectures, reading, writing, and, of course, drinking. Today, in our English Renaissance class, Professor Packer spent most of the time talking about the Seven Deadly Sins. I would have rather watched the film version with Brad Pitt and Morgan Freeman.

"Lust has got to be the worst," Kavita said, as we stepped inside.

"That one doesn't bother me so much," I replied.

"Me neither," Yumi added, pulling her black hair into a ponytail and walking like a soccer player in cleats.

We grabbed a table by the bookcases. I had only been to Tequila Mockingbird a few times, but I was drawn to the real books. Sometimes, I took one off the shelves, just to feel the binding with my fingers and to skim a few pages. The bocce courts were empty today. Two women sat at the bar, and some guys played Monopoly at a nearby table. The jukebox swung with Rosemary Clooney's "Blue Skies."

"I'm trying to decide if I am more of a sloth type or a gluttony type," I said. "I guess it depends on the snack food."

"Big Macs," Kavita practically purred.

"Look," I said, pointing to the chalkboard above the far end of the bar. "'Margarita Mondays.' I'll grab the first round."

As I made my way to the bar, the Monopoly table exploded with activity. Fast rolling dice. Cheers. Theatrical sighs of defeat. From what I could tell, all the guys were named "Dude." As I was passing their table, Dude One spilled a beer on his lap and jumped to his feet. He bumped into me, knocking me off balance, and I fell backward onto a couch—onto another Dude's lap.

"Sorry," I muttered.

We both got to our feet. He had wide shoulders, a thick body, and brown, mischievous eyes.

"How much do you charge for a lap dance?" he asked.

"That one's on the house," I replied. "Hey, you're in my Twentieth-Century European History class, right?"

"Guilty as charged. I'm Doug," he said, extending his hand. "Doug Harrington."

"Ana Shaw."

"I'm heading to the bar. I need another drink, and Mike over there needs a new pair of pants."

"Fuck you, Dude," he mumbled, still inspecting the damage.

"They sell pants here?" I asked.

I followed Doug to the bar and ordered margaritas with salt and the Cervantes "Don't Go Easy on the Cheesy" Nachos. Doug asked for a Capote Cosmopolitan, which had twice the vodka of a standard Cosmo.

"That's very Carrie Bradshaw," I said.

"I'm more of a Samantha, but they're both hot," he boomed. "Aren't your friends in the program, too? I've seen them around."

"We're just getting to know each other, but yes." I glanced over at them. "I'll introduce you."

Doug helped carry the drinks and food. At the table, he gave a round of hellos before sitting next to Kavita on the couch. He waved to the Monopoly guys, but they were too immersed in the game to care.

"Fucking Park Place!" one of the Dudes yelled.

"I just want to say upfront," Doug began with a big voice, "that I am totally cool with foursomes."

"What a coincidence," Yumi replied, fiddling with the straps of her jean overalls. "I was just saying how we're through talking to guys who don't orgy."

"Excellent." Doug took a sip from his pink drink.

After two rounds, we moved to the bocce courts. Yumi and I were team blue, Doug and Kavita team red. No one cared how much I sucked. Doug and Kavita flirted with fleeting touches and sly smiles. Yumi talked earnestly about one of the readings from class. The balls cracked together, and Rosemary Clooney and Benny Goodman sauntered into "Memories of You."

"So, Ana," Doug said as we huddle around each other to toast a new round. "Tell us about the real you."

"As opposed to the fake me?"

"Yeah."

We brought our glasses together. Doug and Kavita stood close, practically touching, and I was happy for her. Sure, I wanted to meet someone. Sure, it would probably take a force of nature—like another hurricane or an earthquake or a car accident—but right now, in that moment, I was convinced that I found something special in this group.

Friends.

•••

The "Help Wanted" sign is scrawled on a small chalkboard in the entryway of Tequila Mockingbird. For the first time, the words strike me as a strange way to describe employment. To need help is an act of vulnerability. A plea. It is an admission that we cannot survive without each other.

So what exactly does this place need? What about me?

The booths by the bocce courts bustle with the lunch crowd. The smell of cooked hamburger meat and French fries fills the room, and the steady buzz of conversation, punctuated with laughter and clanging silverware, obscures the music from the jukebox. I hear drums and a piano, but I can't make out a melody. The front of Mockingbird is empty. The mahogany bar shines as if recently polished, and the surface gets reflected in the tilted mirror behind the colorful bottles of liquor.

I am surprised I don't recognize the bartender. He appears to be in his thirties and smiles like a New Yorker—friendly but not too friendly. He mostly avoids eye contact. He has narrow shoulders, thin limbs, and the kind of short hair you want to run your hand through.

"Are you new here?" I ask.

"Nope."

Apparently, he is not much of a conversationalist.

"I'm Ana," I say. "A regular."

"Samson."

305

"You really need longer hair for that name."

"I've never heard that one before," he replies sarcastically, but a half-smile softens the blow.

I place the "Help Wanted" sign on the counter. "Is the owner here?"

"Why? You interested?" he asks absently, as if he doesn't care one way or the other.

"Maybe. Right now, I part-time at the county morgue. I figure this would be more lively."

He looks up but does not smile. His brown eyes have a kindness and warmth I don't expect. "That is setting the bar pretty low. No pun intended."

"Puns, the lowest form of humor."

"Agreed," he says.

"You want the truth?"

"Sure."

"Those are real books," I say, gesturing to the shelves that line the walls of the lounge. "That's why."

"I don't follow."

"Books read, dog-eared, and underlined. Books loved. They aren't decorations. I want to be around that kind of honesty." I tap my finger on the chalkboard. "Besides, this is the place where new friends became best friends, where I've been sharing my story for more years than I care to admit. That seems as good a reason as any, right?"

"Aren't you a grad student? Most of the people who come in here are."

"Not anymore."

"Graduated?"

"Not until May."

"Then what? Waiting for the right job to come along?"

"Actually, I just turned down the wrong job for the right reasons."

Samson places his hands shoulder-length apart on the countertop. "Again, you've lost me."

"I have that effect on people," I say. "It took me a long time to figure out, but academic life isn't right for me. I lost something of myself along the way, something I need to find again."

"You thinking working here will help with that?"

"I don't know. Maybe."

A waitress approaches the bar and hands him a sheet of paper with a drink order. As Samson pours two glasses of white wine, she tilts her head like a teenager who obsessively chews gum. She checks her phone. It brightens for a moment, then fades away. She takes the wine without a word.

Samson looks at me and stretches out his hand. I take it. He has a warm, strong grip. "You're hired."

"What?"

The front door opens, and Yumi steps inside. She gives me a tentative smile as she makes her way to our usual table. A black trench coat falls loosely to her knees.

"I'm sorry," I continue. "I thought an English PhD owned this place."

"That would be me. If it would make you feel better, you can call me Doctor Samson."

"I'm pretty sure I'll stick with Samson or *garçon*— though I feel *garçon* only works if you're snapping fingers. But I can do that."

He smiles for the first time. "I have a feeling I'm going to regret hiring you."

"You are *totally* going to regret hiring me." I lift up the chalkboard and adjust the strap of my satchel. "Speaking of which, can you bring us margaritas?"

"Sure."

"And make it snappy," I add with a smirk.

Yumi sits at the end of the chair, poised to stand back up. "I can't stay long," she says.

I take a Scrabble "S" tile from my pocket and place it on the table.

"What's this?"

"It's from your Scrabble set. I stole it on the night of the hurricane, not long after we met. I'm sorry."

Yumi looks at the piece and then back at me, her brow wrinkled in confusion. She hooks a strand of her blue-streaked hair behind her ear. "Why the hell would you take a Scrabble piece?"

"It's a long story. The short answer is that I learned to steal from my mom. After she died, I thought that was the only way I could stay connected to her—to keep stealing things like we did together. Eventually, I started taking things to connect with the people I care about."

"O-kay," she says, stretching out the word. "So why give this back now?"

"I have to trust my connection with people. I have to stop taking things that aren't mine."

Yumi nods. "You texted that you turned down the job. Is this why?"

I still have the "Help Wanted" sign in my lap. Without realizing it, my arm has wiped away half the board and only the word "Help" appears.

"I'm thinking of it as reparations," I say.

308

Samson arrives with the drinks, and he places them on the table with care. "This round is on the house," he says.

"That's what I'm talking about," I say with a snap of my fingers. "Employee benefits."

"What?" Yumi blurts. "You work here?"

Samson clears his throat. "Nothing is official yet, and these"—he points to the margaritas—"are the only free drinks."

"Much appreciated, *Garçon.*"

Samson shakes his head before returning to the bar.

"I think he likes me."

Yumi leans forward. "He's kind of cute in a stressed-out, high-school principal kind of way."

"I know, right?"

As we raise our glasses for a toast, Doug and Kavita step inside. They are talking, a bit stiffly but friendly enough to give me hope for the four of us. As they take seats around the table, I feel a big, stupid grin on my face.

They are here simply because I asked, because I want to talk about my decision to leave academia. They are here because I want to return the things I have taken from them. I want to apologize and ask forgiveness. They are here because I want us always to be like this. I am even tempted quote Cicero. "No life is worth living without the mutual love of friends."

No, I'm way too sober to start quoting philosophers.

"To reparations," Yumi says, raising her glass a bit higher, and even though we don't all have drinks, everyone toasts.

"To reparations."

Epilogue

"You have to give this place credit," he says, adjusting the white handkerchief in his breast pocket. "It never stops reminding you how hideous it is. Olive carpets. Oak paneling. And tell me that fake plant isn't a prop from The Golden Girls*? Martha Stewart would fall into a coma—only to fall into another coma when she woke up."*

"You always talk this way when you're nervous, Charlie," Patricia replies, her voice steady and calm.

"You don't die every day."

Charlie flashes one of his easy-going, Robert Redford smiles. She remembers that smile when they met. It was her first year in residency as a medical student in Tulsa. He had an appendectomy a week earlier, and she stood in the room for his follow-up appointment with the attending surgeon, Vlad the Impaler—a Romanian hard ass who had a reputation for making med students cry and for hunting on weekends with a bow and arrow. Even Vlad loosened up in Charlie's presence. Something about Charlie does that to people. Something about the way he tells a story, the way he makes you feel as if you're talking to a lifelong friend, the way he convinces you that you are the reason something is so funny or clever or poignant.

She glances at her outfit—black sweater, black slacks, black shoes. Ridiculous. "Throw in a ski mask, and I can rob a bank," she thinks. "Or I can play an extra in a movie about robbing a bank."

Still, she can't deny the truth of it. She is a criminal. She will be after tonight at least. She adjusts her wide glasses and tightens the grip on her handbag.

"I never took you for the sentimental type," she says as they enter the main office of the Humanities Department. "To do this

where you and Robert met. That's a little sappy, don't you think?"

"I'd prefer the Presidential Suite at the Ritz Carlton, but you know Bob. This will make him happy."

She watches him move to the corner of the room, feet shuffling, legs unsteady. He removes his pinstriped jacket and eases into the chair. It protests with a loud squeak, as if it doesn't want to be here either. He unfastens a cufflink next, before rolling up the sleeve of his powder blue shirt. It is a slow, labored process.

In those Tulsa years, Charlie had a hold on her. She adored him, being out on the town with him, being in his orbit. They confided in each other on the phone, late into the night. They gave each other shit, neither one of them pulling punches. Ever. She loved the banter, the directness, the honesty. Now that she looks back on it, she realizes she fell in love with him long before she admitted it, long before she kissed him on that bridge in Woodward Park. Amid the flowering gardens, above the brook, on a Sunday afternoon. But his lips felt cold, as if drained of blood.

He took her hands and talked about his sexuality with an ease she envied. He loved her. "Kindred assholes," that's how he described them. The best of friends. Just not lovers. For years, they stayed that way. Charlie always managed to be around when she needed him. She was there for him, too.

"It's very Will and Grace *of us," Patricia sometimes joked, but it was the kind of joke that didn't make her laugh or feel better. That was before the trouble started with the law, with Charlie's compulsion to steal.*

She puts on latex gloves, takes the syringe from her bag, and ties the tourniquet around his bicep. Charlie smiles warmly beneath the suede fedora. His favorite hat. He loves dressing as if he just walked off the set of a 1940s movie. He has never cared

312

much for the twenty-first century. Who can blame him? She often worries about the world her boys are inheriting.

She touches the side of Charlie's face. His skin is warm. She takes in the white tufts of eyebrows and watery blue eyes. He is ten years older, and she can see what a big difference that makes now. Charlie has become an old man. The lack of firmness in his skin. The shakiness of his movements. Even his voice slips on occasion, sounding like a violin out of tune.

"Why didn't you tell Robert your real name? After all these years."

"I liked being Payton," he replies. "That's how he knew me. I didn't want to change that. Besides, what good was Charles Redstone Allard to the world? A foster kid whose real dad left before he was born? A foster kid whose mom killed herself when he was five? Payton Wells didn't have that baggage."

"Strange how things worked out," she says, standing there with the syringe, waiting for the okay to inject enough air into his artery to kill him.

"Very strange. Not donut burger strange, but strange."

She laughs. "Not the donut burger again."

"What evil genius thought to himself, 'How do I make the hamburger worse for you than it already is'"?

"What makes you think it was a man?"

"Only a man would be stupid enough to eat a donut burger."

They get quiet again. The yellow light makes the entire room appear sickly, and it reminds her why they are here again. Charlie's cancer. His decision to die on his own terms. Her inability to refuse him.

Patricia took her first and—as it turned out—only job as an Assistant Professor of Internal Medicine at Haverton University Hospital. She moved across the country. She met Bob Green at a dinner party hosted by some colleagues. He was a caring, tender man. Thoughtful and quirky in a way that always made her laugh. The outrageous beard. His ridiculous love of flannel. They became lovers, husband and wife, parents.

It was a balanced life. Work. Marriage. Two beautiful boys. She and Robert did not have sex with fire. They never had. Part of her wondered if all of those years with Charlie ruined her somehow, if she had given her heart away and forgot to get it back. She has always been absent minded. Lost car keys. Misplaced wallets. Maybe one could lose a heart just as easily. She never heard from Charlie after he went to jail. He disappeared from her life, along with her heart, and the hole he left felt bottomless.

One evening, Charlie appeared at the front door with her husband. He seemed just as surprised to see her, but you could never tell with him. If anyone could figure out that she had become Mrs. Patricia Green, it was Charlie. But they pretended not to know each other. She watched him and Robert throughout the meal. She could see a spark between them, even though it would be a long time before Robert had the courage to act on it.

It was odd, not caring about whether her husband and Charlie were or would become lovers. She knew Robert loved her, but something was never right between them. She also knew he would never leave her. That was a comfort, she thought. But it was more than that. She would have Charlie back in her life.

Finally.

The next day, she met Charlie for coffee. It was the start of their friendship again. Coffees and lunches and phone calls. He had come to Haverton because he figured out she had moved there. He wanted to start over, again, and a small town across the country seemed like the perfect fit.

She had Charlie again. Robert had Charlie, too. Charlie made both of them happier. Robert needed his old world charm and ravishing smile. She needed his smart-ass, down-to-earth honesty. And he still made her heart flutter.

That was the thing about Charlie. He could sense what people needed, and he could be that for them. He knew how to be different things for different people. She always wondered how happy that made Charlie, though. To be a blank slate, to be what other people wanted. What about Charlie? Was the real Charlie in there somewhere? Or had the loss of his parents and foster parents scorched it away somehow?

"Thank you," he says. "For this."

"Asshole."

"I asked Bob first."

She shakes her head. "He practically faints when he has blood drawn. He covers his eyes when we watch Jaws on TV, for the hundredth time. He could never—."

"I know." Charlie smiles, and his body seems to relax a little in the boxy chair. Some leaves from The Golden Girls plant touch his shoulder. "I just needed him to know I was serious, to know our last time together was our last."

"What the hell am I going to do without you?"

"You have your hands full with Bob. He has always been one of those Handle-with-Care types. Like us."

They both laugh at the absurdity of being anything like Robert Green—whose soft, gentle nature matches the texture of his flannel shirts. But Charlie's faint laugh carries a trace of sadness.

"I love you, Pats," he says. "It's time."

"Love you more."

She slips the needle into his vein and injects the air. At first, everything is still. He stares at her, waiting, wondering if anything is really going to happen. Then he grips his chest with his right hand. Hard. His body starts to seize. His legs shake. He grabs the armrests fiercely. Saliva spills from the side of his mouth. His head snaps back, and the hat falls to the floor.

315

She pins both of his arms, trying to keep him in the chair. He struggles for air. Short, panicked breaths. His body jerks again. It is not as hard to hold him down as she imagined. He is weaker than she thought.

His head is still back, eyes toward the ceiling. He strains again, his body tightening. Something rattles in his throat.

Then it passes.

He gets still, and she checks his pulse.

Nothing.

The rest feels like a ritual. Putting away the needle and tourniquet. Wiping his mouth and rolling down his sleeve. Restoring his gold cufflink and putting the jacket back on. That is the hardest part—getting his arms into the sleeves and buttoning it up. The dead weight. It leaves her somewhat breathless. She places the fedora gently, snugly on his head. She adjusts his body in the chair before closing his eyes with her fingers. A passerby might think he has just fallen asleep.

She sits at his knees, looking at his marvelous suit and old world hat, his sun spotted hands and lined, handsome face. This isn't part of the plan, lingering with him and crying, chest heaving and nose running. But she stays. For a long time.

After an hour, maybe two, she gathers herself. She is at the door, her gloved hand resting on the handle, when she hears a key slide into the lock. She hurries past the secretary's desk and into the narrow hallway that connects the main office to the copy room.

From here, she watches a young woman enter and snap on the lights. She recognizes her from somewhere. A university function of some kind. A student. Pretty despite her unwashed hair and bloodshot eyes. She wears an oversized puffy jacket and cheap loafers. There is something unusual about this girl. She does not scream or run away or act frightened. She calls out "hello" and approaches the body calmly. Most people don't act this way around death.

316

Then she does something that Dr. Patricia Green, wife of Professor Robert Green and friend of Charlie Redstone Allard, would never have expected.

She kicks him in the shin. Twice.

Patricia has to stifle a laugh as the student storms out of the office, huffing and muttering to herself. The room gets still again in the yellow light. Charlie remains slouched in the chair, the fake fichus resting on his shoulder. This is her chance to slip away.

Patricia walks to the door and takes one last look.

"Don't worry, Charlie," she says. "I have a feeling that girl is going to do right by you."

Acknowledgements

Thank you for purchasing a copy of *Ivory Tower* and supporting the Ivory Tower Writing Scholarship. I have created this fund to help aspiring students in creative writing to thrive, write, and grow into great artists. All of the proceeds will go directly to this scholarship, and I will post updates about the official launch event, the money raised, and the recipients through my website: www.thomasfahy.com Stay tuned, and thank you again!

I cannot possibly name and thank all of the people in my life who have made this book—and all my work—possible. Thank you to my family, my friends from high school, college, and graduate school, teachers and mentors, colleagues at Long Island University, my inspiring students over the years, and so many dear friends around the country. You have all shared your stories, your humor, and your friendship. I am so grateful.

Several people read early drafts and offered insightful, generous feedback that improved this book—particularly Gabby McAree, James MacDonald, Joshua Archibald, Kay Sato, and Mark Graham. Rachel Smith shared her wit, humorous anecdotes, and critical eye at several stages of this project, and she always did so with unwavering enthusiasm and loving support. Susann Cokal lent her incredible editorial skills to this manuscript, and, as always, she challenged me to be a better writer every step of the way. Many thanks to Jennifer Fahy for helping with so many aspect of this book at the eleventh hour.

Lastly, I want to thank my son, Nicolai, whose humor, imagination, and kindness never cease to amaze me. I am so fortunate to be your father.

About the Author

Thomas Fahy is a novelist, nonfiction writer, and professor of literature and creative writing. He has published seventeen books with traditional publishers, including two young adult novels with Simon and Schuster, an adult suspense novel with HarperCollins, and numerous nonfiction titles with university and trade presses.

This new book, *Ivory Tower,* is being published as a fundraiser for the Ivory Tower Writing Scholarship. As a professor of creative writing, I have witnessed firsthand a new generation of great writers, and I am creating this scholarship to support them. I recently launched a national undergraduate journal fully staffed by students, and some of my graduates are in prestigious MFA programs across the country.

Please help me support their efforts. 100% of each sale goes directly to the Ivory Tower Writing Scholarship, and it will be awarded to an outstanding undergraduate who plans to pursue creative writing at the graduate level. For more details and updates on the fundraiser, please visit my website: www.thomasfahy.com Thank you!